Falling Into You

JASINDA WILDER

FALLING INTO YOU

ISBN: 978-0-9891044-0-1
Copyright © 2013 by Jasinda Wilder

Cover art by Sarah Hansen of Okay Creations. Cover art © 2013 by Sarah Hansen.

Copyediting and interior book design by Indie Author Services.

This book is for anyone who has ever lost a loved one, for anyone who has woken up crying and gone to bed the same way, for anyone who has had to learn that it's okay to be not okay. Surviving isn't strength, it's continuing to breathe one day at a time; strength is learning to live despite the pain.

Nell

Chapter 1: BFF...Or BF?
September

I WASN'T ALWAYS IN LOVE WITH COLTON CALLOWAY; I was in love with his younger brother, Kyle, first.

Kyle was my first one true love, my first in every way.

I grew up next to the Calloways. Kyle and I were the same age, our moms having given birth to us in the same hospital, two rooms apart, two days apart. Kyle was the older one, much to my irritation. Only by two days, but that was enough for Kyle to get a big head about it and tease me mercilessly. We played in the same Pack-N-Play in his mom's house as babies. We shared blocks and dolls (Kyle played with dolls as much as I did until we were three or so, which I in turn teased him mercilessly about). We learned to ride bikes together; my dad taught us both, since Mr. Calloway was a congressman and gone a lot. We studied together, did homework together. We were best friends before anything else. It was always kind of assumed we'd end up together, I think.

Not quite arranged, necessarily, just…assumed. His dad, the up-and-coming congressman; my dad, the CEO, the über-successful businessman. Their beautifully perfect children, together? Well, duh. I mean, I know that sounds arrogant or whatever, but it's just the truth. I'm not perfect, obviously. I have some flaws. I'm kind of wide in the hips for my height, and my bust is a little too big for my frame, but whatever. I know what I look like, but I swear I'm not vain about it.

We weren't aware of those assumptions until our sophomore year. We'd been friends until that point, best friends, but *just* friends. I was never a boy-crazy type of girl. My conservative father wouldn't have allowed it, for one thing, and I wasn't permitted to date until I was sixteen anyway. So then, the week after my sweet sixteen, Jason Dorsey asked me out. Jason was the runner-up to Kyle's bid for complete perfection. He was blond where Kyle was raven-haired, a more bulky muscle-builder type to Kyle's lean, cut, lupine grace, and Jason wasn't quite as smart or charming as Kyle, but then I might have been biased.

I didn't even hesitate when Jason asked me if he could take me to dinner after school. I mean, *duh*, right? Just about every girl at my high school dreamed of Jason or Kyle asking them out, and I was BFFs with Kyle, and had a date with Jason. He did it at my locker, which was always a busy spot, so it was a public thing. Everyone saw, and they were all so jealous, let me tell you.

I met Kyle at his souped-up Camaro after sixth period like always, and we took off, tires squealing. Kyle tended to drive like he was in a high-speed chase, but he was a very skilled driver, so I never freaked. His dad had made sure Kyle was given courses in defensive driving by an actual FBI agent, so Kyle could out-drive most of the cops at the local PD.

"Guess what?" I asked, excited, as Kyle drifted a wide left turn onto the dirt road leading to our neighborhood. Kyle shot me a lifted-eyebrow look, so I grabbed his bicep and squeezed, squealing, "Jason Dorsey asked me out! He's taking me to dinner tonight!"

Kyle nearly drove off the road. He jammed on the brakes, spinning the car into a sideways skid on the dirt road leading to our houses. Kyle twisted in the leather bucket seat, one arm braced on the headrest of my seat, brown eyes blazing. "What did you just say?" He sounded angry, which confused me. "'Cause I could have sworn you just said Jason asked you out."

I felt my breath catch at the intensity in his eyes, his voice. "I…he did?" It came out like a question, timid and confused. "He's—he's picking me up at seven. We're going to Brann's. Why are you acting this way?"

"Why am I—?" Kyle snapped his teeth together, cutting himself off, then scrubbed his face with his hands. "Nell, you can't go out with Jason."

"Why not?" Now that I was over the shock of Kyle's sudden anger, I was hurt, more confused than ever, and getting angry. "He's nice, and cute. He's your best friend, so what's wrong with him? I'm *excited*, Kyle. Or I was. No one's ever asked me out before, and I'm finally allowed to date now that I'm sixteen, and you're all mad. I don't get it. You're supposed to be *happy* for me."

Kyle's face twisted, and I watched as half a dozen emotions rippled over his handsome features. He opened his mouth, then closed it again. Finally, he let out a groaned curse and flung his door open, threw himself out of the car, slammed the door behind him, and stalked away through Mr. Ennis's cornfield.

I hesitated, more confused than ever. It looked, just before he stormed away, like Kyle was jealous. Could he be jealous? Then why didn't *he* ask me out? I ripped my hair out of its ponytail and retied it, the wheels in my head spinning so fast I could barely breathe.

Kyle? I'd done everything with Kyle. Everything. We ate lunch together every day. We went on hikes and picnics, long bike rides ending in ice cream at Dairy Queen. We skipped his dad's monthly political soirées to drink stolen wine on the dock behind my house. We even got tipsy once and went skinny dipping.

I had a memory of watching Kyle turn away as he shoved his boxers off and feeling a tingle in my belly at the sight of his naked backside. At the time I'd attributed the feeling to being buzzed. Of course, I'd stripped, too, and Kyle's gaze had taken in my body in a way that had made the tingle even worse. At the time, I'd yelled at him to stop ogling me, and he'd turned away. He'd been in water up to his waist, but now I couldn't help wondering if he'd been hiding a reaction to seeing me naked. He'd been very careful to keep his distance while we swam, when normally we were very physical, hugging, teasing each other, getting in tickle wars, which Kyle always won.

I was starting to look at everything differently, all of a sudden.

Kyle? He was my best friend. I had girlfriends, obviously. Jill and Becca and I got mani-pedis together every week and then went for milkshakes at Big Boy.

But when I was upset or pissed off, when I got in a fight with Mom and Dad or got a bad grade or *anything*, I went to Kyle. We'd sit on my dock or his and he'd talk me out my funk. Hug me and hold me until I felt better. I'd fallen asleep on the dock with him a thousand times, fallen asleep on his couch watching a movie. On his couch, on his lap. Against his chest, his arm around me.

That's not BFF kind of affection, is it? We'd never kissed, never held hands like boyfriend/girlfriend, though. And if anyone asked, which happened a lot, we were always like *no, we're not going out, we're best friends.*

But were we more?

God, what a mess.

I got out of the car and followed after Kyle. He was long out of sight, but I knew where he was going. There was a spot on the ridge on the other side of Mr. Ennis's cornfield where we hung out a lot. You could see our town from that ridge, as well as the silver string of the creek and the dark swath of the forest.

Kyle was halfway up the huge lightning-blasted pine that crowned the ridge. There was a long, thick branch about twenty feet up, easy to climb to, and we frequently sat on that branch together, his back to the trunk, my back to his chest. I stood on the branch beneath Kyle, waiting. He hooked his foot around the branch, reached down and lifted me like a doll, and set me in front of him. This position took on a new significance, suddenly. I could feel his heart hammering in his chest. He was breathing hard and smelled of sweat. He must have run up the ridge.

I leaned my head back on his shoulder and looked at him, his profile chiseled and gorgeous, bathed golden in the late afternoon sun. His brows were knitted together, his jaw clenched hard. He was still pissed.

"Kyle...talk to me. I don't—"

"Don't what? Understand? Yes, you do." He glanced at me, then slid his eyes closed and turned away. As if it hurt to look at me.

"We're best friends, Kyle. If there's something else for you, tell me."

"For me?" Kyle's head thumped back against the tree. "I don't know, Nell. I—yeah, I mean we're best friends, by default, I guess. I mean, we grew up together, right? We spend all this time together, and we tell people that's all we are, but..."

"But what?" I felt my heart pounding in my chest. This could change everything.

He took a lock of my strawberry blonde hair in his fingers and twisted it. "What if there was more? Between us?"

"More? Like, *together*?"

"Why not?"

I felt a rush of anger. "'Why not?' Are you fucking serious, Kyle? That's the answer you give me?" I slid forward on the branch, swung my leg over, and lowered myself to the next branch down.

In seconds, I was out of the tree and running through the cornfield. I could hear Kyle behind me, calling for me to wait, but I didn't. Home was only a mile away at that point, so I ran. I threw open my front door so hard it shook the house, startling my mother so bad she dropped a glass. I heard the smash of the glass hitting the floor, my mother's curse, and then I was slamming my bedroom door and falling onto my bed, sobbing. I'd held it together that long, but in the sanctuary of my room, I could let go.

"Nell? What's wrong, sweetie?" My mom's voice on the other side of the door, concerned and sweet.

"I don't…I don't want to talk about it."

"Nell, open up and talk to me."

"No!"

I heard Kyle's deep male voice behind my mother's. She said, "Nell? Kyle's here."

"I don't want to see him. Make him go away."

I heard my my mom talking to Kyle, telling him she'd talk to me, telling him it would be okay. It wouldn't, though. Why exactly I was crying so hard, I couldn't quite figure out. I was a hundred different kinds of confused.

I was excited to go out with Jason. Or at least, I had been. I tried to picture Jason's hand in mine, his arm around my waist. I tried to picture myself kissing Jason. I shuddered and had to push the image away, almost nauseated. So why had I been so happy? Just because I'd been asked out by a cute boy? Maybe. I mean, it was pretty common knowledge that Nell Hawthorne was off-limits for anyone and everyone. I'd been asked out before, last year when I was fifteen, around homecoming. Aaron Swarnicki. Cute-ish, but boring. Dad had flipped out and told me I couldn't go out. I could go to homecoming, but that was it. It had kind of just spread, unspoken but understood: *Nell is off-limits*. No one asked me out again after that. Dad was a pretty influential figure in our town. Only Kyle's dad was more important, and that was just because he was a congressman. Daddy owned several of the strip mall buildings in town, and several more in the surrounding counties. He was on the city board, had the ear of the mayor, the state governor, too. Through Mr. Calloway, he also had access to national political figures. Meaning, no one wanted to cross Jim Hawthorne. It was all strange, now that I thought about it. Maybe

Daddy had said something to the boy who had asked me out.

My mind spun back to Kyle. To his sudden, extreme reaction to Jason having asked me out. To the way he'd looked at me in the tree.

To my own reaction to his "why not" comment.

'Why not'? That was the best he could come up with? I was angry all over again, and I couldn't stop it, even though I knew it was irrational. I didn't want him to want to go out with me *just because*. I wanted it to mean something.

I tried to picture being with Kyle as *more*, whatever that meant. I could easily picture our fingers tangled together. Candlelit dinners. My face on his chest, his lips descending to mine as the sun set behind us…

I told myself to quit being so melodramatic. But…I couldn't shake the image. I could almost feel Kyle's arms on my back, his hands spanning my waist, brushing dangerously close to my butt. I could feel the secret thrill of wanting his hands to move just a little lower. I could almost feel his lips, warm and soft and wet, slipping over mine…

I blushed and squirmed on the bed, rolling to my back and wiping my face.

What was wrong with me? I was fantasizing about Kyle all of a sudden?

I needed to get outside. I needed to run. I stripped out of my school clothes and put on my running shorts, sports bra and tank top, ankle socks, Nikes, and grabbed my iPod. Running usually cleared my head, and that was what I needed right then.

I stuck the earbuds in my ears as I descended the stairs and rushed out the front door, pretending I couldn't hear my mom calling my name. I put on my running playlist, all the silly, empty, upbeat pop songs that I could push to the back of my head and just run. I stretched briefly and took off, heading for my usual five-mile circuit.

I passed Kyle's driveway and mentally cursed myself for not thinking. He was waiting for me, his own earbuds in, shirtless, in gym shorts. I'd seen him like this a thousand times, his sculpted abs rippling in the sun, a dark line of hair running down his stomach and disappearing beneath his shorts. This time, though, I had to swallow hard at the sight. I mean, I knew Kyle was *hot*. I'd always known that about him, and always appreciated it. I mean, I was a normal, hormonal sixteen-year-old girl with a healthy appreciation for a sexy male body. I just hadn't really thought about Kyle in *that* way. Like, as an object of desire.

I didn't slow down, though, and he fell into step next to me, our footsteps syncing naturally. Even the two-step rhythm of inbreath-outbreath synced immediately.

We didn't speak, didn't even look at each other. We just ran. A mile, then the second, and then we both started to flag. I pushed the pace and he matched it, and then pushed it even faster, and then we had our second wind. We blew past the gnarled tree stump that marked the third mile, breathing hard now, sweating. I forced my gaze to the road ahead, forced my thoughts to emptiness, Lady Gaga in the background. Run, run, run, breathe and focus, swing my arms. Don't look at Kyle. Don't look at the sheen of sweat on his bare chest, don't watch the bead of liquid trickling over one nipple and under the bulge of his pectoral, don't imagine myself licking the droplet away as it touched the rippling field of his abs.

Shit! Where did that image come from? Licking him? *Get a grip, Nell. Get a damn grip.* The self-admonishment didn't help. The image was burned into my brain now. Kyle, on his back, in a grass field. Sweat running over his bronzed skin, hair messy and wet. Lowering my face to his chest, pressing my lips to his breastbone, then licking away a glinting bead of salty liquid.

Oh, god, oh, god…*ohmigod.* This was bad. These weren't good thoughts. Weren't innocent thoughts.

Weren't BFF thoughts. I was a virgin. I'd never licked anyone. Never kissed anyone, even. Sure, I'd watched a few steamy rated-R movies with Jill and Becca, and we secretly watched *True Blood* together all the time. So...we knew how it was supposed to go, and I'd had my own little fantasies and girly daydreams, but...with *Kyle?*

I was just channeling Sookie and Eric. Obviously. Except Kyle looked more like Bill...

I jolted back to awareness, and Kyle was a few steps behind me, and I was full-out running, arms pumping wildly. I pushed harder, ran faster, pushing the images and the sudden ridiculous desire for my best friend away, and just ran. Legs turned to jelly, breathing ragged and burning, vision blurring, desperation in place of blood, confusion in place of oxygen, that kind of running.

Kyle slid into my peripheral vision, pacing me, straining, and then his conditioning took over and he peeled away, faster than I could ever hope to run. All-state football star at sixteen fast. Already being scouted by U of M and Alabama and UNC fast.

I stumbled, slowed, stopped, then slumped forward with my hands on my knees, panting. Kyle was a dozen feet away, doing the same. We were on the crest of a hill, the forest out to our left, our houses a few miles behind us, the ridge with our tree visible off to our right. Wildflowers swayed in a breeze, welcome and cool in the early September evening heat. I made myself walk around, forgot myself and peeled my tank top off and wiped my face with it.

I stopped walking again, head tipped back, trying to slow my breathing, tilted my head back and draped the shirt over my eyes to sop up the burning sweat from my forehead.

"You should stretch out," Kyle murmured, only inches away.

I started at the sound of his voice, his sudden proximity. My heart started pounding again, nerves this time rather than exertion. Which was stupid. This was Kyle. He knew everything about me. He'd seen me naked.

Which was the exact wrong thing to think in that moment. I tugged the shirt off my eyes and looked up to see him gazing down at me, expression intense but otherwise unreadable. He was taking deep, dragging breaths, and I knew if I wasn't careful, I might end up convincing myself it wasn't just post-run panting.

I licked my lips, and his eyes followed my tongue's path. Bad. This was bad.

"Kyle…" I started, then realized I didn't know what to say.

"Nell." He sounded calm, confident. Unaffected. But his eyes…they betrayed him.

He turned away, bent over with his feet together, and began stretching. The moment was broken, and I turned to stretch as well. When we'd both finished, we sat down in the grass, and I knew we couldn't avoid the discussion anymore. To cover my nerves, I tugged my hair free from the ponytail and shook it out.

Kyle took a deep breath, glanced at me nervously, then squeezed his eyes shut. "Nell, listen. When I said 'why not,' that was…it was stupid. It's not what I meant. I'm sorry. I know how that must have sounded to you. I was just so upset and confused—"

"Confused?"

"Yes, confused!" Kyle said, almost yelling. "This whole thing between us today, it's *confusing*. When you told me Jason asked you out, I just—it was like something in my head just…snapped. I pictured you out with him, maybe even kissing him, and I…no. Just no."

He scrubbed his face, then lay back on the grass, staring up at the blue sky scattered with shreds of white and stained orange by the lowering sun.

"I know how this is gonna sound but—when I pictured Jason's arms around you, his lips touching you…I couldn't handle it. I thought, 'Hell, no! Nell is mine.' That's when I ran off. I couldn't figure out why I was so possessive suddenly. I still…I don't know where this is coming from."

"I don't, either. I mean, I was surprised by the way you reacted, but then I went home and thought about actually going out with Jason, and…it just didn't fit. I couldn't imagine it."

"So are you still going out with him, then?"

I paused. "I don't know. I guess not."

Kyle glanced at me, then pulled out his iPhone, the earbuds trailing from it. "Does he know that?"

I sucked in a breath. I hadn't called him to cancel. "Shit, no, he doesn't."

Kyle's lip quirked up in a grin. "You'd better call him, then, huh? He'll be wondering where you are, I imagine."

I glanced at my iPod: 6:54 p.m. "Can I use your phone?"

He scrolled through his contacts, yanked the earbuds free, and handed it to me. I hit "Send" and pressed it to my ear, the rubber case still damp and warm from Kyle's grip.

Jason's exuberant voice came through the phone. "Hey, Kyle, my man! Whassup!"

I sucked in a hesitant breath. "Actually, Jason, this is Nell. I'm calling from Kyle's phone…I—I forgot mine."

"Forgot yours? Where are you? I'm pulling up to your driveway right now." His friendly, excited voice took on a confused tone.

"Listen, I'm sorry, but I can't go out with you."

A long silence. "Oh, I gotcha." His voice drooped, and I could picture his features falling. "Everything okay? I mean —"

"I just—I may have said yes too quickly, Jason. I'm sorry. I don't think…I don't think it'd work."

"So this isn't a rain check, is it." His words implied a question, but his tone was a statement, flat, tense.

"No. I'm so sorry."

"It's fine, I guess." He laughed, a forced bark. "Shit, no. It's not. This is kinda shady, Nell. I was all excited."

"I'm so, *so* sorry, Jason. I just realized, after really thinking about things…I mean, I'm flattered, and I was excited that you asked me, but—"

"This is about Kyle, isn't it? You're with him, on his phone, so of *course* this about him."

"Jason, that's not—I mean, yeah, I'm with him right now, but—"

"It's fine. I get it. I think we all knew this was coming, so I shouldn't be surprised. I just wish you'd told me sooner."

"I'm sorry, Jason. I don't know what else to say."

"Nothing to say. It's all good. I'll just…whatever. See you in chemistry on Monday."

He was about to hang up, and a flash of inspiration jolted through me. "Jason, wait."

"What." His voice was dead, flat.

"I probably shouldn't tell you this, but…Becca has had a crush on you since seventh grade. I guarantee she'll go out with you."

"Becca?" I could hear him considering the idea. "Wouldn't that be weird? I mean, what would I say? She'd think she was my second choice, or something. I mean, I guess that's true, but not like *that*, you know?"

I thought about it. "Just tell her the truth. I backed out on you, last minute. You already have reservations, and I thought she might like to go with you instead of me."

"Think it'll work? Really?" His voice took on a new life, excited once more. "She is pretty hot."

"It'll work. Just call her." I rattled off her number, and he repeated it.

"Thanks…I think. But, Nell? Next time you're gonna break a guy's heart, give him a bit more notice, would you?"

"Don't be ridiculous, Jason. I didn't break your heart. We hadn't even gone out yet. But I *am* sorry for standing you up like this."

"No worries. Besides, maybe something will work out with Becca and me. She's almost as hot as you. Wait, shit, that didn't come out right. Don't tell Becca I said that. You guys are equally hot, I was just—"

I couldn't help laughing. "Jason? Shut up. Call Becca."

I hit "End," handing Kyle his phone back. He stared at the phone. "That was pretty slick, Nell. I gotta hand it to you." He glanced at me quizzically. "Does Becca really have a crush on him?"

I laughed again. "Hell, yes. She's been mad in love with Jason Dorsey since…well, I told him seventh grade, but it's been longer than that. Way longer. Like…since fourth grade. Forever. Another reason why I should never have said yes to him, I was just…I was excited, Kyle. Getting asked out by cute boys is a big deal, and you and Jason are the two cutest guys in the whole school."

Kyle grinned at me, rakish and mischievous. "You think I'm cute?"

Oh, god. Oh, god. This was trouble. I couldn't meet his eyes. The grass was suddenly really, *really* interesting.

"You know you're hot, Kyle Calloway, so quit fishing for compliments." I tried the flirty, joking tack, hoping to distract him from the fact that I was blushing hot red from forehead to cleavage.

It didn't work. "You're eight shades of red, Nell." His voice was all too close. His breath was hot on my neck.

What was going on? What was he doing?

I looked up, and Kyle's eyes were centimeters from mine. He was lying on his side, and his fingers were reaching for me. I couldn't breathe suddenly. He was brushing my hair behind my ear, and I couldn't focus on anything but his sculpted body and his fiery eyes and his hand in my hair and his mouth, his lips, so close, his tongue tip running over his lower lip. Suddenly Kyle was someone else, someone different. Not the little boy I'd grown up with, but a young man with his features, his eyes, his strong jawline, but an intense, grown-up, almost hungry gaze.

I didn't know this Kyle, but I liked him. I wanted to know him.

Electricity surged through me, startling my eyes shut, shock dragging a gasp through my lips as Kyle pressed his mouth to mine. Wet heat and soft power thrilled through me, surprise giving way slowly to wonder, to delight.

Kyle was *kissing* me. Oh, god, oh god...*ohmigod*. I liked it, *so* much. My first kiss.

I was breathless, unable to move for the incredible feeling of lips touching lips. Foreign but perfect, questing and hesitant. He pulled away, leaving me even more breathless and mourning the loss of the kiss.

"Nell? I—you…?" He seemed unsure of himself, of the kiss.

I smiled at him, our faces still so close I felt my lips curving against his. My hand drifted from my lap to his arm, then to his face, my fingers splaying around his ear, my palm against his cheek. He let out a sigh of relief, and this time the kiss was mutual. I pressed in, moving my lips against his, breathless in wonder again…or still.

A thousand questions that had cropped up in my mind when watching movies showing people kissing were answered. What did you do with your noses? What nose? All I knew was his mouth against mine, slightly tilted. Hands? They seemed to know where to go on their own. To his face, to his nape, to his arms. I could breathe even as we kissed, obviously. When I was younger I'd wondered if I would have to hold my breath. Now I was delighted to understand that I could kiss Kyle forever, I'd never have to break for breath. I didn't want to.

I wasn't sure how much time passed while we kissed there in the grass on the hill. I didn't care. Nothing mattered but the delirious joy of Kyle, of my first kiss, of making out with my best friend, the only guy I'd ever really cared about.

This wasn't just perfectly natural, it was the only thing I could imagine happening, and I couldn't figure out how it hadn't happened before now.

Then, suddenly, I was lying down in the grass, blades crushed and tickling my bare back beneath the strap of my sports bra. Kyle was above me, weight partially on me, partially supported by his arm. His palm planted into the grass next to my face, and I curled my hand around his arm, the other on his nape, making sure he didn't pull away, didn't stop kissing me.

Suddenly I understood so many things.

I understood the danger in a kiss. The heat and the power and the lightning. I felt something hard pressing against my hip, and I knew what it was in a flash of heat. The kiss broke, and Kyle shifted away, pulling his hips back. His gaze flickered over my body, and I blushed, both from his attention and from the knowledge of what I'd felt.

He blushed, and I realized I'd been gazing at him, at his body, his sculpted abs and further down, to where a bulge gave away what we were both aware of.

"Shit—" Kyle said, and rolled away, covering his face, clearly embarrassed. "Nell, I'm sorry, I don't know what happened—"

I giggled. "Kyle, I'm pretty sure we both know that's bullshit. I know what happened, and so do you. We kissed. We made out. And you got…excited."

He pulled the the waistband of his running shorts away from his body briefly, adjusting himself. "Yeah, but…it's just embarrassing."

I rolled to my stomach and leaned over him, as he had me. "Kyle, it's fine. We're not kids. I'm…I know—I mean, yeah, it was a little odd for a second, but—"

"This changes things between us, doesn't it?" Kyle asked, interrupting me.

I cut the words short, stunned silent by his abrupt question. "I guess it does, yeah," I said.

"Are we still friends?"

I panicked. "I—yes? I mean, I hope so. I don't know what happened, why we kissed like that, why you got so jealous and why I couldn't go out with Jason. I mean, I *know*…but I don't understand why *now*. You know? Kissing you, it felt…right. And you're still you. I'm still me. We're still us, Kyle and Nell. But…just more, I guess."

Kyle sighed in relief. "I was afraid…I mean—I didn't mean to kiss you. It just kind of happened. It was amazing, and I didn't want to stop." His gaze finally met mine, his fingers toying with a lock of my hair. "I want to kiss you again, right now. But…I'm afraid I'd never stop."

"Who said I wanted you to stop? I kissed you back, Kyle. I don't know what this means for us, what this makes us. I mean, are we boyfriend-girlfriend now? I don't know. What will our parents say? Everyone has always thought that's what we are anyway, right?"

Kyle's tongue ran over his bottom lip, and I knew he was thinking about kissing me. I beat him to it. I leaned down, my hair draping over our faces and blocking out the world, everything except the kiss. Kyle's hand skated up my arm, rested awkwardly on my shoulder, and then down my back. He hesitated, and I did, too. The kiss broke, but our lips barely parted. Our eyes met, and I could see him wondering, thinking, wanting but unsure. I moved slightly, but enough so more of my weight was on him, my hands resting on his chest. I'd seen this position in a movie before, and now I understood it. It was intimate. Comfortable, but…suggestive.

I felt worldly. Adult. Grown-up. Full of desires I didn't quite understand and didn't know what to do with. I felt the hardness between us, and Kyle's hesitant gaze told me he was as achingly aware of it as I was. What was I supposed to do? Move away? In the movies, this was where the kiss would naturally and easily move to other things. In *True Blood*, this was where Eric would skillfully get Sookie's clothes off, and then the scene would change and he would be above her, all male muscle and long lines and motion, and they would be making love...*fucking*...and they'd both know exactly what they were doing.

I wasn't so sure about all that. Seeing him without his shirt on was suddenly enough to have me blushing. Feeling the skin of his chest beneath my hands, his palms on my flesh beneath the strap of my sports bra had me tingling. But...the rest?

I wasn't ready.

Kyle must have sensed my turmoil, or felt the sudden hammering of my heart. He pulled away and sat up, forcing me to do the same.

"We should slow down, Nell."

"Yeah...yeah." I shot to my feet and picked up my shirt from the grass.

It was sopping wet, so I didn't put it back on. I felt my muscles pulling, my back twingeing. I stretched, arching backward, my arms above my head with my palms facing the sky. As I eased out of the stretch, I felt Kyle's eyes on me. On me in a guy way. Seeing me, really looking. I blushed.

"What?" I asked, even though I knew.

"Nothing." Kyle's eyes darted away, and I couldn't help my own gaze from raking over his sweat-gleaming muscles, the still-apparent telltale bulge in his shorts, which only made me blush harder.

I remembered the one time Jill and I had watched a porno she'd found on the Internet—simply out of curiosity and the rush of knowing we shouldn't watch it. All I could think of was how the men had looked, huge and veiny and hairy and...*shudder*. It hadn't been fun, or hot, or attractive. The women hadn't looked real. It had been ugly and shocking and kind of scary. We'd turned it off not even halfway through and vowed to never talk about it again. We'd turned on a *Jersey Shore* repeat and tried to pretend we both didn't have those awful images burned into our brains.

And now, of course, six months after Jill's and my failed experiment with porn, all I could think as I tried to force my eyes away from Kyle's crotch, was whether he'd look like them, if I'd be turned on by how he looked naked, if he and I were to do it together.

"We should head back," Kyle said. "We've been gone a long time."

The sun was setting as we struck out across the field back toward the main road. I jogged down the steep hill ahead of Kyle, and again I felt his eyes on me, and this time I knew he was staring at my butt. I ignored my blushing embarrassment and twisted to look at him over my shoulder, trying to look coy and sultry. I swayed my hips at him as I slowed at the bottom of the hill.

"You were staring at me, Kyle," I said in a low voice when Kyle approached.

"No, I wasn't." He was fighting a grin, but his cheeks were pink, giving away his lie.

"Yes, you were. You were staring at my ass."

"I—" He ducked his head and rubbed the back of his neck, then looked back up at me, grinning lopsidedly. "You know what, yeah, fine. I was. Okay? I was staring at your ass. Is that a problem for you?"

I shrugged. "I didn't say I had a problem with it." I wasn't about to admit that I liked it.

We walked side by side in silence after that, a little awkward, a little hesitant. Kyle broke the silence finally.

"You know, I've been trying not to look at you like that for-fricking-ever. Every time we ran together, I had to run in front of you so I wouldn't stare at your ass. Or watch your boobs bounce. Even when you wear that bra, your boobs bounce a lot, and it's really fricking distracting."

"Kyle!" I nearly fainted, I blushed so hard, and I couldn't stop giggling, suddenly.

"What? I'm just telling you the truth. You're my best friend, and it felt wrong to be looking at you like any other girl. I mean, I try not to ogle girls anyway 'cause that's rude or whatever, but you're different. But…goddamn, Nell. It's so hard to not look at you. You're hot."

I stopped walking and turned to face him, abruptly. "You think I'm hot?"

He threw my words from earlier back at him. "You know you're hot, Nell Hawthorne, so quit fishing for compliments." His grin faded into an intense gaze, serious and rife with emotion. "But…'hot' isn't the right word. I mean, every guy in school thinks you're hot—except Thomas Avery 'cause he's gay. But I think you're beautiful. You're lovely."

I shifted uncomfortably under the intense scrutiny and prickling heat in his eyes. "Thanks?"

He thinks I'm…lovely? The idea that Kyle thought I was not just hot, but lovely, sent pangs of something like fear through me, an intense pressure in my heart.

We walked home, and at some point his hand ended up tangled in mine, fingers threaded as if they'd always been there. We arrived at his driveway first, and his mom was at the end of the driveway flipping through the mail, her cell phone stuck between her ear and shoulder, probably talking to my mom.

She saw us stroll through the motorized wrought-iron gate, hand in hand. Her eyebrows shot up to her hairline, and she trailed off mid-sentence, mouth open in a shocked "O." I knew my hair was a ragged, sweaty mess, my shirt was off and so was Kyle's…and suddenly my lips tingled with the memory of his kiss, and

I wondered if she could tell we'd been kissing, if she thought we had been—

"Rachel? I'll have to call you back. Our children just walked in…holding hands. Yes. I know. Already." Olivia Calloway hung up and turned to us. "So. You two were gone a while."

She glanced down at our joined hands. We looked at each other, exchanged a long, meaningful glance. I squeezed his hand, indicating I wasn't going to let go. I wasn't ashamed of this, or trying to hide anything.

Kyle nodded at me subtly, then turned to his mom. "Well, we went for a run, then stopped up by Keller's Ridge to talk."

Mrs. Calloway narrowed her eyes at us, taking in our state of undress and the tangled mess of my hair. "To talk, hmmm? And this?" She gestured at our hands.

Kyle lifted his chin. "We're together now."

We hadn't exactly decided that, per se, since we'd started kissing without actually agreeing to anything official. But I wasn't about to say any of that, not here, not now. And we were together, even if we hadn't made it "official."

"I see," Mrs. Calloway said. "You're together now. Are you sure that's a good idea? You're both so young."

Kyle frowned at his mom. "Seriously? Colt had a girlfriend at sixteen and I don't remember you guys saying shit to him about it."

"Watch your language, young man," she said, her voice hard. "And for the record, we *did* say something to him. The same thing I'm saying to you now. Just because you didn't hear the conversation doesn't mean it didn't happen. You were, what, eleven? Your father and I would not have had that conversation with your brother in front of you, Kyle."

Kyle sighed. "Yeah, I guess you're right. But—"

"Just be careful, okay?" Mrs. Calloway cut in over her son.

"Mom, no, we weren't—I mean we haven't—"

"I'm *not* having that talk with you, Kyle. Especially not in front of Nell. All I'm going to say is, now and going forward, whatever you do or don't do...be careful." She turned away, tucking the mail under her arm, then stopped and glanced back at us. "And I mean that in an emotional sense, not just physical. You two have been best friends your whole life. Crossing the line into more...that's a line you can't uncross." Something in her tone of voice and the way she stared into middle distance had me wondering if she knew what she was saying from personal experience.

"We know that, Mom. That's what we were talking about, actually."

"Well...good." She vanished into the house, nose already buried in her phone.

I stood with Kyle in his driveway. "That wasn't so bad."

"No, but that was Mom. She'll call Dad, and he'll call me, and we'll have 'the talk.'"

I contorted my face into an expression of commiseration. "Yeah, I've probably got that talk waiting for me at home right now."

He laughed. "Didn't we already have this talk with them when we were kids?"

"No, that was different, I'm pretty sure. Then, they were explaining what's what and what goes where and why. This is…" I trailed off, unsure how to finish the statement.

"Why we should wait? And how to be responsible if we don't?"

"Exactly." I was almost absurdly relieved that we'd gotten through that discussion without having to say anything overtly embarrassing.

Again, not ready. So not ready.

But then I felt his hands sliding onto my back to pull me into an embrace, and suddenly the idea of more with him didn't seem so absurd.

More…eventually.

Chapter 2: Lucky I'm in Love
January

KYLE AND I HAD SETTLED INTO A COMFORTABLE but exciting relationship. In a very significant way, not much had changed between us. We were the same as we'd always been—we just held hands at school and kissed in the hallways, in his car, on the couch in front of the TV. Our parents did indeed have "the talk" with both of us about being safe, which was beyond mortifying. They didn't even give me a chance to tell them we hadn't even gone past kissing, or that sex wasn't on our horizon as yet.

At least, it wasn't on mine. Kyle seemed to be taking his cues from me, and I was content to let things stay where they were. I liked kissing Kyle. I liked making out with him on the couch. It was maybe a little like how I hadn't wanted to push our relationship from friendship into dating, simply because I hadn't wanted to change something I enjoyed.

In reality, deep down, I was scared. I might have psyched myself out a bit with all the shows and movies I'd watched with Becca and Jill that had sex in them. I was afraid the reality wouldn't live up to my expectations. I mean, I knew in my head, logically, that TV and movies don't portray things with any degree of accuracy to reality. Even the way characters kissed on screen wasn't like kissing in real life. I couldn't explain the difference, even to myself.

I couldn't say any of this to Kyle, though. I wasn't sure he'd understand, and I knew it would sound silly. It sounded silly even to me. But I just couldn't shake the fears. I knew the facts, sure. I knew a girl's first time wasn't always that awesome, and that it hurt. I had plenty of friends at school who'd already had sex and had gotten the details from them. Becca, for example. Setting her up with Jason turned out to be exactly what I'd hoped. They'd been going steady ever since, and Becca had come over late one night, flushed and excited and glowing and fighting tears.

I sat with her on my bed and clicked the volume up on my TV so the sounds of *Teen Mom* would drown out our conversation. I waited, fiddling with the draw-strings of my pajama pants, knowing Becca would tell me what was on her mind once she'd gathered the right words. Becca was like that: She never spoke until she'd thought through what she was going to say. She'd struggled with stuttering as a child, and as a result of the speech therapy, she'd learned to plan out every word, every sentence before she spoke. It had a way of making her sound as if she was reading a script sometimes, which not everyone understood about her.

I did, though, because I'd known her since before she went through ST. I'd learned to listen past the stut-tering to the words she meant to say, and learned not to rush her. Even after ST, you couldn't rush Becca. She'd say what she meant to say when she was ready, and not before.

"I s-slept with Jason," she said. And yeah, Becca still stuttered occasionally in moments of extreme emotion.

I jerked my head up, hair bouncing across my shock-wide eyes. Becca was half-smiling, tight black curls obscuring part of her face. I could see her blush-ing, which was tricky since she was half-Italian and half-Lebanese, and thus had dark, dusky skin and didn't often flush.

"You *what*? For real? When? Where? What was it like?"

Becca twisted a curl around her finger and tugged on the springy lock of hair, a sign she was agitated. "It was everything we'd ever heard, Nell. Amazing, awkward, intense, and kind of painful at first. I mean, just like a pinch, not really bad or anything, and after it's— it's pretty incredible. Jason was very careful and very gentle. It was his first time, too. He was very sweet. It didn't last long, though. Not like in *True Blood*, that's for sure. It was good, though."

"Did you bleed?" I asked.

She nodded. "Yeah, a little. We told our parents we were going to Great Lakes Crossing to shop, but we actually went to a hotel. It wasn't like I gushed or anything." She grinned at me. "The second time was even better, and less awkward."

I frowned. "What's awkward about it?"

"Remember when you kissed for the first time? I mean, *really* kissed. Like, made out. Remember how it was completely natural, like you knew what you were doing somehow, but you still had to sort of figure out how to do it right? Where your hands went, and all that? Well, it's kind of like that." She looked out the window at the oak tree branches swaying in the winter wind, and I could tell her mind was back in that hotel room with Jason.

I sat with her in silence, watching Jenelle argue with her mom on the TV. "Do you feel different?" I asked, eventually.

She nodded. "Yes. A lot. Like, it's hard to explain how you see everything differently. Physically I don't feel much different. A little sore down there, but that's it. Inside my head, I feel older. Wiser. But that's not it really, though. I don't know. This part is the hardest to explain. I guess it's like I finally understand what the big deal is."

"Do you feel like you were ready?"

She didn't answer right away. "I guess. I don't know. I mean, I wanted to. I really did. We talked about it for weeks, planned out when and where. We went to dinner first, and it was romantic. But I was scared. Jason was, too, but I think not as much as I was."

I met her eyes and saw the hesitation. "Did he pressure you, Becca?"

She looked away, then back to me. "A little? I wouldn't have done it if I didn't want to. I just might have waited a bit longer, if it was only up to me."

I wasn't sure how to respond to that. "You were… safe, right?"

She nodded vigorously. "My cousin Maria is twenty-three, and she took me to get birth control from a clinic. And we used a-a—you know. Protection."

"Could your cousin take me, too?"

Becca met my eyes. "I can ask her, if you're sure. But wait until you're sure you're ready."

She took a couple deep breaths, and then her shoulders shook and I pulled her into a hug. "Are you okay?"

She shrugged, shook her head, but said, "Yeah, I guess. I'm overwhelmed. I mean, I can't believe I did that." She pulled away and met my eyes. "I'm not a virgin anymore, Nell. I'm a woman now." She laughed, the sound almost a sob.

"You weren't ready, were you?" I whispered.

She collapsed onto me. "N-no. But I love him, Nell. I do." She took a long shuddering breath, and then composed herself, sitting back and wiping her face. "I love him, and I didn't want to disappoint him. And-and I knew we couldn't keep skirting the line like we had been, you know?"

"What do you mean?"

"Oh, come on, Nell. You know what I'm talking about. You make out, and it gets more and more intense. And eventually, you just know where it's going, and you have to keep stopping yourselves before it goes there accidentally. Like I said, I really truly did want to. Please don't think Jason was putting all this pressure on me. It wasn't that, and it wasn't that I didn't want to, because I did. I just…I don't know how to explain it."

"I think I understand," I said. "Making out with Kyle is starting to reach that point of having to stop ourselves before we get carried away."

She took my hands in hers. "Well, just do what we did. Talk about it. If it's going to happen anyway, we figured it would be best to plan it, make sure it happens on our terms, you know?"

I nodded, but I had to push away the dizzying storm of thoughts rushing through my head from the conversation. Becca hung out for a while longer, finished *Teen Mom*, which suddenly took on a whole new level of meaning, and then went home.

It took me a long time to fall asleep after Becca left. All I could think of was how I'd had to push myself away from Kyle that evening, how I'd felt like I was drowning in him, losing myself in his kisses. How easy it would be to just let go and let myself be swept away.

I didn't want to have any doubts, though. I didn't want to show up at Becca's house afterward and cry because I hadn't been a hundred-percent ready to have sex with Kyle.

A voice whispered deep in my head, though, and asked me if I'd ever be completely ready, if it was even possible to be a hundred-percent ready for something like that.

Two weeks later, late on Friday night, I was sitting in the passenger seat of Kyle's Camaro as we carved through a thick blanket of drifting snow. Our favorite song, *our* song, was playing on the radio: Jason Mraz's "Lucky," and I sang along. Kyle was frowning in concentration, the brights on and still barely able to pierce the pall of falling white. He was going barely thirty on a dirt road near our houses which I knew he knew like the back of his hand.

"This snow is effing crazy," Kyle said. "I can't see ten feet in front of me, and my back tires keep slipping."

"Maybe we should pull over and see if it lets up a little," I suggested.

"No, I'll be fine. We're not far from home anyway. I'll just take it slow."

I rolled my eyes, having known even as I suggested it that he wouldn't pull over and wait. We rounded a curve, and Kyle let out a curse as the back tires fishtailed. I peered through the snow ahead of us and saw the reason for Kyle's panic: a huge doe standing in the middle of the road, eyes gleaming blue-green-silver in the headlights, stock still and frozen and getting larger by the second. He cursed again and downshifted, trying to get the car under control, but the Camaro only fishtailed worse before twisting into a flat spin.

"Move, goddamn it, you stupid deer!" Kyle shouted as we spun closer to the animal.

Kyle knew how to drive in the snow, however, and he pumped the brakes, turned into the spin, and touched the gas. The Camaro went through a third complete three-sixty, but it was slowing on the dirt, gravel, and snow mixture. The front quarter of the car thudded into the deer, and the car shook violently on the impact. I screamed and braced my hands on the dashboard but was unable to look away as the deer was knocked backward, stumbling and falling to its side in the snow. Kyle was able to get the car to a stop, the lights bathing the motionless deer in the middle of the road, snow like a curtain of white all around us. We were both panting, Kyle's hands clenching the wheel in a white-knuckle grip.

I sucked in a deep breath and let it out, glancing at Kyle. He met my eyes, and we both cracked up in semi-hysterical laughter. I lunged over the gearshift and wrapped my arms around his neck, trembling now that it was over, and the rush of adrenaline hit me. The seatbelt was cutting into my chest, so I clicked it free and held tighter to Kyle. He shoved the shifter into Park and then pulled me closer. I clumsily clambered across the console so I was straddling him, clinging to his neck. He took my face in his hands and pulled me into a deep, heated kiss.

I lost myself in him then, gave myself over completely. Adrenaline was coursing through me, powering me with lightning-hot energy. I clenched my fists in the hair at the back of his head, then clawed my hands across his shoulders. My fingers caught the neck of his shirt, and my palm slipped under the cotton to stutter over bare flesh. I gasped at the heat of his skin, at the electricity zinging through my body at the feel of his skin.

And then he touched me. Oh, god. His fingers curled under my coat and under my shirt and palmed the hot flesh of my back. I arched into his touch, felt his tongue dart out to taste mine, and I felt dizzy, subsumed, drowning wonderfully. I brought my hands around, feeling the ridges of his abs and the slabs of muscle on his chest. He mimicked my motion, sliding his hands around to trace my belly with his fingers, and then our kiss broke, leaving our lips touching, eyes open and sparking intensity between us. I held my breath as he brought his palms upward, bit my lip and drew a deeper breath as his hands cupped the lace of my bra.

I felt my nipples harden under his touch, even through the bra, not looking away from him, giving him tacit permission to keep touching me. I shifted backward so my weight was on his knees and my back against the steering wheel. He hesitated with his hands cupping both breasts, and I could see him thinking, wanting to push the moment. He wanted to touch bare skin. I wanted to let him. I liked his hands on my flesh, liked the lightning thrill of his hands on my skin.

I reached up and under my shirt, brushed the strap of my bra off one shoulder, then the other. Kyle curled his fingers under the edge of the cup, tugged it down and lifted my breast free. My shirt was still hanging between us, my coat unzipped and dangling open. The heater was still blasting, overheating both of us. I fumbled with one hand and cut the heater off, then returned my gaze to Kyle. He was watching me with a hooded gaze, warring with himself, his desire fighting reason.

I felt the same war. I wanted this with him. Here and now, I wanted him. Nothing else mattered. A voice in the back of my head reminded me of my conversation with Becca a couple weeks before. I pushed the voice aside. Kyle's hands were roaming my belly, my sides, and returning to my breasts. He had both of them free of the cups now, and was exploring my breasts with his palms and fingers.

I shrugged out of my coat, and then, before I could second-guess myself, I pulled my shirt over my head. Kyle sucked in a breath, a giddy smile curving his lips.

"God, you're so hot," he breathed, taking in my pale skin and the dark circles of my areolae and the pink buttons of my nipples.

I bit my lip as he cupped one breast, rubbing the nipple in circles with his thumb, squeezed my eyes shut in a rush of nerves, feeling suddenly exposed, shame fighting with desire. I wanted this. I liked this. It was okay, right? This was Kyle, my boyfriend and best friend, and I loved him.

The last thought came a shock, drawing a gasp from me. *I love him?* Did I? My heart swelled and ached every time I was near him, and the thought of not being with him scared me. That was love, right? I wanted to be with him all the time, every moment.

"I wish I could see all of you right now," he said, caressing my breast.

A bolt of need shot through me. I wanted him to see all of me. But here, now? Like this? I opened my mouth to speak, but he beat me to it.

"Not here, though," he said, squeezing his eyes shut and gritting his teeth. "I want you, Nell. I'm not gonna lie."

He withdrew his hands from my skin, and I nearly whimpered at the loss of his touch. I stuffed myself back in my bra but didn't put on my shirt. Kyle's eyes were bright and intense.

"I want you, too," I said.

"But I want it to be right. I want it to be special." He seemed to be struggling with himself.

I felt my heart squeeze at his words and leaned forward to kiss him, taking his face in my hands. "And that's why I love you," I whispered, not thinking.

He froze, his eyes wide, searching mine. "What?"

I bit my lip, worried it was too soon. "I—" My eyes slid closed as I fought for the right words. I decided to own it. "I said, that's why I love you. I do. I love you, Kyle."

His hands slipped around to skate up and down my back before coming to rest on my hips in a familiar, sensual, incredible touch. I suddenly loved his hands there, wanted them there forever. His hands on my hips above the waist of my low-rise jeans felt perfect.

"I'm not gonna say it yet," he said, then frowned. "I don't want you to think I'm just saying it back because you did. But I do."

The thought had crossed my mind. "You do?"

He shook his head, thumbs rubbing in circles on my hipbones. "Yep."

I smiled and leaned in for another kiss. "Good. You should love me."

He chuckled into my lips. "Oh, I do." His hands roamed up my sides, and I arched my back out to allow him access to my breasts. "Especially these. I really like these."

It was my turn to laugh. "Oh, really? Especially those? Just those? You only love me for my boobs?"

"Hmmm." He pretended to consider, then slid his hands around to my back, hesitated, then descended to cup my backside. "And this. I like this, too."

I slid my palms up under his shirt and pinched his nipples, eliciting a squawk from him. "Try again, buster."

He laughed and pulled me into a hug, whispering into my hair. "I'm teasing, Nell. I love you for you. For who you are."

I turned my face up to kiss his jaw. "I know. I was teasing, too."

With the heater off, cold had sneaked into the car, and I felt goosebumps cover my skin. Kyle felt it, too, and handed me my shirt, cranking the heat back up. I slid off his lap and put my shirt on.

"I wonder if the deer is dead," Kyle said.

I peered over the hood at the shape in the still-falling snow. "It's not moving." I glanced at him as I zipped my coat. "Should we check?"

"I'll look," he said. "Stay here."

I snorted. "No way! I wanna see, too."

He shook his head, huffing a laugh. We both got out, stepping softly through the powdery snow. Flakes settled on my nose and in my hair, covering me almost instantly in a cold dusting of white. I wrapped my arms around my middle and leaned into Kyle's side. He stopped a few feet away from the deer, put a hand on my shoulder to keep me in place, then moved forward again. A tense silence stretched between us, the engine rumbling behind us, headlights bathing us in a swath of brightness that pierced the otherwise dark winter night.

I watched as Kyle carefully approached the deer. He extended a toe to touch the animal's side, nudging gently. Nothing. I let out a breath. Kyle moved forward a bit more, crouched, extended a hand to touch the doe's side.

He turned back to me, surprised. "She's still alive. Still breathing."

"What do we do?" I asked. "We can't just leave her here."

He held his hands out in an "I don't know" gesture. "She might just be unconscious, or if she's hurt somehow…I don't know, Nell."

At that moment, the deer's hoof twitched, and then her flank shuddered and she huffed out a breath. Kyle scrambled backward, cursing in shock as the doe flailed wildly, gathered her feet under her, and trotted a few steps away, stopping to regard us with doleful eyes and swiveling ears. Kyle was on his butt in the snow, watching the deer as she gazed at us for a long moment, then bounded off across the road.

"Shit!" Kyle said, standing up and brushing himself off. "That honestly scared the crap out of me. I think I might've peed a little."

I laughed so hard I had to clutch his arm to stay upright.

We drove home the rest of the way without incident, but the memory of the moment we'd shared in the car was foremost in our minds. We didn't kiss for as long as we normally did before I got out at my driveway. I knew the power of getting carried away now, and out of the heat of the moment, I knew I still wasn't ready. I didn't think Kyle was, either.

Chapter 3: Going to the Hotel
Valentine's Day

I WAS A LITTLE JITTERY DURING SCHOOL, absentminded, wondering what Kyle had planned for us. I knew he knew it was Valentine's Day, and I knew he had something planned, as he'd hinted at something special. We'd been careful the last couple of weeks, keeping our kisses calm and under control. We both knew, in an unspoken way, that if we let ourselves get carried away, it would be too easy to simply not stop.

We had to talk about it at some point. I knew we had to. He knew we had to. But we kept avoiding it. Which was weird in a way, because we were both horny, hormonal teenagers. I knew he wanted it, and I did, too. But we were both scared, I think, because we knew that would be another line crossed, a more significant line.

Just in case, though, I'd gone with Becca's cousin to get birth control, and I'd been taking it for about a week. I hadn't told Kyle, though. Another thing I figured I probably should do, but couldn't ever seem to find the right time for.

Sixth period finally ended, and I met Kyle at his car. He grinned at me as he opened my car door and closed it behind me.

"Are you gonna tell me what we're doing tonight?" I asked.

He wrinkled his brow, as if confused. "Tonight? What's tonight?"

I stared at him, trying to decide if he was joking, or if I had misinterpreted his hints. "You're kidding, right?"

At the warning tone in my voice, he burst into laughter. "Yes, Nell, I'm kidding. No, I'm not gonna tell you. Both of our parents know we're going to be out late, though. I've already cleared everything with them. Our temporary curfew for tonight is two a.m."

I cut my eyes at him. "Two? Planning on keeping me out that late, huh, Kyle?"

He blushed. "Maybe."

I took a deep breath, knowing I had to broach the subject. I didn't think he would. "About tonight. Are we…I mean…if we're staying out late, does that mean you're planning on us—" I couldn't get the words out.

Kyle fiddled with the gearshift, chewing on his lower lip. Finally he glanced at me as we pulled to a stop at a red light. "Look, I know what you're getting at, and…I've made arrangements. You know, in case that's what we want. But we don't have to. I want it to be right."

"You've made arrangements? What does that mean?"

He blushed again, redder than ever. "We have a room at the Red Roof Inn. It's just down the road from where we're having dinner."

I tried to joke. "Getting a bit presumptuous, are we, Mr. Calloway?"

Kyle grinned at me, but we both knew the joke had fallen flat. "Just…in case."

A thought struck me, and I blurted it out before I had a chance to over-think it. "Kyle? Have you thought that maybe we're not ready if we can't even talk about it without getting uncomfortable?"

He laughed, a nervous sound. "Yeah, that thought has crossed my mind."

"Are we doing this because it's what all our friends are doing?"

He glanced at me in irritation. "No! I mean, Jason told me about him and Becca, and I know Aaron and

Kyla have done it, too, but no. No. And we're not doing anything, necessarily. I just wanted to have the option available."

I laughed, more at myself than anything else. "I don't know if I'm touched that you thought ahead, or weirded out that you assumed we would."

"I didn't assume anything, Nell." Kyle sounded almost angry. "I just—you know what, yeah. I did assume. I mean, I really want to be with you, Nell. I know we're young, but I love you. I think we're ready."

I stared at him: he'd said the words. "We're sixteen, Kyle." I quirked an eyebrow at him. "And aren't you supposed to wait until a romantic moment during dinner to tell me you love me? The middle of an argument doesn't seem like the best time for it, you know?"

"Is this an argument?"

I shrugged. "Kind of? I don't know. I don't want it to be."

"Me, neither. And I guess you're right, but it's out there now. I do love you. I've been wanting to say it to you for weeks now, but I've been too chicken. I was planning on telling you tonight. I had the whole thing scripted. Like, actually written out." He dug into his pants pocket and pulled out a folded piece of lined notebook paper, edges ragged with ripped-out spiral-bound tags.

I know we're young, it read. And I know most people would say we're just kids, or too young to know what love is. But screw that. I've known you my whole entire life. We have shared everything together. Every important thing in our lives has happened together. We learned to ride bikes together and we learned to swim together and we learned to drive cars together. We failed 8th grade algebra together. (Remember how nasty Mr. Jenkins was? How many times were we sent to the office that semester?). And now we're learning how to fall in love together. I don't care what any one else says. I love you. I'll always love you, no matter what happens with us in the future. I love you now and forever.

Your loving boyfriend,
Kyle

I read the note through several times. I wasn't aware that I was crying until something plopped onto the crinkled, much-folded page, spreading a wet blue stain over the ink. This changed everything.

"I love you, too, Kyle." I laughed, even as I sniffled. "This note is so sweet. So perfect. Thank you."

He shrugged. "It's true. I know this wasn't maybe the most romantic way for me to tell you I love you, but—"

"It's perfect, Kyle." I refolded the note and tucked it into my wallet in my purse.

That note would become my greatest comfort, and the reminder of my deepest heartache.

The restaurant Kyle had chosen was insanely busy. Even with reservations, we waited almost an hour for our table to be ready. There were dozens of couples ranging from our age to old married couples. We took our time, sharing a salad, soup, and an entrée, as well as a huge piece of cheesecake for dessert.

We were oddly relaxed, now that the declaration of love was out of the way. We chatted easily about everything from teachers at school to gossip regarding who was sleeping with whom and who wasn't. Eventually Kyle paid the tab, and we went back to his car. Kyle pulled out of the restaurant parking lot and wound his way slowly around town. He was killing time, I knew, giving us a chance to talk before we broached the issue of going to the hotel or not.

Kyle circled town on the dirt back roads as we talked, and after about half an hour, he pulled back onto the main road, approaching where I knew the hotel was located. He glanced at me, reached out, and took my hand in his.

"Do you want to go home? There's a couple movies playing at the theater, too, in case you wanted to see a movie." He fidgeted with the steering wheel as we sat at a stoplight, then finally turned to meet my eyes, his gaze serious. "Or we can go to the hotel."

Decision time.

Oh, god. His eyes were liquid brown, mocha sprinkled with cinnamon-red highlights, little specks of topaz and flecks of tan. He was so serious, so sweet. Offering up the idea without pressuring me. I squeezed his hand as we approached the signature red tile roof of the hotel. I swallowed hard.

"Let's go to the hotel," I said.

We were still skirting the issue. Talking about it in code. *Going to the hotel*. Meaning, let's go have sex. I blushed as the blunt thought crossed my mind. But then I looked at Kyle, at his carefully spiked black hair, his strong jawline and high cheekbones and soft lips. His long black eyelashes blinked rapidly, and then he glanced at me, offered me a nervous but brilliant smile, flashing straight white teeth. My nerves receded, just a little bit. My heart continued to pound a million miles a minute, though, and the hammering in my chest only ratcheted up faster as we pulled into parking lot and approached the check-in counter.

The woman behind the counter was older, with graying blonde hair and steel-blue eyes. Knowing eyes. She gave us each a long, hard stare, as if daring us to continue. Her lips pursed in a disapproving frown as she handed Kyle the keycard, and I knew she wanted to say something to us. She didn't, though, and Kyle and I both fought laughter as we boarded the elevator to our third-floor room.

"God, she was intense," Kyle said, snorting in laughter.

"Yeah, she was," I agreed. "I think she knew what we were doing, and she didn't like it one bit."

"Well, no shit she knew," Kyle said. "There's only one reason two sixteen-year-olds would get a hotel room on Valentine's Day without any luggage."

"Think she would tell anyone?" I asked.

"Who would she tell? It's not like we're running away."

I had no answer for that besides a shrug and a nod. We were at our room, 313. Kyle slid the card in, and the light turned green with a click, audible in the silent hallway. He pushed the door open, led me into the darkened room, clutching my hand tightly.

He flipped a switch, bathing the room in too-bright light. He seemed to sense the feeling of the overhead light being too bright and immediately left my side to click on the lamp affixed to the wall next to the queen bed. I turned off the overhead light, and we both sighed in relief.

Kyle sat on the edge of the bed, fidgeting with the end of his tie. I smiled at him. He was so handsome in his black suit, a daring pink tie the only splash of color against his black dress shirt. He unbuttoned his blazer and rubbed his palms on his knees.

I licked my lips, twitching the hem of my sleeve-less coral knee-length dress. Our eyes met and skidded past each other, nerves rushing back in spades now that we were alone in a hotel room.

At my house or his, in his car on the back roads, everywhere we'd ever kissed, there had been the knowledge that someone could find us. The back roads were regularly patrolled by county sheriffs, and at least one of our parents were always home. This was the first time we'd ever been truly alone, in private, with no possibility of being interrupted.

My heart was beating so hard I was sure Kyle could hear it from across the room.

My eyes flicked back to his face, watched his tongue slide across his lower lip, and I mimicked the action, almost unconsciously. That was the break-ing point. Kyle lunged off the bed and was pressed up against me before I could react, one of his large, strong hands cupping my cheek, the other resting on my waist just above my hip. He didn't kiss me immedi-ately, though. He hesitated, his lips an inch from mine, his eyes hot and soft on mine.

"Are you afraid?" he whispered, his breath huffing softly on my lips.

I shrugged, a tiny roll of one shoulder. "Yes, a little."

"We can leave."

I shook my head. "I want to be here with you," I breathed.

I lifted my hands to tangle my fingers in his hair. I pushed my fingers through his hair, gel-spiked locks prickly but soft, then curled my hand around his nape and pulled him into a kiss.

"Let's just start with this," I said, pulling away. "One step at a time."

"That's what I was thinking."

We stood in the middle of the hotel room, kissing, hands grazing faces, pawing at shoulders and backs. We didn't try to push it, initially. I felt his heart pounding in his ribs, my hand on his chest, and the knowledge that he was as nervous as I was gave me courage.

I pulled back from the kiss, met his gaze, then brushed his suit coat from his shoulders. It fell to the ground behind him, and I pulled his tie loose with both hands, slid the silk free, and dropped it on the blazer. He searched my eyes, waiting. I fumbled with the tiny top button, finally got it open with a nervous laugh. Kyle laughed with me, resting his hands on my hips, lower now. Our eyes were locked together as I undid his dress shirt one button at a time, my hands shaking. Finally, the shirt hung open, revealing a stark white wife-beater tank top that hugged his muscular torso.

I took one of his hands in mine, unbuttoned the cuff, then the other, tugged the sleeves down past his wrists so the shirt billowed to the floor at his feet.

He reached behind me for the zipper of my dress, but I stopped him. I wasn't done yet. I was determined to do this right, to do this as I'd imagined. See, I'd pictured this moment over and over in my mind. I would slowly undress him, and then wait, heart in my throat as he unzipped my dress and let it fall away. I never got past that moment in my imagination, though.

He kicked off his shoes and then stood still once more, waiting, smiling hesitantly. I licked my lips, watching his eyes follow my tongue. I put my hands on his waist, hesitated, then pushed up the cotton tank top, baring his torso slowly, one inch at a time. He lifted his arms over his head and we removed the shirt together, leaving him standing shirtless in his suit pants, gloriously beautiful.

Now came the hard part. I drew in a deep breath and reached for his belt. His eyes widened and his fingers tightened on my hips, curling into the fabric of my dress and into the flesh beneath. My hands were trembling like leaves in a long wind as I unbuckled the belt, drew it free, and then reached for the slip-catch of his pants. He held his breath and drew in his belly as I opened the top. His eyes closed briefly as I tugged the tab of his zipper down. His pants fell around his ankles, and he stepped out of them. His tight boxer-briefs were tented in front, and we both blushed and looked away.

He kissed me, pushing my hands to my sides. "My turn," he whispered.

I nodded, and now my heart crashed wildly in my chest. I had a lot less for him to take off. He slid his hands up my bare arms, leaving goosebumps in his wake. I held my breath as he pinched the zipper pull in his fingers, bit my lip as he drew it down agonizingly slowly. A whisper of fingers against flesh, and then my dress was pooling around my feet, leaving me standing before him in my bra and underwear.

He'd seen me in a bikini before, but this was different somehow.

"You're beautiful, Nell." His voice was a husky breath in the silence.

"So are you."

He shook his head, giving me a lopsided grin. His fingers skated over my shoulders, toying with the bra straps. His grin faded as I reached up behind me to unhook the bra. He stopped me, his hands stilling mine.

"Are you sure?" His eyes searched mine, tender and hesitant.

Hesitant. A voice in the back of my head murmured doubts, but I pushed them away.

I nodded. He brought my hands around to rest on his shoulders, and then took the bra hooks in his hands. He fumbled a bit, and his tongue darted out. I stifled a laugh against his shoulder.

"Shut up," he muttered. "It's not like I've ever done this before."

"I know," I said. "It's cute."

He growled under his breath as he freed one hook, then a second, mumbling a curse as the third and final hook defied him. "It's not supposed to be cute," he said, peering over my shoulder to try to see what he was doing. "It's supposed to be hot and erotic and romantic."

I giggled again as he cursed, fighting the last hook and eyelet. Finally it came free, and then my laughter faded, replaced by nerves and desire. I did want this. I was nervous, yes, and afraid a little, yes. But I wanted it. There was no one else I could imagine doing this with but Kyle.

The bra joined our clothes on the floor, and then Kyle stepped back to look at me. I shifted my weight from foot to foot as he scrutinized me. I knew he thought I was beautiful, and I wasn't uncomfortable in my own skin usually, but his blatant perusal of my nearly naked body was difficult to bear gracefully.

I bit my lip as I summoned the courage to do what came next; Kyle's thumbs hooked in the elastic of his boxers, and I mirrored the action.

"Together?" he said.

I nodded, my voice stuck in my throat. He hesitated a beat, then pushed his boxers down to his knees and stepped out of them. I froze, unable to move, paralyzed by the sight of him, completely nude now.

It was his turn to shift in discomfort as I stared at him. He was beautiful. I had no real-life experience to compare it with, but he was big down there. He looked nothing like the images I had burned into my head, thank god. He was proportionate, and his proud, tall member seemed to beckon me.

His voice distracted me. "I thought we were doing that together."

"Sorry," I said. "I was going to, but then I saw you, and—" I couldn't finish.

He lifted his chin, rolled his shoulders, flexed his fingers, summoning his confidence. He took a step toward me, and I forced myself to relax.

"How about you do it for me?" I said, shocked a little by my own daring.

"I like that idea." His hands went for their favorite spot, just on the outward bell of my hips.

I was wearing lacy red underwear to match the bra, and Kyle's hands drifted over the top of my butt, tracing the lace, following the line of the elastic. I forced myself to breathe as he pushed them down to my thighs, forced my eyes open and up to his as he palmed my buttocks.

I wiggled my hips and thighs, and then the scrap of lace was on the floor and we were naked together. My heart was a wild drum in my chest, in my ears. I was trembling from head to toe, fear and excitement and desire. His skin was hot against mine where his hands touched my bare hips, my ribs, his thigh against mine. The tips of my breasts brushed his chest, sending little thrills of lightning through me. His palms arced across my back, then dared downward to my ass, cupping and kneading, a little too hard, but I didn't mind.

My hands moved of their own accord, palming the knots of muscle on his back, following the ridges and ripples of his spine. He sucked in a breath as I touched his backside, marveling at the cool hardness of it. I cupped it as he had mine, then clawed my fingernails lightly over the firm half-globes.

I felt something twitch against my belly as I touched him. I looked down between us to see his erection, the tiny hole at the very tip leaking clear fluid.

Glancing up at him, I saw his eyes widen as my hand delved down between us, and then his breath caught when my fingers touched him.

"God, Nell. You have to let go…it's too soon."

I released him and brushed my palm across his chest, and cupped his nape and drew him down into a kiss. The slow burn of our usual kisses smoldered, then burst into a blaze. I found myself pressed against his body, his hardness against my softness, and the fire burned hotter with the feel of his muscular physique flush against me.

He backed me up against the bed and I crawled backward, feeling the pound of nerves resume as Kyle followed me.

"Are you—" Kyle started.

I interrupted him. "Yes. I'm sure. I'm nervous and scared, but I want it more than I'm scared." I bit my lip, then admitted, "I'm on birth control. I got it a week ago, just in case."

Kyle's eyes widened. "You did? Why didn't you tell me?"

I shrugged. "I don't know. I just…it never felt like the right time. I was embarrassed, I guess."

Kyle slid off the bed and dug his wallet out of his suit coat, withdrew two condoms, and set them on the table beside the bed. "I got those."

"Are *you* sure?" I asked him. He seemed nervous now.

"Yeah, I'm sure. Like you said, I'm a little nervous. I mean, I don't want to hurt you, or do anything wrong."

"You won't do anything wrong. You won't hurt me. Just…we'll go slow, okay?"

He nodded, then ripped open the condom and rolled it over himself.

He knelt over me, his hands on either side of my face, knees between mine, eyes locked on me, searching me.

I pulled him toward me and rested my hands on his back, then leaned up to kiss him. The heat of the kiss erased both of our fears, or eased them at least. He moved into me, slowly.

I felt stretched, then a pinch, sharp and quick. I winced, and Kyle froze. His breathing was ragged already, and I could feel tension in his muscles. I was biting my lip hard now, feeling the pricking pain ease and the wonder of foreign fullness take over. I touched his backside, pulled him against me, encouraging him to move.

It wasn't long before he stilled, groaning.

There were no fireworks, no screaming, no wild sweaty thrashing, but it was still amazing.

Kyle got up, disappeared into the bathroom, and came back. I cradled my head against his chest. Minutes passed in silence. His body felt hard and hot beneath me, and the feeling of being held by him this way, naked skin against naked skin, was almost better than what had gone before.

I felt a tear trickle down my cheek and drip onto Kyle's chest. I wasn't sure where the tear had come from, or what it meant. I blinked, trying to keep back the others that threatened, not wanting Kyle to think I hadn't enjoyed it.

"Are you crying?" Kyle asked.

I nodded, and let the tears spill. "It's...I'm not upset or anything. Just emotional."

"Emotional how?"

I shrugged. "It's hard to explain. I'm not a virgin anymore. We can't go back now. Not that I'd want to take it back, because it was a wonderful experience. But...it's a big deal, you know?"

"Yeah, I know what you mean."

I tilted my head up to look at him. "I love you, Kyle."

"I love you, too."

The second time was incredible. I felt a fire blossom low in my belly, a feeling like I might explode, or implode. I'd brought myself past that point on my own, obviously, but this was different.

I wondered what it would be like to be brought to that point with Kyle.

Chapter 4: A Proposal; A Tree Falls
August, Two Years Later

IF OUR PARENTS KNEW THAT KYLE AND I were having frequent sex, they didn't say or do anything about it. We were careful of when and where we did it, of course. Kyle's mom had started going to a scrapbooking club two or three evenings a week, and his dad was in Washington much of the year, so we spent a lot of time in his room. My mom was home more frequently, as was my dad, but they didn't seem to care how much time I spent with Kyle at his house. Of course, we claimed to be studying, doing homework, or watching movies most of the time. We *did* do those things, just not as much as we led my parents to believe.

We'd both turned eighteen the previous week. Our parents had decided that, instead of giving us an extravagant party, they'd let us go to Kyle's family's cabin on the lake up north for the weekend. We'd been petitioning for this all summer, and they'd hesitated, telling us they'd think about it. We'd almost given up on the idea when our parents called a meeting with us.

"You guys are eighteen now, and legally adults," Kyle's dad said by way of introduction. "You two have been dating for what, two years now? We know what this trip of yours means, and we get it. We were young once, too."

Everyone shifted awkwardly at the implication.

"Yes, well." Kyle's dad cleared his throat and continued in his stentorian congressman's voice. "The point is, we've decided to allow you to make this trip together. Now. The hard part. I realize this is tricky and uncomfortable for everyone, but it must be said. You're young adults now, and capable of making your own decisions. We've raised you well, raised you to be smart young people capable of making good decisions. I know we've spoken about this before to each of you, as parents, but I believe it must be said to you both together as a couple."

"Just say it, Dad," Kyle sighed.

"We've spoken of being careful. Of using protection." Kyle and I exchanged glances but kept silent. "I am a public figure, as is your father, Nell. It is imperative that you take this seriously. I *cannot* afford scandal at this point in my career. There's talk of nominating me for the presidential race in two years, and I know I don't need to remind you how important image is in such a situation."

"Dad, we're careful," Kyle said. "I promise. We're protected."

My parents were staring hard at me, so I felt the need to speak up. "I'm on birth control, okay? I have been since we…you know, started. And we use protection. No unplanned pregnancies here, okay? Can we stop talking about this now, *please*?"

"God, that would be great," Kyle muttered.

"How long has this been going on?" my dad asked.

Kyle and I exchanged glances again.

"I don't know if that's important or not, sir," Kyle said.

"Of course it's important," Dad said, his voice gruff and threatening, fixing Kyle with his sternest CEO-glare. "She's my daughter. How long?"

I was glad I wasn't on the receiving end of that look; it was scary as hell.

Kyle lifted his chin and squared his shoulders. "I'm sorry, Mr. Hawthorne, but I really feel like that's between Nell and me." Kyle stood up, and I stood with him, and of course everyone else followed suit. Kyle addressed my father once more. "I haven't discussed my relationship with Nell with any of my friends, and with all due respect, sir, I'm not going to discuss it with you. It's private."

My father nodded and extended his hand to Kyle, and they shook. "Good answer, son. I don't like it, because that means it's probably been going on longer than I care to think about. But I do respect you for keeping your business private. Protecting my baby's reputation and all that."

Kyle nodded. "I love your daughter, sir. I'd never do anything to hurt her, or embarrass her. Or you guys and my parents."

I threaded my fingers through Kyle's, proud of him. My dad could be intimidating. I'd gone with Dad to work a few times recently, as I was planning on majoring in business at Syracuse, and I'd seen him use that same hard glare and gruff voice on his employees. Invariably, the unfortunate person on the receiving end had been quaking in their boots and had fairly tripped over themselves to do exactly as my dad asked. Glancing at Mr. Calloway, I could see he was proud of Kyle, too, for the way he'd handled the situation.

We discussed our plans briefly, and then Kyle and I were dismissed to pack. When we were alone in my room, Kyle slumped back on my bed, scrubbing his face with his hands.

"Holy shit, Nell. Your dad is scary."

I knelt astride him, leaning down to kiss him. "I know he is. I've seen grown-ass men almost piss themselves when Dad does that." I bit his chin lightly. "I'm proud of you, baby. You did good."

He cupped my backside and moved me against him. "Do I get a reward?"

I laughed and moved off him. "When we get up north."

We packed quickly, putting all of our things in one of Kyle's extra football gear bags. It felt worldly and adult to be packing together in one bag, my things mixed with his.

As we packed Kyle's things into the bag, I noticed him dig something out of his sock drawer and shove it into the hip pocket of his jeans. It was small, whatever it was, and I couldn't make out the shape. I met Kyle's eyes inquisitively, but he just shrugged and grinned at me. I didn't push it. I'd never known Kyle to lie to me or keep anything from me, so I wasn't worried.

We got in the car, and Kyle drove while I sorted the junk out of my wallet. I pulled out old receipts, ticket stubs from concerts and movies, half a dozen Starbucks and Caribou gift cards either empty or with a few cents left. I came across the note Kyle had written me over a year and a half ago. I reread it, smiling to myself. It seemed like such a long time ago now. I remembered the girl I was then, and how full of trepidation I'd been. In the year and a few months since, Kyle and I learned about each other, discovered a wonderland of pleasure in each other. He'd learned to bring me to that shivering edge and push me beyond. I'd learned the joyful comfort of lying in his arms afterward, and the drowsy drug-like high of making love in the sleepy afternoon on a summer Sunday in the sun, on a picnic blanket high up on our ridge beneath our tree.

Kyle glanced over at me and grinned when he saw what I was looking at. "Aren't you gonna get rid of that old thing? It's embarrassingly sappy, if I remember right."

I clutched the paper to my chest, a look of horror on my face. "I'll never get rid of it, you callous brute. I love it. It's cute and wonderful, and it makes me smile."

He just shook his head and smiled at me, then turned up The Avett Brothers' "I and Love and You," and we held hands, listening to the song we'd made love to more times than I could count. We looked at each other and then away, sharing mutual memories of the things we'd done to that song.

The cabin was several hours away, and of course I ended up falling asleep, not waking up until Kyle's lips brushed mine and his voice whispered "we're here" in my ear.

Kyle was leaning in my car door, stroking my cheek with the backs of his fingers. I stretched languorously, ending with my arms around Kyle's neck. "I'm too sleepy to walk. Carry me."

Kyle's lips pressed kisses along my neck as I stretched, sending me into a paroxysm of giggles, and then he swept me up into his arms and lifted me effortlessly out of the car and up the three steps onto the cabin porch.

"Keys are in my pocket," he said.

I dug in his pocket, pulling his keys out and sorting through them until he indicated the correct one. I unlocked the door quickly, still in Kyle's arms. He wasn't showing any signs of strain except for tightening in his lips. He carried me over the threshold and in through living room, then stopped at the stairs to the second floor.

"Hold tight, baby," he said. "We're going up."

I kicked and tried to slip out of his arms. "You're crazy. You can't carry me upstairs!"

He let me down, but as soon as my feet hit the stairs, he leaned into me, pressing me back into the stairs. I landed on my butt and kept going, pulling him down to my mouth. I lost myself in his kisses then, and forgot about the step gouging into my back, or the fact that my hair was caught under one shoulder against the next stair. Next thing I knew, I was in his arms again and we were moving up the stairs. I heard the strain in his breathing, but he carried me up into the master bedroom and laid me on the bed. He crawled on with me, pushing my shirt over my head, his palms stuttering on my ribs, palming my breasts. I arched into his touch and fumbled with the button of his jeans.

We christened the hell out of that bed.

As we lay in the afterglow, Kyle's fingers tracing patterns on the expanse of flesh between my breasts, he turned to meet my gaze, a serious look in his eyes. "Have you decided on college?"

We'd been discussing it on and off for a while now. We'd both taken the SAT and ACT, and had sent applications off to a dozen colleges and universities each. We'd talked about where we wanted to go, what we wanted to do. What we hadn't done was talk about whether we were going to go to the same place. Our conversations on the subject had a kind of unstated assumption that we'd stay together and choose colleges based on somewhere we'd both go.

I shrugged, not liking the topic. "I was thinking Syracuse. Maybe Boston College. Somewhere on the East Coast, I think. I want to major in business."

He didn't answer for a few moments, which I took to mean he didn't like my answer. "I got accepted to Stanford. They offered me a huge scholarship."

"Football?"

"Yeah."

That much was obvious. His grades were good, but not scholarship good. He'd been approached by several different universities over the last few months. He expected more as our senior year wound down, though.

"Stanford is in California." My voice was unattractively flat.

"And Syracuse is in New York." His hand stilled on my skin. "I did get an offer from Penn State."

I nodded. "I guess the question is, are we making these decisions together? I mean…what if you decide Stanford is the best place for you, and I really want to go Syracuse?"

"I don't know," Kyle said, not quite sighing. "That's what I've been wondering. The offer Stanford has on the table is *really* enticing. Penn State is pretty good, but Stanford is…Stanford." He shrugged, as if to say there simply wasn't any comparison.

Long minutes passed. I wasn't sure what to say, how to get us past this. Eventually I sat up. "I don't want to talk about this anymore. I'm hungry."

Kyle sighed, as if the relief of leaving the discussion aside was a weight off his shoulders. We fired up the grill and had a lovely domestic moment grilling burgers and corn on the cob together. There was an unopened case of Budweiser cans in the pantry left over from a party held here over the summer, and we drank beer together. Neither of us were hard partiers. We would go to our friend's get-togethers and we'd have a drink or two, but we weren't the type to get obliterated. I'd only been drunk once, and that had been with Kyle over this past summer. We'd convinced Becca's cousin Maria to buy us a fifth of Jack, and we'd taken it to the dock while our parents attended some political soirée.

Being drunk had been fun up until the shots started catching up to me. I ended up puking and passing out on the dock. Kyle carried me to bed and watched me until he was sure I wasn't going to choke on my own vomit. After that, I decided getting hammered wasn't my thing. I had friends who seemed to live for the weekend parties, for getting drunk and hooking up.

I had Kyle, and that was enough.

After dinner, we built a fire in the fire pit out by the lake and went skinny dipping once the sun went down, laughing and chasing each other around the inlet. There was an island about a quarter mile out into the bay, a tiny bump of land with some scrub pines and bushes and a thin beach. Kyle and I had been swimming out to that island together since we were kids. This time, we swam out and made love on the sand, lay naked in the warm late summer air, watching the stars twinkle and shimmer, talking about nothing and everything.

Talking about everything, but avoiding the heavy topic of the future and colleges. It was heavy on my heart, because something told me we wouldn't come to an easy or pleasant decision. Kyle was set on Stanford. I could see it in his eyes, hear it in his voice. I really wanted to be on the East Coast, close to the financial center of New York City. The plan was to major in business finance and get a killer internship in New York, then get a job with Dad's company, but legitimately, working my way up with no strings pulled, no favoritism showed.

Dad really wanted to just bring me into the boardroom as soon as I had my degree, but I was determined to do it on my own. Kyle was having a similar problem with his parents. His dad wanted Kyle to follow in his footsteps and intern in Washington, pull some strings to get him a lush political gig. Kyle wanted to stay in the athletic world. Play college ball, try to go pro, and, barring that, get into coaching. It was a sore spot, but Kyle was like me, and determined to do things his own way.

I knew I wasn't willing to ask Kyle to compromise on his school of choice for me. I could get the degree I wanted at a lot of different colleges, and I knew between Mr. Calloway and my dad, I could get strings pulled to get me into any college I wanted.

I loved Kyle enough to shift my plan. Kyle was locked into accepting the best offers. He had a wealth of them choose from, so I wasn't worried about that as much.

I sat by the fire, wrapped in a towel, watching Kyle idly strum a guitar, staring into the middle distance, knowing I had to decide. Did I follow Kyle for love? Or did I follow my plan for the future?

Little did I know that choice would soon be stripped away from me.

Saturday was a lazy day spent on the pontoon boat, drinking beer and eating sandwiches, making love and listening to music on my iPod. We avoided heavy conversation and just enjoyed each other, enjoyed the rippling blue of the lake, the pale expanse of the clear sky, and the lack of expectations of each other.

Back home, we were both chased by the image of our parents. My dad was considering running for the mayorship of our town. Kyle especially had to be careful of what he did now. With his father angling for a presidential nomination, every facet of the Calloway family was examined on a regular basis by the media. Kyle and I had to be careful not to be caught in any compromising positions, not to do or say anything to cast doubt on Mr. Calloway.

Here, up north, no such expectations existed. It was just us.

Sunday was stormy, so we spent the day inside watching movies. We went for an early dinner to the only nice restaurant within an hour's drive, a fairly swank Italian place where the Calloways were well known. Kyle was greeted by name and given a table immediately, despite the crowd of waiting vacationers.

It was another nice but slightly awkward dinner, with the coming conversation weighing on us both. I knew I had to send my official acceptance to Syracuse soon, or have our dads start pulling strings to get me into Stanford with Kyle. Time was running out. We'd put this off for too long, to the chagrin of both of our parents, and now the time had come. It was August, and the universities were starting their academic year in September.

I opened my mouth to bring it up several times, but Kyle always seemed to head me off, as if he knew what I was about to say. We drove home in a tense silence. Kyle had his hand in the pocket of his Dockers while he drove, and he kept glancing at me, a deep, inscrutable expression on his face. We pulled up to the cabin and sat for a moment, watching fat drops of rain splatter on the windshield, listening to the wind howling outside. The huge pine trees surrounding the cabin were bending and swaying in the wind, which was approaching gale force, it seemed to me. I watched with my heart hammering as one tree in particular seemed to be bending almost double in the gusts, and I found myself tensing for the moment when it would snap and fall. With the direction the wind was blowing, if the tree did break, it would hit the house and the car we sat in.

Kyle looked at me, and I noticed beads of sweat on his face, despite the coolness in the car. His hand gripped the steering wheel and smoothed the leather across the top, a gesture he only made when nervous or upset. I waited, knowing he'd speak up when he was ready.

He glanced at me again, took a deep breath, and withdrew his hand from his pocket. My heart pounded in my chest as realization dawned on me. *Oh, god. Oh, god*. He was about to propose. No, no. I wasn't ready for that.

He opened his hand, and, sure enough, there was a black box, *Kay Jewelers* written in gold thread across the top. I bit my lip and tried not to hyperventilate.

"Kyle? I—"

"Nell, I love you." His hand trembled slightly as he opened the box, revealing a half-carat princess-cut diamond ring, simple and beautiful. And terrifying. "I don't want to spend a moment without you. I don't care about college or football or anything. All I care about is you. We can figure out the future together."

He withdrew the ring and held it out to me between thumb and forefinger. Rain blatted on the windshield, and the wind howled like a banshee, gusting so hard the car rocked on its suspension. *Why now?* I wondered. *Why here?* In a car, in a rainstorm? Not in the restaurant during dinner? Not out at the fire pit where we had so many memories? My heart juddered in my chest and my eyes stung, sight wavering and blurring. My lip hurt, and I tasted the tang of blood. I forced myself to release my lip before I bit straight through it.

"Nell? Will you marry me?" Kyle's voice broke at the end.

"Ohmigod, Kyle." I choked out the words, forced the rest out. "I love you, I do. But...now? I don't—I don't know. I can't…we're barely eighteen. I love you, and I was going to tell you I'd follow you to Stanford. Dad can get me in last minute…" I shook my head and scrunched my eyes closed against the confused hurt in Kyle's eyes.

"Wait…" He shook his head, withdrawing the ring slightly. "Are you saying no?"

"It's too soon, Kyle. It's not that I don't love you, it's just…" Doubts assailed me.

I'd never dated anyone else. It wasn't that I wanted to, necessarily. But I felt so young sometimes. I'd never been away from my parents for more than a week. I'd never left home. This was the first time I'd gone somewhere without them. I wanted to experience life. I wanted to grow up a bit. I wasn't ready to be married.

But I couldn't get any of this out of my mouth. All I could do was shake my head as tears fell, mimicking the rain. I pushed the car door open and stumbled out, ignoring Kyle's shouts to wait. I was drenched to the skin in moments, but I didn't care.

I heard Kyle behind me, chasing me. I wasn't running from him, but from the situation. I stopped, high heels slipping and digging into the wet gravel.

"I don't understand, Nell." His voice was thick and rough with emotion, but the rain on his face obscured his features, so I couldn't tell if he was crying or not. "I thought…I thought this was the next step for us."

"It is, just not yet." I wiped my face and took a step toward him. "I love you. I really do. I love you with all my heart. But I'm not ready to get engaged. *We're* not ready for that. We're just kids still. We just graduated high school a few months ago."

"I know we're young, but…you're what I want. All I want. We could live in married housing, and…be together. Experience everything together."

"We can still do that. We could get an apartment together. Maybe not right away, but soon." I turned away, frustrated with my inability to express why I wasn't ready. "Kyle…it's just too soon. Can't you see that? I don't want to be apart, either. I'll go to Stanford with you. I'll be with you wherever you go. I *will* marry you, just not yet. Give it a few years. Let's get through college and get careers going. Grow up a bit."

Kyle was the one to turn away this time. He brushed his palm over his wet hair, sending a spray of water flying. "You sound like our parents. You sound like your dad. I asked him first, you know. That's why they let us come up here. He said he wasn't sure we were ready and he thought we needed some time to experience a bit more life, but you were legally an adult now, and if you said yes, he had no problem with us getting engaged."

The rain let up then, but the wind blew harder than ever. The trees around us swayed like stalks of grass. Even over the harsh cry of the wind I could hear the trunks creaking. A streak of lightning lit up the night sky, then another. Thunder crashed overhead, so loud I felt it in my stomach, and then the rain blew over us again, cold and stinging.

"I love you, Kyle." I stepped toward him, reaching for him. "Please don't be mad at me. I just—"

He turned away from me, pinching the bridge of his nose. "I thought—I thought this was what you wanted."

"Let's go inside now, okay? We'll talk about it inside. It's not safe out here." I reached for him again, but he pulled away.

Lightning struck again, closer this time, so close I felt the hair on my arms stand on end and tasted ozone, felt the crackling of energy all around me. The trees creaked and bent, the wind gusting hard enough to buffet the car and send me stumbling sideways.

I shook my head and stalked past Kyle toward the house. "I'm going inside. You can stay out here and be unreasonable, then."

I heard a deafening *crack* then, but it wasn't lightning. It was like a cannon booming, like a firework detonating mere feet away. My stomach churned, fear bolting through me. I froze with my foot on the first step to the porch, looked up, and saw death coming for me.

The tree had snapped. Time slowed as the mammoth pine fell toward me. I heard the roof crunching and giving way, heard siding pop and split, heard bricks disintegrating. I couldn't move. All I could see was the trunk wet and glinting black against the sky, the green needles fluttering in the wind.

Kyle shouted behind me, but his words were lost in the wind, in the haze of terror. I was frozen. I knew I needed to move, but my limbs wouldn't cooperate. All I could do was watch the tree descend. I couldn't even scream.

I felt something hard impact me from behind, and I was thrown to the side. I heard the crash of the tree hitting the ground. My ears rang, and my breath was knocked out of me, leaving me gasping. I was on my side, my arm twisted beneath me. Then pain shot through me, agony like lightning in my arm. It was broken, I thought. I flopped to my back, letting a scream loose as the jarring thud sent another shard of pain through me. I looked down at my arm cradled to my chest, saw blood streaming in the rain, red slicking down my flesh. The forearm was bent at an unnatural angle, a white spike protruding from the elbow. I had to roll over again to vomit at the sight of my ruined arm.

Then awareness struck.

Kyle.

I twisted and scrambled to my knees, arm cradled against my stomach. Another scream resounded, loud even over the wind and thunder. The tree was a fallen giant in the clearing. The house was crushed, the right side obliterated by the tree trunk. Kyle's Camaro was crushed as well, windshield splintered, hood and roof and trunk flattened. The branches were like spikes and splinters piercing the earth, green needles obscuring the ground and the sky and the world beyond the tree.

I saw a shoe without a foot. A black dress shoe. Kyle's shoe, knocked clean off his foot. That image, the black shoe, leather wet from the rain, a smear of mud on the toe, would be burned into my mind forever.

Kyle was beneath the tree trunk, his legs scrabbling for purchase in the mud and the gravel. I screamed again, not hearing myself. I felt the scream in my throat, scraping my vocal chords raw.

I scrambled across the gravel driveway on my hands and knees, agony lancing through me as I unheedingly used my shattered arm to drag myself toward Kyle. I reached his feet, draped myself over the trunk between foot-thick branches broken into jagged spears.

"Kyle? *Kyle?*" I heard the words, his name, drop from my lips, desperate pleas.

I saw his chest move, saw his head twist, looking for me. He was on his stomach, face down. Mud caked his cheek. Blood dripped from his forehead, smeared around his nose and mouth. I pulled myself over the tree with my one arm, struggling against the bite of the bark on my bare knees, feeling sap stick to my calves and thighs. My dress caught on a branch and ripped, baring my flesh to the angry sky. I fell free, landed on my shoulder, felt something snap further in my arm. Pain stole my breath, left me trembling and unable to even scream. My eyes fluttered open, met Kyle's brown gaze. He blinked slowly, then squeezed his eyes shut as a pink stream of blood and rain dripped into his eye. His breath was labored, whistling strangely. Blood trickled from the corner of his mouth.

I twisted my torso, trying to get my weight off my broken arm. Then I saw it. The tree hadn't just fallen on him. A branch had spiked through him. Another scream ripped through me, this time fading into silence as my voice gave out.

I reached out and brushed the rain from his face, the blood from his cheek and chin. "Kyle?" This was a whisper, ragged and barely audible.

"Nell…I love you."

"You're gonna be okay, Kyle. I love you." I forced myself to my feet, put my shoulder to the tree and pushed, pulled. "I'm gonna get you out. Get you to a hospital. You'll be fine....We're gonna go to Stanford together."

The tree shifted, and Kyle groaned in pain. "Stop, Nell. Stop."

"No...no. I have to...have to get you out." I pushed again, slid in the mud, and my face bashed into the bark of the tree.

I slumped to the ground next to Kyle. I felt his hand snake through the mud and latch onto mine.

"You can't, Nell. Just...hold my hand. I love you." His eyes searched my face, as if memorizing my features.

"I love you Kyle. You're gonna be fine. We'll get married...please..." The words tripped out, broken by sobs.

I forced myself to my feet. Ran stumbling to the car, red paint and black racing stripe battered and shattered, reached in through the broken window for my purse. A shard of glass cut a long line of crimson across my arm, but I didn't feel it. I clutched the purse awkwardly against my chest with my hurt arm, dug my phone out from my purse, frantically slid my finger across the screen to unlock it, nearly dropped it as

I punched the green and white phone icon. My purse fell forgotten to the mud.

A calm female voice pierced my shock. "Nine-one-one, what is your emergency?"

"A tree fell...my boyfriend is trapped under it. I think he's hurt bad. I think a branch...please...please come and help him." I didn't recognize my voice, the abject terror and incoherent tone.

"What is your address, miss?"

I spun in place. "I don't—I don't know." I did know the address, but I couldn't summon it. "Nine three four..." I choked on a sob, fell to the ground next to Kyle, gravel biting into my knees and backside.

"What is your address, miss?" The operator repeated herself calmly.

"Nine...three....four...one...Rayburn...Road," Kyle whispered.

I repeated the address to the operator. "Someone will be there as soon as possible, miss. Do you want me to stay on the phone with you?"

I couldn't answer. I dropped the phone, heard her voice repeat the question. I stared absently as rain pebbled and beaded and smeared the screen, the red "End Call" bar, the white icons for "Mute," "Keypad," and everything else turning gray as the operator hung up, or the call disconnected. I reached for the phone again, as if it could help Kyle. I grabbed it, but with the wrong hand. My fingers wouldn't work, and red liquid mixed with rain on the darkened screen, trailing down my forearm and trickling from my fingers.

I turned to Kyle. His eyes were glassy, distant. I took his hand in mine. Fell forward into the mud to lie face to face with him.

"Don't leave me." I barely heard my own voice.

"I…I don't want to," he whispered. "I love you. I love you." Those were the only words he seemed to know now. He repeated them over and over, and I said them back, as if those three words could hold him here on earth, hold him to life.

I heard distant sirens.

Kyle dragged in a ragged breath, squeezed my hand, but it was weak, a distant touch. His eyes fluttered, searched for me.

"I'm right here, Kyle. Help is coming. Don't go. Don't let go." I sobbed as his eyes skittered past me as if he didn't see me.

I pressed my lips to his, tasting blood. His lips were cold. But he was in the rain, so he'd be cold, right? That's all it was. He was just cold. I kissed him again.

"Kyle? Kiss me back. I need you. Wake up." I kissed him a third time, but his lips were cold and still against mine. "Wake up. Wake up. Please. We have to get married. I love you."

I felt hands lift me, pull me away. Heard voices saying something to me, but the words were lost. Someone was screaming. Me? Kyle was still, too still. Only cold, only frozen. Not gone. Not gone. No. *No.* His hand was curled as if holding mine, but I was far away, gliding away, carried by the wind. Blown away by the wind.

I felt nothing. No pain, even when my arm was jostled as I was laid onto a stretcher. I saw Kyle, far away, farther now, heard more voices asking me questions, handling my arm carefully. Pain was like the thunder, distant now. Like the rain, cold and forgotten.

I love you. I wasn't sure if the words were spoken aloud.

I felt a hand trying to pry my fist open. I was clutching something in my uninjured hand. A round middle-aged face hovered in front of me, speaking silent words, mouth moving. My eyelids slid closed, blanketing me in darkness, and then light returned as I opened them again. I drew a breath, let it out. Then again. I wondered idly why I had to breathe anymore. Kyle was gone. So why breathe?

Something cold and hard and clear was placed over my mouth and nose, and I was breathing again anyway.

I looked at my closed fist. What was I holding? I didn't know.

I forced the fingers to fall open, revealing a silver band with a sparkling diamond. I tried to put in on my left hand, where the ring should go. I would tell Kyle when they let me out of the hospital. *I love you, yes, I'll marry you.* But first I have to wear the ring. A thick hand, black hair on the knuckles, took the ring from me and slid it onto my third finger of the right hand, the wrong hand. Something red stained the silver, and I wiped my hand on my lap, on the wet dress. There, the redness was gone.

A kind face, pale blue eyes set deep in a fleshy face. Mouth moving, but no sounds. He held something out to me. A phone. My phone? I pressed the circular button with the square symbol. There was Kyle, so handsome, his face pressed to mine as we kissed. My phone.

I looked from the phone to the man. Confused. The man seemed to want something from me. He pointed at the phone and said something.

My ears popped, and sound returned.

"Miss? Is there anyone you can call?" His voice was deep and throaty.

I stared at him. Call? Who did I have to call? Why?

"Can you hear me?"

"Y-yes. I hear you." My voice was faint, distant, slow.

"What's your name, sweetheart?"

My name? I stared at him again. He had a pimple on his forehead, red and angry and needing to be popped.

"Nell. My name is Nell Hawthorne."

"Can you call your parents, Nell?"

Oh. He wanted me to call my parents. "Why?"

His face twisted, and his eyes shut slowly and then opened, as if summoning courage. "There was an accident. Remember? You're hurt."

I looked down at my arm, which was throbbing distantly. Then to the man again. "Accident?" My mind spun and whirled, hazy and fogged. "Where's Kyle? I need to tell him I love him. I need to tell him I'll marry him."

Then it all came back. The tree falling. Me, unable to move. Kyle, his eyes turning vacant as I watched.

I heard a scream and a sob. The phone fell from my hands, and I heard a voice speaking far away.

Darkness swept over me.

My last thought was that Kyle was dead. Kyle was dead. *He saved me, and now he's dead*. Sobs echoed, echoed, wrenched from a ruined heart.

Chapter 5: Liquid Heartbreak
Two Days Later

I SWEPT THE LAST LOCK OF HAIR BACK and fixed it in place with the bobby pin. I barely recognized myself in the mirror. I was pale, ghost-white with dark rims under my eyes. My eyes looked back at me from the mirror, gray as the wintry sky and just as empty.

"Nell?" My mother's voice came from behind me, soft, hesitant. Her hand closed around my arm. I didn't pull away. "It's time to go, honey."

I blinked hard, blinked back the nothing. I felt nothing. I felt no tears. I was empty inside, because emptiness was better than agony. I nodded and turned on my heel to sweep past my mother, ignoring the bolt of pain when my cast bumped the doorframe. My dad was holding the front door open, eyes watching me carefully, as if I might explode, or crumble.

Either was possible. But it wouldn't happen, because you had to feel for that. And I didn't feel. Nothing. Nothing. Nothing was best.

I descended the steps, clicked across the blacktop driveway to my Dad's boxy Mercedes SUV. I slid into the back seat, drew the buckle across my torso, and waited in the silence. I saw my mother stop in the doorway, facing my father, watched them exchange worried glances at me. After a moment, my dad locked the front door, and they both got into the car. We drove away in silence.

My father's eyes met mine in the rearview mirror. "Do you want some music on?"

I shook my head but couldn't find the voice to speak. He looked away and kept driving. My mother twisted in her seat to look at me, opened her mouth to say something.

"Don't, Rachel," Dad said, touching her arm. "Just leave her be."

I met my dad's eyes in the rearview mirror, tried to express my gratitude silently, with dead eyes.

Rain fell. Slow, thick drops through still, warm air. Nothing like the storm that stole Kyle. Gray, heavy clouds, low in the sky like a broken ceiling. Wet cement, glinting grass and puddles on the sidewalks.

I clutched a crumpled, folded piece of paper in my hand. The note. I had it memorized now. I'd read it and reread it so many times.

The viewing, a small room filled with too many people. I stood next to the casket, refusing to look in. Stood next to a tastefully created collage, pictures of Kyle, of us together. Strangers in the pictures, I thought, seeing happy me, happy, living him.

Words spoken, empty condolences. Hands squeezing mine, lips brushing my cheek. Weeping friends. Cousins. Becca, hugging me. Jason standing in front of me, not speaking, not hugging me, his offered silence the best thing he could have given me.

Then, oh, god…Mr. and Mrs. Calloway, standing in front of me. They'd been here all the while, but I couldn't see them. Couldn't bear to meet their eyes. But now they were here, hands clasped and threaded between them, two sets of brown eyes so much like Kyle's, pinning me, searching me. I'd said little about what happened. There was a storm, a tree fell. Kyle saved me.

Nothing about the proposal, the ring on my finger, the wrong finger. Nothing about the fact that we were arguing. That it should have been me.

That if I had done…*god*, so many things differently, their son would still be alive.

Nothing about his death being my fault.

If I had said yes, he would still be alive. We'd have gone up to the bedroom. Made love. The tree would have crashed through the house, but not near us.

I stared into their eyes and tried to find words.

"I'm so sorry." It was all I could say, and even that was barely audible, shattered words falling like shards from my tongue.

"Oh, Nell…me, too." Mrs. Calloway wrapped me in a hug, bawled onto my shoulder.

I stood stiff, the physical contact too much. I had to suck in air through my nose and let it out through my mouth into her straight black hair, trembling and tense. I couldn't let myself feel. If I felt, I would break.

I don't think she understood that I was begging her forgiveness for killing her son. But those three words were all I could dredge up out of myself. Eventually her husband pulled her away and tucked her into his side while she shuddered.

People came and went, words were spoken. Faces passed in front of me in a blur. I nodded at times, mumbled things. Just so they would know I wasn't catatonic, that I was physically alive.

I wasn't, though. I breathed. My synapses fired, my blood pumped in a circle. But I was dead, dead with Kyle.

Dad slipped to my side, held me in a one-armed hug. "It's time, Nell."

I didn't know what it was time for. I pivoted in his embrace and glanced up at him, brows scrunched.

He saw the question. "To have the service. To close the casket and…bury him."

I nodded. He pulled me to a chair, and I sat down. Mr. Calloway stood with his back to the casket and spoke. I heard his words, but they meant nothing. Words about Kyle, about how wonderful he was, how great he was, how much promise he had, cut short. Cut short. True words, but empty in the face of things. Nothing mattered. Kyle was gone, and words meant nothing.

Mrs. Calloway couldn't say anything. Jason talked about how Kyle was such a great friend, and those words were true, too.

Then it was my turn. Everyone was looking at me. Waiting. I stood up and walked to where everyone else had stood, behind a little podium with a disconnected microphone. I picked at the wood with my fingernails, which were painted a dark plum by my mother.

I knew then that I was changed. The old Nell would have known what to say, would have found polite and well-meant words, would have spoken about how incredible Kyle was, how loving and thoughtful, how we had a future together.

But none of that came out, because I wasn't that Nell anymore.

"I loved Kyle." I stared at the blond wood of the podium, because the eyes of the people in the seats would have pierced my armor of numbness, would have spiked through to the river of magma deep inside me that was my emotions.

"I loved him so much. I still do, but...he's gone. I don't know what else to say." I pulled off the ring from my right hand and held it up. A few people gasped. "He asked me to marry him. I told him we were too young. I told him...I would go to California with him. He was going to go to Stanford and play football. But I said no, not yet...and now he's gone."

I couldn't hold it in anymore, but I had to. I choked the breakdown back, sucked it in and forced it down. I slipped the ring back on my right hand and walked out of the viewing room without looking into the casket. I knew, from when Grandma Calloway died, that the thing in the casket wasn't Kyle. It was a shell, a husk, an empty clay gourd. I didn't want to see that. I wanted to see Kyle in my mind as the strong, gloriously gorgeous Adonis, the way his muscles moved and rippled, the way his hands touched me and the way his sweat mingled with mine.

The problem was, all I could see when I closed my eyes was that one shoe, his eyes hunting for me as the life bled out of him, his hand curling around my fingers and then falling empty and limp as I was carried away.

I left the funeral home, bolting out a back exit and making a beeline across the wet grass for a huge spreading oak that stood behind the building. By the time I was leaning against the rough bark, my black dress was soaked through and sticking to my skin. My hair hung in damp strings past my shoulders. I shuddered, struggling to hold it in. I breathed, choking on my tongue as I tried to literally bite down on sobs.

I turned in place and pressed my forehead to the bark, clenching my teeth and panting, whimpering through my lips. Not crying, not crying. Because I couldn't. I couldn't let myself.

I felt a warmth descend over my shoulders, the soft silk of a suit coat. I pushed away from the tree and turned to see a pair of sapphire eyes gazing at me, stunning, piercing, breathtakingly blue. The face was haunting, familiar, chiseled and achingly beautiful like Kyle's, but more rugged. Older, harder. Rougher. Less perfect, less statuesque. Longish, shaggy black hair, messy and thick and lustrous and raven-black.

Colton. Kyle's brother, older by about five years.

I hadn't seen Colton in a long, long time. He left home when Kyle and I were just kids, and he hadn't been back since. I wasn't even sure where he lived, what he did. I didn't think he got along with Mr. Calloway, but I wasn't sure.

Colton didn't say anything, just settled his suit coat over my shoulders and leaned back against the tree trunk, white button-down soaking through to show his skin, and the dark ink of a tattoo on his arm and shoulder. Something tribal, maybe.

I stared at Colton, and he met my gaze, level and calm but still fraught with unspoken pain. He understood my need for silence.

I felt something hard in the inside pocket, stuck my hand in, and withdrew a pack of Marlboros and a Zippo. Colton lifted an eyebrow, taking them from me. He flipped open the top and withdrew a cigarette, flicked the Zippo and lit it. I watched, because watching kept the magma at bay.

He put the filter between his lips and sucked, and I felt something odd happen inside me as his cheeks hollowed. A feeling as if I knew him, although I didn't. As if I'd always watched him drag on a smoke and blow it out slowly through pursed lips. As if I'd always looked on in disapproval, but never voiced my thoughts.

"I know, I know. These things'll kill me." His voice was rough and gravelly and deep, but still melodic somehow.

"I didn't say anything." That was the most I'd spoken in over forty-eight hours.

"You don't have to. I can see it in your eyes. You disapprove."

"I guess. Smoking is bad. Maybe it's an inherited dislike." I shrugged. "I've never known anyone who smokes."

"Now you do," Colton said. "I don't smoke much. Socially, usually. Or when I'm stressed."

"This counts as stress, I think."

"The death of my baby brother? Yeah. This is a chain-smoking occasion." He spoke the words casually, almost callously, but I saw the crushing agony in his eyes as he looked away, stared at the glowing orange cherry of his cigarette.

"Can I try?"

He glanced at me, eyebrow lifted, silently asking if I was sure. He held the white tube toward me, the bottom pinched between two thick fingers. He had grease under his fingernails, and the tips of his fingers were callused, the mark of a guitar player.

I took the cigarette and tentatively put it to my lips, held it there for a moment, then sucked in. I tasted harsh air, something like mint, and then I inhaled. My lungs burned and protested, and I blew it out, coughing. Colton laughed, a low chuckle.

I got so dizzy I almost fell over. I put a palm to the tree trunk to balance myself. Colton wrapped a huge hand around my elbow.

"First drag'll make you dizzy. Even now, if it's been a while, I'll get dizzy." He took the cigarette back and drew on it, then blew it out of his nostrils. "Just don't get addicted, okay? I don't need that shit, knowing I got you hooked on smoking. It's a nasty habit. I should quit." He puffed again, putting the lie to his words.

He was slumped back against the tree, hunched over, as if the weight of grief was too much to stand up under. I knew the feeling. I took the cigarette from his fingers, ignoring the strange, unwelcome spark of feeling that shot up my arm when my fingers touched his.

I took a drag, tasted the smoke, blew it out, coughed again, but less this time. I felt the airiness in my head spread. I liked the feeling. I took another, then handed it back. I saw my mother standing in the door I'd left through, watching.

Colton followed my gaze. "Shit. Guess it's time to go."

"Can I ride with you?"

He paused in the act of pushing away from the tree. He stood more than a foot taller than I did, his shoulders like a football player's pads, arms corded thick. He was huge, I realized. Kyle had been lean and toned. Colton was…something else. Obviously powerful. Hard. Primal.

"Ride with me?" He seemed puzzled by the request.

"To the cemetery. They'll…want to talk. Ask me questions. I can't…I just can't."

He took one last drag, then pinched the cherry off with his fingers and stepped on it, stuffed the butt in his pocket. "Sure. Come on."

I followed him to a Ford F-250 with huge tires and diesel exhaust pipes behind the cab. It was splattered with mud and had a lockbox in the bed. He walked next to me, not touching me, just there. I heard my mom's voice in the distance but ignored her. I couldn't handle the questions I knew she'd have.

Colton opened the passenger door, offered me his hand, and lifted me up. Again I felt an awful, powerful lightning bolt of energy zap through me at his touch. Guilt assailed me.

I passed close to him as I stepped up into the cab. He smelled of cigarettes and cologne and something indefinable. I saw him swallow hard and look away, letting go of my hand as soon as possible. He wiped his palm on his pants leg, as if to erase the memory of a thrill from the touch.

He was in the cab next to me a moment later, twisting the key to start the truck with a throaty rumble. The leather seats vibrated under my thighs, not unpleasantly. I slipped out of his coat and set it on the seat between us. As the truck started, music blared from the speakers, male and female voices raised in haunting harmony: "…if I die before I wake…I know my soul the Lord won't take…I'm a dead man walking…I'm a dead man walking…"

Something snapped in my chest, and I had to clench my teeth until my jaw hurt to keep from crumbling. "What—who is this?" I asked, the words raw and rasped.

"The Civil Wars. The song is called 'Barton Hollow.'"

"It's amazing."

"You've heard thirty seconds."

I shrugged. "It…speaks to me."

He touched something on the dashboard, and the song started from the beginning. I listened, rapt. The next song grabbed me, too, and Colton drove, unspeaking, letting me listen. The burgeoning pressure in my chest lessened with the power of the music.

All the while, I felt Colton's presence in the truck like a hot spike of awareness. He filled the four-door cab until I felt almost claustrophobic. Almost. Except…his presence was—somehow—a balm on the open wound of my heart.

This fact alone was enough to cause a river of guilt. I shouldn't feel this. Shouldn't feel anything. There should be no balm, no comfort.

I didn't deserve it.

There was an awning set up over the open grave, two rows of chairs. The rain had turned cold. I shivered as I stepped down out of the cab, and Colton was there again, opening the door and extending his hand.

He seemed too rough, too big, too hard around the edges to be such a gentleman. He was a contradiction. Grease under his fingernails. Hand hard and callused, like gritty concrete under my soft palm as I stepped down from the cab.

His eyes skittered over mine, held on me for a brief moment, wavered as if searching, as if memorizing. His adam's apple bobbed as he swallowed. His eyes narrowed and he licked his lips, releasing my hand after holding it for a beat too long.

He sucked in a deep breath, stuck his hand in his pants pocket, and jingled his keys. "Let's do this," he said with a sigh.

I followed him. I didn't want to do this. I wanted to run away. I didn't want to watch the wooden box containing the corpse of my first love lowered into the ground. I nearly turned and ran.

Then Colton stopped, startling blue eyes piercing me. He just nodded, a brief dip of his chin, but it was enough to put one of my feet in front of the other, carrying me to the grave. He knew my thoughts, it seemed. He knew I wanted to run. But he couldn't know that, shouldn't know that. He didn't, couldn't know me. I'd met him twice in my life. He was Colton's older brother.

I felt my mother's eyes on me as I stopped at the dark cherrywood casket. I put my fingers to my lips to keep in the sounds, the emotions. I felt my father's eyes on me. I felt Mr. and Mrs. Calloway's eyes on me. Everyone's eyes on me. I put my hand to the cold wood, since that seemed to be expected of me. I wanted nothing more than to climb into the box with him and quit breathing, find him in whatever came after life.

I stumbled as I turned, high heel catching in the grass. Colton's hand shot out and steadied me, yet again. Electric touch, ignored. He let go immediately, and I sat down. A preacher or minister in a black suit with a black shirt and the little white thing at his collar stood over the grave, intoning Bible verses and rote words of supposed comfort.

I couldn't breathe. I was choking on the bottled-up emotion. I had a flower in my hand somehow, and the casket was being lowered into the awful black chasm. I stood over the hole and tossed in the flower, as expected.

"I'm sorry," I whispered. No one heard, but it wasn't for anyone but Kyle anyway. "Goodbye, Kyle. I love you."

I turned then, and ran. Kicked off the heels and ran barefoot through the grass, across the gravel parking lot, ignoring the voices calling me.

The cemetery was only a few miles away from my parents' house, from home, from Kyle's house. I followed the dirt road, ignoring the stabbing pain when rocks dug into my feet. I welcomed the pain, the physical pain. I just ran. Ran. Off-balance with one arm in a cast. Each step jostled my broken arm, adding to my pain. I turned on the correct street and ran some more. I heard a car pull up next to me, heard my father's voice pleading with me. Rain pelted on my head, still the rain, always the rain, nonstop rain since the day he died. I ignored my dad, shook my head, wet hair slapping my chin. I think I was crying, but the rain mingled with the hot salt.

Another car, another voice, ignored. Run, run, running. Dress wet against my skin, clinging, flapping against my thighs. Feet aching, burning, stabbing. Arm excruciating, jolted with every step. Then footsteps taking space-eating strides, rhythmic, unhurried, the pace of a runner. I knew who it would be. He didn't try to keep up, and I tried to pretend, just for a moment, that it was Kyle behind me, letting me run ahead so he could stare at my ass. That thought, that image, that memory of Kyle's easy lope behind me had me struggling for breath, fighting against the swell of tears.

I ran harder, and his stride behind me increased. I shook my head, hair slapping into my mouth, wet. After a few more strides, he was next to me, shirt wet and transparent, tie gone, buttons open to mid-chest. He kept pace with me easily. He didn't speak, didn't even look at me. Just ran next to me. Our breathing began to sync, huffing in two steps, huffing out two steps, a too-familiar rhythm.

A mile from home, I stepped on a large rock in the road and twisted my ankle, flying forward. Before I could hit the ground, I was in Colton's arms. He slowed to a walk with me in a fireman's carry, one arm beneath my knees, the other around my shoulders. He was breathing hard, and there was a hitch in his step.

"I can walk," I said.

Colton stopped and let me down. As soon as I put weight on my ankle, however, it gave out, and I had to hop to stay upright.

"Let me carry you," Colton said.

"No." I gripped his bicep in my hand, gritting my teeth and taking a step. It hurt, but I could do it.

I would not be carried. There would be too many questions if I showed up at home in Colton's arms. There would already be a barrage, I knew.

The real reason, though, was because it had felt too right, being nestled in his arms. Too comforting. Too natural. Too much like home.

Guilt assailed me once more, and I intentionally put too much weight on my twisted ankle, sending pain throbbing through my leg. The pain was good. It distracted me. Gave me a reason to whimper past clenched teeth and brush away the tears. I was crying from the pain in my ankle, and that would pass. I wouldn't cry from the pain in my heart, because that wouldn't fade. It only grew heavier and harder and sharper with every passing minute, hour, day.

I stumbled, and Colton's hand steadied me. "At least lean on me, Nell," he said. "Don't be stubborn."

I stopped, foot lifted slightly. Hesitating. Considering.

"No." I shook his hand off, lowered my foot, and took a natural step. No limping, no hobbling.

It hurt so bad I couldn't breathe, and that was good. It pushed away the guilt. Pushed away the hurt in my soul. Pushed away the waking nightmare, the knowledge that Kyle was gone forever. Gone. Dead. Lost.

Killed, saving me.

I took another step and let the agony wash through me. I ducked my head so my hair fell around my face, obscuring my vision to either side. I heard Colton's step beside me, heard his breathing, smelled the acrid, faded scent of cigarette smoke and the fainter cologne and the ripe sweat of exertion. Man smell. Uniquely Colton, and entirely too comforting, all too familiar.

It took a long, long time to walk the mile home, and my ankle was swollen, throbbing, lances of pain rocketing up my leg and into my hip. I pushed open the front door, ignored my parents in the den, who shot to their feet and called my name. Colton had followed me in.

"She twisted her ankle," he told them. "I think it's sprained."

"Thank you for going with her," Dad said. I heard the suspicion in his voice as I listened from the top of the stairs.

"No problem." I heard Colton's foot squeak on the marble, and then the door open.

"I'm sorry for your loss, Colton." My mom's voice.

"Yeah." That was it from him, just that one word, and then the door closed and he was gone. I hobbled into my room, letting myself limp now that I was alone. I shut my door and stripped off my dress, my rain-soaked panties, then wrapped plastic around my cast and stepped into the shower. Hot water, scalding on my lower back, scouring away the pain, but not the guilt.

When the water ran lukewarm, I stepped out, toweled off, wrapped myself in my robe, and curled on my bed under a pile of blankets. The silence in my room was profound.

I closed my eyes and saw Kyle, crushed under the tree, spiked through, bleeding, breath whistling. I heard his voice whispering "I love you…I love you…" over and over again, until he had no more breath and the sirens in the distance hailed his passing.

I heard my door open, felt the bed dip as Mom sat down next to me. I squeezed my eyes shut, felt something hot and wet trickle down my cheek. It wasn't a tear. I wouldn't cry. Couldn't. To let it go would be to open my soul. It would never stop. I would break… just shatter. The liquid on my cheek was blood, surging out from my ripped and tattered heart.

"Nell…sweetheart." Mom's voice was soft, tentative. I felt her shift the blankets and probe my ankle with a finger. "Oh, god, Nell. You need to see a doctor. Your ankle is swollen and purple."

I shook my head. "Just wrap it. Ice it. It's not broken."

She sighed, sat silent for a long minute, then came back with an ice pack and an ACE bandage. When I was iced and wrapped, she sat down again.

"I didn't know you knew Colton."

"I don't."

"You were smoking." I didn't answer. I had no reason or excuse to give her. "Talk to me, baby."

I shook my head. "And say what?" I pulled the blanket over my head.

Mom tugged it down and brushed my damp hair out of my eye. "I can't say it will stop hurting. It'll just get easier to deal with it."

Her older brother had died in a car accident when Mom was in college. She still got choked up when she talked about him. They had been very close, I think.

"I don't want it to get easier."

"Why?" She took the brush from my nightstand and tugged on me until I sat up. She brushed my hair with long, smooth strokes, reminding me of when I was a girl. She would sing to me and brush my hair before bed.

"Because if it gets easier...I'll forget him." I still had the note clutched in my cast-clad hand. I took in in my free hand and opened it, read it. The paper was damp, the blue ink faded but still legible.

I heard Mom sigh, something like a sob. "Oh, honey. No. I promise you, you'll never forget him. But you have to let yourself heal. It's not a betrayal of his memory to let go of the pain. He would want you to be okay."

I strangled on something thick and hot in my throat. I had thought exactly that. If I stopped remembering, if I tried to let go of the pain, it would be a betrayal of him. Of us.

"It's not your fault, Nell."

I shuddered, and my breath failed me. "Sing to me? Like you used to?"

I had to distract her. I couldn't tell her how it was my fault. She would just try to convince me it wasn't.

She sighed, as if seeing through my tactic. She took a breath, stroking my hair with the brush, and sang. She sang "Danny's Song" by Kenny Loggins. It was her favorite song, and I knew all the words from having listened to her sing it to me at night, all as I was growing up.

When the last note quavered from her throat, I shuddered again, feeling more heart-blood leak out from my eye. I didn't wipe it away, just let it slip into my lips, down my chin.

Mom set the brush down and stood up. "Sleep, Nell."

I nodded and lay down. Eventually I slept, and dreamed. Haunted dreams, tortured dreams. Kyle's eyes on me, dying; Colton's eyes on me, knowing.

I read the note again, seven times. Recited the words under my breath like a poem.

I woke up, and the clock read 3:38 a.m. I couldn't breathe from the pressure of grief. The walls of my room closed in around me, pressed in on my skull. I took off the melted bag of ice and rewrapped my ankle, then put on my favorite loose sweatpants and a hoodie. Kyle's hoodie. It smelled of him, and that only made the pressure on my chest worse, but the smell comforted me as well. It pierced through the numbness and touched my heart, pinched it with hot fingers. I descended quietly, slowly, awkwardly, not able to use my foot much. Out the back door, down the steps, onto the cobblestone path leading to the dock.

Quiet guitar strains floated to me from the Calloways' dock. I knew who it was. The grass was wet with dew and old rain under foot, cold, bracing. The night air was thin and cool, sky a black blanket strewn with silver. My bare feet were silent on the smooth-worn wood of the dock. The guitar chords didn't falter, but I knew he knew it was me.

He was leaning back in an Adirondack chair, feet stretched out in front of him, guitar held on his stomach. A bottle of liquor sat next to him.

"You should have shoes on," he said, picking a slow, lilting melody.

I didn't answer. A second chair sat a few feet away from Colton's, and he held the guitar by the neck as he reached out to drag the chair closer. I eased into it, aware of his tension, his hand waiting to reach out to help me.

"How's the foot?" He lifted the bottle to his lips, took a long sip, then handed it to me.

"Hurts." I took a hesitant sip. Whiskey burned my throat. "Ohmigod, what *is* that?" I hissed, rasping and coughing.

Colton chuckled. "Jameson Irish Whiskey, baby. The best whiskey there is." He reached down to the other side of the chair and handed me a beer. "Here. Chase it with that."

I took it and cracked the tab, sipped. "Trying to get me drunk?"

He shrugged. "You can always say no."

"Does it help?" I asked.

He sipped from his own beer. "I don't know. I'm not drunk enough yet." He took another shot from the Jameson. "I'll let you know."

"Maybe I'll find out on my own."

"Maybe you will. Just don't tell our parents you got the alcohol from me. You're underage."

"What alcohol?" I took another fiery slug from the whiskey.

I felt lightheaded, loose. The pressure of guilt and grief didn't dissipate, but it did seem to be pushed to the back by the weight of the whiskey.

"If you don't drink much, I'd hold off on any more. It tends to sneak up on you."

I handed the bottle back and clutched the cold beer can in my fist. "How do you know I'm not a hard drinker?"

Colton laughed openly. "Well, I guess I don't know for sure. But you're not."

"How can you tell?"

"You're a good girl. Kyle wouldn't have dated a party girl." He lifted his hips up and dug in his jeans pocket for his smokes and lighter. "Besides, your reaction when you took the first shot told me enough."

"You're right. I'm not a drinker. Kyle and I got hammered once. It was awful."

"It can be fun if you do it right. But hangovers always suck." He blew a plume of gray, dissipating into the starry sky.

We sat in silence for a while, and Colton kept drinking. I let the buzz roll over me, helped it along with a second beer.

"You can't hold it in forever," Colton said, apropos of nothing.

"Yes, I can." I had to.

"You'll go crazy. It'll come out, one way or another."

"Better crazy than broken." I wasn't sure where that came from, hadn't thought it or meant to say it.

"You're not broken. You're hurting." He stood up unsteadily and strolled to the edge of the dock. I heard a zipper, then the sound of urination.

I blushed in the darkness. "Did you really have to do that right in front of me?" I asked, voice tremoring with irritation and laughter.

He zipped up and turned to face me, swaying in place. "Sorry. Guess that was kinda rude, huh? I wasn't thinking."

"Damn right it was rude."

"I said I'm sorry. Didn't take you for the squeamish type, though."

"I'm not squeamish. I just have to pee, too, and I can't do it like you did, right off the dock."

He chuckled. "Oh…well…I don't know what to tell you. You could try squatting off the edge?"

I snorted. "Sshh-yeah. That'd work real well. I'd either fall in or pee on my ankles. Probably both."

"I wouldn't let you fall in."

"I don't doubt that." I levered myself to an upright position, struggling to find my balance without putting too much weight on my ankle. Colton's hand settled on my shoulder, steadying me.

"Going up?" Colton asked. I nodded. "Coming back?"

I shrugged. "Probably. I couldn't sleep any more if I tried."

Colton left my side to screw the cap on the bottle of Jameson. I waited until he was next to me again, and then we made our way up the path. When I started to veer left toward my house, Colton tugged on my arm.

"Mom and Dad have a bathroom in the basement. It's a walkout, so you wouldn't have to go up any stairs."

I knew this from years spent shuttling between my house and Kyle's, but I didn't say so.

He went in ahead of me, turning on the lights. Waited for me outside, and helped me back down to the dock, offering a silent, stabilizing presence when my feet slipped in the wet grass.

We settled back into our chairs, and he picked up his guitar, strummed a few chords, then began to play a song. I knew the song within a few chords: "Reminder" by Mumford & Sons. I thought he'd only play, so I was stunned when he took a breath and began to sing the words in a low, melodic, raspy voice. He didn't just play the song as it was, though. He twisted it, changed it, made it his. It was already a beautiful, haunting song, but Colton's version touched something in my soul.

I closed my eyes and listened, feeling the pressure lessen, just a little. I didn't open my eyes when he finished. "Will you play something else? Please?"

"Sure. What do you want to hear?"

I shrugged, leaning my head back against the chair. Colton strummed a few times, then cleared his throat. I heard the liquid glug as he took a shot from the bottle. I felt the cold glass touch my hand, and I took it and drank without opening my eyes. The burn was welcome now. I was feeling a measure of peace, tipsy and floating. The guilt and the grief were still there, banked coals burning underneath the alcohol haze.

Colton began another song, and I recognized this one too. "This is 'Like a Bridge Over Troubled Waters' by Simon and Garfunkel." The way Colton announced the song and artist made me think he'd done this before, that he was falling into a habit. Was he a performer? He again seemed just too big, too rough, too primal and hard of a man to sit in coffeehouses behind a microphone playing indie folk songs. Yet…hearing him play and raise his voice to sing the high opening notes, it seemed only natural.

I was stunned by the rough beauty of his voice. He turned the song into a poem. I wished desperately, in that moment, to find my own bridge over the troubled waters of my grief.

But there was none. Only the raging river of unshed tears.

When the song ended, Colton shifted into another song, one I didn't know and he didn't announce, rolling and low and soft, a circular melody that drifted up and down the register. He hummed in places, a deep bass throb in the bottom of his throat. Something about the song struck through the alcohol and the numb armor around my grief. There were no words, but it was an elegy nonetheless. I couldn't have explained it, but the song just exuded grief, spoke of mourning.

I felt thick heat at the back of my throat, and I knew I wouldn't be able to contain it this time. I tried. I tried to choke it down like vomit, but it came up anyway, spurting past my teeth in ragged whimpers. I heard myself gasp, and then keen high in my throat, a long, tortured moan.

Colton clapped his hands over the strings, silencing them. "Nell? You okay?"

His voice was the the impetus that pushed me over the edge. I shot up out of the chair, hopping away off the dock, limping. I ran, hobbling desperately. I hit the grass and kept going. Not for the house, not for the road, just…going. Away. Anywhere. I ended up in the sand, where my feet sank deep and slipped. I fell to my knees, sobs clattering in my throat, shivering in my mouth.

I crawled across the sand, pulled myself to the softly lapping water's edge. Agony bolted through my arm as it slid over the sand. Cold liquid licked my fingertips. I felt tears streaming down my cheeks, but I was silent still. I heard Colton's feet crunching in the sand, saw his bare feet stop a foot away, toes curling in the sand, rocking back on his heels, digging deep as he crouched next to me.

"Leave me alone." I managed to grate the words past my clenched teeth.

He didn't answer, but he didn't move, either. I dragged deep breaths in and out, fighting to keep it in.

"Let go, Nell. Just let it out."

"I can't."

"No one will know. It'll be our secret."

I could only shake my head, tasting sand on my lips. My breathing turned desperate, ragged, puffing into the grit of the beach. His hand touched my shoulder blade.

I writhed away, but his hand stayed in place as if attached. That simple, innocent touch was fire on my skin, burning through me and unlocking the gates around my sorrow.

It was just a single sob at first, a quick, hysterical inhalation. Then a second. And then I couldn't stop it. Tears, a flood of them. I felt the sand grow cold and muddy under my face, felt my body shuddering uncontrollably. He didn't tell me it was okay. He didn't try to pull me against him or onto his lap. He kept his hand on my shoulder and sat silent next to me.

I knew I wouldn't be able to stop. I'd let go, and now the river would flow un-dammed.

No. No. I shook my head, clenched my teeth, lifted up and let myself fall down hard, sending a spear of pain spiderwebbing out from my arm. The pain was a drug, and I accepted it greedily. It was a dam, stemming the tide of tears. I panted, a whine emitting from my throat. I forced myself up, scrambling in the sand like a madwoman, hair wild and caked with grit. Colton stood up, caught my arm, and lifted me to my feet. I landed hard, too hard, and I couldn't stop the cry of pain as my ankle jarred. I fell forward, into Colton.

He caught me, of course.

He smelled of alcohol, cologne, cigarettes. His arms circled my shoulders and held me in place. The sobs rose and fell within me, brought up by guilt from finding pleasure and comfort, doused by the same.

I let my forehead rest under his chin, just for a moment. Only a moment. Just till I caught my breath. It didn't mean anything.

It's just a moment of comfort, Kyle. I found myself talking to him, as if he could hear me. *It doesn't mean anything. I love you. Only you.*

But then he shifted, looking down at me. So of course, I had to tilt my head up and meet his eyes. Damn his eyes, so soft, so piercing and bright and blue and beautiful. His eyes… they drowned me. Sucked me in. Dark sapphire laced with cornflower blue, sky blue, ice blue, so many shades of blue.

I fell forward, into him. I tasted Jameson on his breath, heat on my lips, moist soft heat and scouring power of his lips. It was only a moment, the briefest instant of contact. A kiss, an instant of weakness like the inevitable pull of gravity.

Awareness rifled through me, struck me like a dagger to the heart.

I threw myself bodily backward, out of his arms, away from the drowning comfort of his arms, his lips.

"What am I doing?" I stumbled back, back. "What am I doing? What the *fuck* am I doing?" I turned and limped away as fast as I could, barely hanging on to my sanity, barely keeping the guilt from eating me alive.

Colton followed, ran around in front of me and stopped me with his hands on my shoulders. "Wait, Nell. Wait. Just wait."

I wrenched free. "Don't *touch* me. That…that was wrong. So wrong. I'm sorry…so sorry."

He shook his head, eyes boiling with emotion. "No, Nell. It just happened. I'm sorry, too. It just happened. It's okay."

"It's not okay!" I was nearly yelling. "How can I kiss you when he's dead? When the man I love is gone? How can I kiss you when…when I—when Kyle—"

"It's not your fault. I let it happen, too. It's not your fault. It just happened." He kept saying that, as if he could see the guilt, the secret weight of awful knowledge.

"Stop *saying* that!" The words were torn from me before I could stop them. "You don't *know*! You weren't *there*! He's dead and I—" I chomped down on the last two words.

Thinking them, knowing them to be true was one thing; saying them out loud to Kyle's brother, whom I just kissed, was another.

He was close to me again, somehow. Not touching, but only an inch separating us. That sliver of air between us crackled, sparked, and spat.

"We're not talking about the kiss anymore, are we?" His voice throbbed low, wired with passion, understanding.

I shook my head, my only answer for so many things. "I can't—I can't—I can't…"

I could only turn away, and this time Colton Calloway let me leave. He watched me; I could feel his eyes on me. I could feel him knowing my thoughts, delving deep into my secret soul, where guilt and grief festered like an abscess.

I made it to my room, to my bed. My eyes closed, and all I saw was Kyle dying, over and over again. Between the images of his last indrawn breath, I saw Colton. His face growing closer, his mouth on mine.

I wanted to cry, to scream, to sob. But I couldn't. Because if I did, I'd never stop. Never never. There would only be an ocean of tears.

Hot heart-blood leaked from my face. From my eyes and my nose and my mouth. Not tears, because those would never stop. This was just liquid heartbreak seeping from my pores.

The mountain of pressure, the weight of grief and guilt…it was all I could feel. It was all I would ever feel. I knew that. I knew, too, that I would learn to be normal once again, someday. To live, to be, to seem okay.

Okay would only ever be skin deep, though.

The note was under my pillow. I unfolded it, gazed at it.

…And now we're learning how to fall in love together. I don't care what anyone else says. I love you. I'll always love you, no matter what happens with us in the future. I love you now and forever.

I saw the splotch where my tear had fallen, staining the blue pen strokes black in a sudden Rorschach pattern. Another wet drop splatted on the paper, just beneath the writing this time. I let it sink in and stain. The slanting downstroke of the "Y" in his scrawled signature blurred and became blotted.

Eventually the slow leak stopped, and I fell asleep. I dreamed of brown eyes and blue, of a ghost beside me, loving me, and of a flesh and blood man sitting on a dock, drinking whiskey, playing guitar, and remembering an illicit kiss. In the dream, he wondered what it meant. In the dream, he stole into my room and kissed me again. I woke from that dream sweating and shaking and nauseous with guilt.

Colton

Chapter 6: Old Man Jack
Two Years Later

I'M SITTING ON A PARK BENCH on the edge of Central Park, busking. I've got my case on the ground next to my feet, a few bucks as seed money bright green against the maroon velvet. I haven't busked in months. The shop has been too busy, too many orders, too many rebuilds and custom jobs. But this, the open air and the lack of expectations, this is where I live. Where my soul flies. Like my weekly gig at Kelly's bar, it's not about the money, although I usually make a decent chunk of change.

It's about letting the music flow out of my blood and into the guitar, letting it seep through my vocal chords.

I'm adjusting a string, tweaking the tuning for my next song. My head is down, tilted to the side, listening for the perfect pitch. I get it, bob my head in approval.

I start in on "I and Love and You" by the Avett Brothers. This is a song that always draws a crowd. It's the song more than me, really. It's such brilliant piece of music. So much meaning stuffed into the lyrics. I look up after the first verse and scan the sidewalk in front of me. An older man in a business suit, a phone against his ear, another clipped to his expensive leather belt; A young woman with bottle-blonde hair in a messy bun, a sticky-faced boy-child gripping her hand, both stopped and listening; a gay couple, young men holding hands, flamboyant, bouffant hair and colorful scarves; three teen girls, giggling, whispering to each other behind cupped hands, thinking I'm cute.

And her.

Nell.

I could write a song, and her name would be the music. I could sing, strum a guitar, and her body would be the melody. She's standing behind the rest of the crowd, partially obscured, leaning against a parking meter, a patchwork-fabric purse slung over one shoulder, pale green dress brushing her knees and hugging her curves, strawberry blonde hair twisted into a casual braid and hanging over one shoulder. Pale skin like ivory, flawless and begging to be caressed. Kissed.

I'm no saint. I've hooked up with other girls since then, but they've never been enough. Never been right. They've never stuck around long.

Now, here she is. Why? I tried so hard to forget her, but still her face, her lips, her body, glimpsed beneath a wet black dress...she haunts me.

She's biting her lip, worrying it between her teeth, gray-green eyes pinning me to the bench. Shit. For some reason I can't fathom, that habit, the biting her lip...I can't take it. I want to throw down the guitar and go over to her and take that perfect plump lower lip into my mouth and not let go.

I almost falter at that first meeting of our eyes, but I don't. I meet her gaze, continue the song.

I'm singing it to her, as I reach the final chorus. "I...and love...and you."

She knows. She sees it in my eyes. It's utter madness to sing this song to her, but I can't stop now. I watch her lips move, mouthing the words. Her eyes are pained, haunted.

The person standing in front of her moves, and I see a guitar case resting against her thigh, the round bottom planted on the sidewalk, her palm stabilizing the narrow top. I didn't know she played.

The song ends and the crowd moves away, a few people tossing in ones and fives. The businessman—still on the phone—tosses in a fifty and a business card announcing himself as a record label producer. I nod at him, and he makes the universal "call me" gesture with his free hand. I might call him. I might not. Music is expression, not business.

She approaches, bending at the knees and lifting her guitar case, slides onto the bench next to me. Her eyes never leave mine as she sits, zips open her case, withdraws a beautiful Taylor classical acoustic. She bites her lip again, then plucks a few strings, strums, begins "Barton Hollow."

I laugh softly, and see that the pain has never left her. She's carried it all this time. I weave my part in around hers, and then I'm singing. The words fall from my lips easily, but I'm barely hearing myself. She plays easily and well, but it's clear she hasn't been playing too long. She still glances at her fingers on the fretboard as she switches chords, and she gets a few notes wrong. But her voice…it's pure magic, dulcet and silver and crystalline and so sweet.

We draw a crazy crowd together. Dozens of people. The street beyond is blocked from view by the bodies, and I can tell she's uncomfortable with the attention. She crosses her leg over her knee, bounces with the rhythm, ducks her head as if wishing her hair was loose so she could hide behind it. She slips up a

chord, loses the rhythm. I twist on the bench to meet
her eyes, lock gazes and nod at her, slow down and
accentuate the strumming rhythm. She breathes deep,
swelling her breasts behind her Taylor, and finds the
rhythm with me.

The song ends, eventually, all too soon. I half expect
her to rise and put away the guitar and float away again,
without a word exchanged, just gone again as mysteri-
ously as she appeared. She doesn't, though. Thank god
for that. She glances around at the crowd, chews her lip,
glances at me. I wait, palm flat on the strings.

She takes a deep breath, plucks a few strings, idly,
as if deciding, then nods to herself, a quick bob of the
head as if to say, "Yeah, I'm gonna do it." Then she
begins to strum a tune I know I know, but can't place.
Then she sings. And again, her admittedly mediocre
guitar playing fades away, replaced by the shocking
beauty of her voice. She's singing "Make You Feel My
Love" by Adele. The original is simple and powerful,
just the piano and Adele's unique voice. When Nell
sings it, she takes it and twists it, makes it haunting
and sad and almost country-sounding. She sings it low
in her register, almost whispering the words.

And she sings it to me.

Which makes no sense whatsoever. But still, she
watches me as she sings, and I can see the years of pain
and guilt in her gaze.

She still blames herself. I always knew she did, and hoped time would cure her of that, but I can see, without having even spoken to her, that she still carries the weight. There's darkness in this girl now. I almost don't want to get involved. She'll hurt me. I know this. I can see it, feel it coming. She's got so much pain, so many cracks and shards and jags in her soul, and I'm going to get cut by her if I'm not careful.

I can't fix her. I know this, too. I'm not going to try. I've had too many goody-goody girls hook up with me, thinking they can fix me.

I also know I'm not going to stay away. I'm going to grab onto her and let myself get cut. I'm good at pain. I'm good at bleeding, emotionally and physically.

I let her sing. I don't join in; I just give her the moment, let her own it. The crowd whistles and claps and tosses dollars into her open guitar case.

Now she waits, watches. My turn. I know I have to choose my song carefully. We're establishing a dialogue here. We're having a conversation in music, a discussion in guitar chords and sung notes and song titles. I strum nonsense and hum, thinking. Then it comes to me:

"Can't Break Her Fall" by Matt Kearney. It speaks to me, and it's unique, a song people will remember. And I know she'll hear me, hear what I'm not saying

when I sing it. Half-sung, half-rapped. The verses tell
such a strong, vivid story, and suddenly I can see her
and me in the lyrics.

She listens carefully. Her gray-green gaze hardens,
and her teeth snag her lip and bite down hard. Oh yeah.
She heard me. I catch the tremble in her hand when she
sets her guitar in the case, zips it closed, and tries not to
stumble as she runs from me. Her braid trails behind
her, bouncing between her shoulder blades, and her
calves flash pale white in the New York sunlight. I let
her go, finish the song, two more chords, and then I
click the guitar case closed and jog after her. Across
the street, Yellow Cabs honking impatiently, city noise,
and then down to a subway. She swipes a card and
struggles with the turnstile, guitar held awkwardly by
the handle. She swipes the card again, but the turnstile won't budge and she's cursing under her breath.
People are lining up behind us, but she's oblivious to
them, to me mere inches away. She tosses her head,
stops struggling, takes a deep breath. At that moment,
I reach past her, swipe my own card and gently push
her through the gate. She complies as if in a daze, lets
me take her guitar from her and slip the straps over
my shoulder, holding my own hard-case by the handle. The palm of my free hand cups her lower back,
prompts her onto the waiting subway car. She doesn't

look me, doesn't question that it's me. She just knows. She's breathing deeply still, gathering herself. I let her breathe, let the silence stretch. She won't turn in place to look at me, but she leans back, just slightly, her back brushing my front. She doesn't put her weight against me, merely allows a hint of contact.

She steps off after a few stops, and I follow. She catches another line, and we continue in silence. She hasn't met my eyes since she ran from the Central Park bench. I've stayed behind her, just following. I follow her to an apartment building in Tribeca, follow her up the echoing stairwell, trying not to stare at her ass swaying as she ascends the stairs. It's hard not to, though. It's such a fine ass, round and taut and swinging teasingly under the thin cotton of her sundress.

She unlocks door number three-fourteen, shoves it open with her toe and goes straight to the kitchen, not watching to see if I follow her in uninvited, which I do. I close the door behind me, set her guitar case on the floor beneath a light switch, just inside the doorway, next to a small square table stacked with sheet music and guitar books and packets of nylon strings. My case goes on the floor next to me in the entryway to the open kitchen. I watch her jerk open a cabinet next to the refrigerator, pull out a bottle of Jack, twist the cap off, and toss it to the counter. Her fist shakes, and she tilts the bottle up to her lips and sucks three times, long hard drags straight from the bottle. Damn. She sets the bottle down violently and stands with her head hanging between her arms braced on the counter, one foot stretched out behind her, the other bent close to the counter in a runner's stretch. She shudders in a breath, straightens, wipes her lips with the back of her hand. I cross the space between us, and I don't miss the way she tenses as I draw near. She stops breathing as my arm dives over her shoulder, and my hand grabs the bottle and brings it to my lips, and I match her three long pulls. It burns, a familiar pain.

She turns in place, finally, retreating to the counter edge, staring up at me, eyes wide and searching. She looks like an anime character suddenly, so wide-eyed and full of depthless emotion. I want to kiss her so badly, but I don't. I don't even touch her, even though I'm mere inches from her. I hold the bottle, my other hand propped against the counter beside her elbow.

"Why are you here?" she asks. Her voice is a harsh whisper, whiskey-burned.

I let a lopsided smile tilt my lips. "Here in your apartment? Or here in New York?"

"In my apartment. In New York. In my life. Here. Why are you here?"

"I live in New York. I have since I was seventeen. I'm here in your apartment because I followed you from Central Park."

"But why?"

"Because we weren't done talking."

She scrunches up her nose in confusion, a gesture so absurdly adorable my breath stutters in my chest. "Talking? Neither of us said a word."

"Still a conversation." I tilt the bottle to my lips and take another pull, feeling it hit my stomach.

"About what?"

"You tell me."

"I don't know." She takes the bottle from me, drinks from it, caps it, and puts it away. "About...that night on the dock."

I shrug, tip my head side to side. "Sort of, but not really."

"Then what do you think we were talking about?"

"Us."

She pushes past me, tilts her head to the side, and peels her hair free from the braid, kicking off her flip flops. "There is no us. There never was and never will be."

I don't answer that, because she's right. But so wrong. There will be an us. She just hasn't seen it yet. She'll resist it, because it's wrong on so many levels. I'm her dead boyfriend's older brother. And she knows nothing about me. I'm bad for her. She's underage, and I shouldn't encourage her drinking. She's obviously using Old Man Jack to cope, and I understand that all too well. But she's still only twenty, which is just too young to be drinking like that, straight from the bottle like a jaded alcoholic.

She finishes unbraiding her hair and shakes it out, combs through it with her fingers. "You should go," she says, disappearing into the bedroom. I hear cloth rustling and hit the ground. "I have class."

I'm a shameless asshole. I know this, because only a shameless asshole would move around the counter to see into her room. Which is what I do. She's in a matching bra and panties set, pink with black polka dots. Facing away from me, tight round ass so delectably perfect in the boy-short panties. Oh, god, oh, god. She feels my presence, twists her neck to glare at me.

"Well you're an asshole."

"Should've closed your door."

"I told you to leave." She reaches into a drawer and unfolds a pair of jeans, steps into them.

Watching a girl dress is almost as hot as watching her strip.

"But I didn't, and you knew it."

"I didn't think you'd blatantly watch me change. Fucking pervert."

I grin at her, the smile my buddies call the panty-dropper. "I'm not a pervert. I just appreciate art."

She smirks. "Smooth, Colton. Very smooth."

I grin. No one calls me Colton. No one. I'm Colt. "It wasn't a line, Nell. It was the truth." I turn up the wattage on the smile, stepping toward her.

She tenses, clutching a pale blue T-shirt in white-knuckle fists. "What are you doing?"

I don't answer. I continue toward her, step by deliberate step. I feel like a predator, a lion stalking its prey. Her eyes grow wide, doe eyes. Her nostrils flare, her hands twist the shirt, her breasts swell as she breathes deeply, swelling until they threaten to spill out. God, I wish they would. Like I said, shameless. She's just inside the room, which is tiny. Barely space for the bed and dresser. I'm inches away from her again, and I could see her nipples if I looked down, probably. At the very least, I'd be treated to a huge expanse of porcelain cleavage. I don't look, though. I meet her eyes, let my raw desire, my weltering boil of emotions, show in my gaze as I reach past her. My hand brushes her shoulder just beside her bra strap as I grasp the edge of the door. I'm so close now. Her breasts are touching my chest, my arm touching both her shoulder and ear. Her eyes slide closed, breaking the contact, and I hear her breath catch. She wilts slightly, the tension bleeding out of her, and she tilts her head to rest against my arm.

Her eyes flick open, bright with renewed determination, and she straightens so she's not touching me. I pull the door closed between us. Just before I step out of her front door, I take one of my business cards from my wallet and set it on the table, on top of the packet of guitar strings. I close her apartment door with deliberate noise, so she'll know I left.

The walk back to the subway and the subsequent ride to my apartment in Queens is long, providing me with too much time to ask myself exactly what the fuck I'm getting myself into. Nell is bad news. She's got major damage, a baggage train a mile long. And so do I.

I toss my guitar on the bed and go downstairs to the shop. I set my phone in the dock and blast Black Label Society's "Stillborn" loud enough to drown my thoughts as I throw myself in the 396 big-block I'm rebuilding. It's for a classic '69 Camaro, which didn't mean shit to me until Nell showed up, and then all I can think of is Kyle's Camaro, which I restored from a bucket of rust in a junk heap to mint condition, and then left behind when I moved here.

I loved that car, and it hurt so bad to leave it behind, but Dad had paid for it, so I couldn't take it. Never mind that every penny of the parts came from me, or that I'd spent the blood, sweat, and tears to restore it. The seed money came from Dad, and if I moved to New York instead of attending Harvard, then I brought nothing but what I bought myself. That was the deal.

At least Kyle took care of it.

I snorted as I thought of Dad's expectation that I go to Harvard. He'd actually thought that would happen. Fucking ridiculous. Even now, almost ten years later, I can't fathom what went through his head. I'd fit in at Harvard like a bull in a china shop.

My thoughts return to Nell. Sanding piston rings is boring busywork, so of course I can't help but think of her. Of her sweet crystalline voice and her piercing green-gray eyes and her fine, fine body. Goddamn it, I'm in trouble. Especially when I think of the deep-seated ache in her gaze, in the desperate way she drank that whiskey, as if the numbness was a friend, as if the burn was a welcome respite from reality. I know that pain, and I want to take it from her. I want to know her thoughts, know what haunts her.

I mean, of course I know. Kyle died, and she saw it happen. But that's not really it. Something else drives her. Something else eats at her, some guilt. And I want to know what, so I can absolve her of it. Which, of course, is impossible and stupid and reckless.

I set the 400-grit sandpaper down and inspect the ring, finding it ground down to my satisfaction. The headers are the next item of business, and those, too, only take a portion of my attention, so my thoughts are free to roam back to the way she leaned her head on my arm for a split second, as if wishing she could let herself go, let herself lean farther. But she didn't, and I can't help but respect her for that, even I know her strength is false, propped up by the shaky girders of Old Man Jack.

One day soon, those girders will collapse, and her world will crumble, and I know I have to be there when that happens.

Chapter 7: Cuts; Pain for Pain
One Week Later

I'M PERCHED ON A BARSTOOL in a midtown hole-in-the-wall bar, strumming my guitar and playing an original song. No one is listening, but I don't care. It's enough to play for the love of the music, for the chance to feel the notes fly out and bounce off minds and hearts. I take that back—there is one person listening: the bartender, a girl I knew for a long time and finally hooked up with a couple times a few months ago. We weren't really compatible, and it turned into an odd sort of friendship, wherein she gets me to play on Thursday nights in return for a hundred bucks and free drinks and some harmless flirtation that never goes further. Kelly, her name is. Beautiful girl, good in bed, funny, and slings a damn good Jack and Coke. But we just didn't click in the bedroom. We never really figured out what it was, other than just…not quite right. But we enjoy each other's company and have some good, much-needed laughs. So she's listening, and I'm playing for her. It's a song about her, actually, about a girl with long black hair and bright brown eyes and coffee-colored skin and a sweet smile and a rocking body who will never be more than a friend. It's an odd song, kind of lonely and sad but touched with humor.

Then *she* walks in. I strum a wrong note, and Kelly frowns at me from across the bar. Then her eyes follow my gaze, and her eyes widen and she's smirking knowingly. Nell is surrounded by people, four girls who could all be sisters, quadruplets or something with their identical blonde hair pulled into a ponytail with that stupid bump on top and their yoga pants and Coach purses. Each girl has a boy on her arm, and they're matching sets as well, muscle-bound juiceheads with idiotic tribal tattoos and dead eyes and cocky swaggers. These guys have their hands on their girls possessively, and the girls seem to enjoy it.

Nell has one, too, and this pisses me off. He's huge. I mean, I'm a big guy, but he's massive. And his eyes aren't dead. They're quick and alert and full of latent aggression. He's got the hottest girl in the bar on his arm, and he knows and he wants someone to make a move so he can destroy them.

His hand is on her lower back, on her ass, really, curling around her hip as he guides her to the bar. I see green, and then red. Which is stupid.

This is bad.

I'm gonna end up in jail. I make it through the song, but barely. Kelly sends over a shot of Jameson with a waitress. I down it, nod at Kelly. She gives me a questioning thumbs-up. *Am I good?* I nod, lying.

I'm not good. I'm really, really bad. I'm gonna start a fight tonight. I'm gonna get hurt, and Nell is gonna be pissed and Kelly is gonna be pissed.

I should leave. I owe Nell nothing. I don't own her. I don't have a claim on her. Sure, she never said anything about a boyfriend, but then, we didn't really talk much, and I didn't ask. It didn't cross my mind.

I start a cover of Matt Nathanson's "Come On Get Higher" because I can do that song without thinking. I'm watching, waiting. She'll realize who's singing any second, and that's when things'll get interesting.

He's pushing her impatiently toward the bar, and she writhes her back away from his touch, twists her torso to snap something at him. I can't see her lips to read them, but I can imagine. She steps away from him, but he follows and curls his arm around her waist, tugs her against his side and leans down to whisper in her ear. Whatever he says has her stiffening but acquiescing. Staying tucked against his side. I see her face, and she's unhappy, but in a long-suffering sort of way. This isn't new.

But it only sends my rage burning hotter.

I finish that song, then decide to up the ante. I clear my throat into the mic and do an intro. I usually just play through without any theatrics, especially when no one is really paying attention, but this is a unique situation.

"Hey, everybody. I hope you're all having a great time. I know I am. I'm Colt, and I'm gonna be playing a mix of covers and original songs." She swivels toward my voice as if pulled by a wire. Her eyes go wide, and she stops breathing. "That was Matt Nathanson I just sang, by the way. If you don't know his stuff, you should give him a listen. He's great. Anyway, I'm gonna do another cover. This is 'I Won't Give Up' by Jason Mraz."

It's a little high for my voice, but it works. I don't take my eyes off her, and it's then, when I've got real reason to sing, that the crowd starts paying attention. Maybe something in my voice shifts, but the chattering quiets and heads turn toward me.

I'm not sure she breathes at all. She's still held tight against Brick-shithouse's ribs, and she's growing impatient. She wiggles to get away, and he resists. Eventually she elbows him, hard, and he lets go, frowning. She disappears into the bathroom; when she comes back, she's wiping her lips with the back of her hand, and I know exactly what she did in there. I never take my eyes from her through several more songs. Eventually I have to take a break, so I thank the crowd and step off the stage. She's been trying to ignore me, pounding shots of Jack and chasing them with Rolling Rock. Obviously she's got a fake ID, or she's older than I thought. Then I hear the group of girls and their guys all converge around her and sing "Happy Birthday dear Nell" hideously off-key. Her ogre boyfriend pulls her against him for a kiss, which she submits to limply, hands at her side, not kissing him back. At length, she pushes him away and turns to the bar. I'm to her side, so I see her wipe her mouth as if disgusted, and suppress a shudder. Ogre doesn't see, since he's too busy ogling the waitress, who is in turn leaning over for him so he can see down her shirt as she flirts with him.

I'm puzzled by this exchange, especially when he slips his hand—the one that isn't on Nell's hip—down to openly grope the waitress' ass. I'm even more confused when Nell swivels in place and watches the entire thing, hints of amusement and disgust playing on her lips and eyes.

Nell turns away, shaking her head, but leaves his hand on her. She meets my eyes, and I lift an eyebrow. Her eyes take on an almost guilty expression for a split second, but then it's gone. I wave Kelly over and tell her to pour two big shots of Jameson, one for me and one for Nell.

When Nell has her shot in hand, I lift mine to my lips and tip it back. Nell matches me. Ogre watches this, and his face darkens. He leans down and whispers in her ear. She shrugs. He latches his hand on her bicep, and I see him squeeze, see Nell wince.

Fuck that.

I set my glass down and weave through the crowd toward them. Nell is watching me, shaking her head at me. I ignore her warnings. Ogre straightens as he sees me approaching, and his mouth turns up in a ready smile. He flexes his fist and steps past Nell.

"COLT!" Kelly's voice snaps out from my left, from behind the bar. "I don't fucking think so. Not in my bar."

I turn to Kelly, who is glaring daggers at me. Kelly knows a bit about me, knows some of the people I used to run with. She knows what I can do, and she doesn't want any part of it here. I don't blame her.

She reaches beneath the bar and lifts a collapsible police baton, flicks her wrist to extend its weighted head. She points it at Ogre and company.

"Get out. All of you. Now." She also lifts her cell phone from her purse and dials a number, then shows the screen to them. "I'll fuck you all up, and then I'll call the police and you'll be arrested, because I have that kind of understanding with them. So get the fuck out."

You don't fuck with Kelly. She knows the people I used to run with because she used to run with them, too. What she doesn't say is that the red bandana tying her dreadlocked hair back isn't just for fashion. It's colors. The kind of colors that say she can make one phone call, and Ogre and company will vanish. Bloodily.

Nell glances at me one last time, then leads the way out, tossing a bill on the bar. Her vapid friends and asshole boyfriend follow her, but the Ogre stops in the doorway to stare holes in my head. I stare back until he turns away and leaves.

I get back on the stage and fiddle with the tuning on my guitar.

Kelly comes out from behind the bar and faces me. "What the hell was that, Colt?"

I shrug. "Someone I know."

"You were ready to throw down."

"He was hurting her."

"She was letting him."

"Doesn't make it right." I fish my capo out of the case and fit it on the strings.

Kelly eyes me warily. "No, it doesn't. But if she lets him, it's her business. I don't need trouble in my bar. *You* don't need trouble, period." Kelly's hand touches my arm, a rare moment of contact between us; part of our post-coital friendship contract is no touching. "Colt...you're doing really good. Don't fuck it up. Okay?"

"How would I do that?"

Kelly gives me a *what are you, stupid?* look, hand on her popped-out hip. "I've never seen you look that pissed, Colt. You don't get pissed. Which means she means something."

"It's complicated." I scrape the pick along one of the strings, not looking at Kelly.

"It's always complicated. My point is...you've got a good thing going. You've left all that behind," she waves at the bar, at the street beyond, meaning our shared past of violence, "and you don't need to make trouble for yourself over a girl."

"She's not just a girl." Well, shit. I did *not* mean to say that.

Kelly narrows her eyes at me. "I ain't said that." Her street accent is coming back, which I know how hard she works to disguise. "I'm jus' sayin'—I'm just

saying. Don't mess it up. Do what you gotta do, but…
you know what, whatever. Do whatever you want."

I sigh and finally look up at her. "I hear what
you're saying, Special K." I grin at her old nickname.

Kelly does the neck-roll *I don't think so* thing. "You
did *not* just call me that."

"I sure did, sister." I flash the panty-dropping grin
at her, which always works.

Kelly pretends to swoon, then socks me in the
arm, hard. Hard enough to make my arm sting. "Shut
up and play a song, asshole." She swaggers away, and I
don't mind watching. We may not hook up anymore,
but it doesn't mean I can't appreciate the view.

Immediately after that thought, I feel an odd
twinge of guilt. I see Nell's face in my mind, as if I
owe her fidelity. Which I don't. But I can't shake the
thought. So I play the music, and try to forget Nell and
her Ogre and Kelly and trouble and memories of old
fights.

I walk the streets a lot. I always have. When I
was an angry, homeless seventeen-year-old lost on the
mean streets of Harlem, it was all I had to do. I didn't
know shit about living on the streets, so I walked. I
walked to stay out of trouble, to stay awake, to stay
warm. Then, when I met T-Shawn and Split and the

boys, the streets became our livelihood, our life, our turf. So I walked the streets doing business. Now I walk the streets because it's familiar, and comforting. When I have to think through shit, I walk. I slip my guitar into the soft case and tie on my Timberlands and walk. I might start at my apartment above the shop in Queens and end up in Harlem or Astoria or Manhattan. I walk for hours, no iPod, no destination, just mile after mile of crowded sidewalks and cracked blacktop and towering skyscrapers and apartment blocks and back alleys where old friends still sling and smoke and fight. Old friends, old enemies, people I don't associate with anymore. But they leave me alone, friend or enemy, and let me walk.

It's 2 a.m., I'm sober, mostly, and I've got nowhere to be, and I'm walking. I'm not ready for the cold, quiet apartment, not ready to finish the big-block. I'm trying to convince myself that I should forget Nell. It's what I've been doing for the last two years, only now it's even harder because I have fresh images of her, the scent of her shampoo in my nose, the memory of the tingle of the silk of her bra against my T-shirt. Fresh knowledge of her seductive beauty, the harsh chasm of pain in her heart.

So I'm not entirely surprised when 3 a.m. sees me approaching her building in Tribeca. The door to the building isn't locked, oddly. For reasons I don't care to examine, I'm pushing through and up the stairwell. I hear her voice first.

"Dan, I'm going inside. *Alone*. I'm tired."

His voice is low, but audible. "Come on, babe. Watch a movie with me."

She sighs in exasperation. "I'm not stupid, you know. I know what you want. And the answer is no. That hasn't changed."

"Yet I keep hoping." His voice was amused but irritated. "Then why are we even dating?"

"You tell me. I've never encouraged you. I never said we were dating. We're *not*. You just won't go away. I'm not going to sleep with you, Dan. Not tonight, not tomorrow night."

"What can I do to convince you?"

"Be someone else?" Her voice is sharp and biting.

I'm on the landing of the first flight of stairs, hand on the railing, head tilted up, as if I could see them through the stairs.

He snorts in laughter at the barb. "You're such a fucking tease, Nell." The amusement is gone.

"I am not."

"You are, too. You'll kiss me, you'll let me grope you, you'll go out with me and all that other shit, but then we get here, and you close down." His voice is rising, getting angry. "I've put up with this shit for three months. I'm tired of it."

"Then stop putting up with it. Leave me alone. I have never promised you anything. You're a nice enough guy. You can be funny when you're not being a douchebag. But this isn't going anywhere, and it never was." The silence is palpable. He's pissed; even I can feel it from a flight of stairs away. I hear a key in a lock, a doorknob twist. "Goodbye, Dan."

Then a hiss from her, contained pain.

"I don't think so, babe. I haven't put three months of work into you, buying your drinks and your lunches and your coffee, just to get dumped now with nothing to show for it."

"Sorry, Dan. I never asked you to do that stuff. In fact, I told you not to, and you insisted."

"It's called being a gentleman."

"No, it's called expecting me to put out in exchange for free drinks. Now let *go*."

I hear a foot thump against wood and door hinges creak open, shuffled, stumbling steps. "Like I said, Nell. I don't think so. I feel like watching a movie. I'll even let you pick."

"Say what you mean, Dan." Her voice is hard, but I can hear the fear.

"Is that how you want it? Fine, then, babe. We're gonna go inside, and we're gonna have a good time together. You're gonna show me how sweet your body is, and how nice you can be."

"No. Get out."

A scuffle. A smack of hand on flesh.

Dan's laughter, amused and cruel. "Smacking me isn't going to help, bitch."

A whimper of pain and fear, and then I'm seeing red, creeping up the stairs. Old habits die hard; I've got brass knuckles on my fist, which I never really needed, but they came in handy and I always carry them because you never know what could happen on the streets of New York, even to me.

I'm at her door, closed now. I hear struggles, muffled.

"Quit fighting me, and I'll be gentle."

Motherfucker is gonna die.

The knob twists silently in my hand, and the hinges creak, but the sound is lost beneath Nell's whimpers and Dan's laughter as he holds her in place and fumbles roughly with her skirt and panties.

She sees me, and her eyes widen. Dan sees her reaction, turns and straightens in time to meet my fist. He's a tough sonofabitch, I'll give him that. Not many men can stand up after I've hit them, especially with brass knuckles adding force. His face is a mask of blood, and bone shows white on his forehead. His mouth spreads in a rictus of primal glee.

"Colton! NO! He'll kill you!" Nell is panicked, shrieking.

He wipes his eyes with his arm and takes a step toward me, assumes a fighting stance.

"You don't watch UFC, do you?" He smiles at me, and I know I've bitten off a pretty big chunk in tangling with him. I do recognize him, now. Dan Sikorsky, heavyweight UFC contender. Brutal bastard. Rumors are he killed a guy in a back alley bare-knuckle boxing match.

I grin back at him. I was scouted by the UFC, too. I turned them down. I don't fight for money anymore. The brass knuckles go back in my pocket.

I glance at Nell. "I'll be fine. But what the fuck are you doing with a guy like him?"

She seems puzzled. As if she can't quite believe my nonchalant tone in the face of a bruiser like Dan. I flash her a cocky grin that I don't quite feel.

He rushes me, and Nell screams. It's a slow, clumsy rush, though. He telegraphs his punch with his eyes and his whole demeanor. He's used to crushing with the first blow, and that's that. I am, too, so I know the feeling when it doesn't work. Took a few ass-beatings before I learned to counter it.

Duck...*whiff.* I'm not fighting fair. This isn't UFC. I plant my knee in his diaphragm, clutch his head in my palms, and pull his face down to my rising knee. Shove him back. Kick him in the balls, twice, hard. Crush his kidney with a pair of jackhammer punches, mash his already broken nose with my forehead.

He gets his fist in my shirt, and I know I'm in for pain. He's a berserker. I block the first few blows, but then they're coming in too fast, and god*damn* the guy can hit hard. Nell is still screaming. Ogre-boy is a bloody mess, and now so am I. But he's working on rage and berserker fury, which will fade soon. I'm in the cold fury phase. I'm in pain, but I've taken worse beatings and still won the fight. By which I mean, walked away on my own power.

He won't be.

I finally get his fist out of my shirt by virtue of ripping the shirt off.

I spare a glance at her. "Nell. Shut up."

She goes silent immediately, sucks in a breath as if realizing where she is, what's happening. Then she spins on her heel, digs in a kitchen drawer, and slinks up behind Dan with a giant knife in her hand. She presses the blade to Dan's throat.

"Enough." She doesn't need to yell. The knife speaks loud enough.

Dan goes still. "You don't want to do that, Nell." His eyes are deadly.

Her dress is ripped open down the front, her panties torn partially off. Her lip is bleeding, and she has
bruises on her arms and throat.

I don't want her to kill him. That's a lot of trouble
neither of us need. "Strangely, I agree with the Ogre
here," I say. "Let me finish this."

Nell snickers at the name. "Ogre. Fitting." She
meets my eyes, then relaxes the knife.

Which was a mistake. The instant the blade moves
away, Dan bats her hand to the side, spins in place, and
punches her, knocking her flying.

"Bitch," he growls, and turns to me.

Of course, I didn't spend those moments idle,
either. Brass knuckles go back on, and I'm not holding
back anymore. The second I saw those bruises on her,
I was gone.

I'm a street thug again, an enforcer. Except this is
different; he hurt Nell.

He doesn't stand a chance. Within moments, he's
a bloody, broken mess on Nell's floor. I've got some
tender ribs, a broken nose, split lips and cuts on my
cheekbones, a loosened tooth. Blood is everywhere.

I pull my phone out, dial a number, wipe my face
clean with a paper towel. "Hey, Split, it's Colt. I have
a problem." I explain the problem and spit out the
address. "Yeah, in Tribeca. Shut up, motherfucker. Just

come get the bastard and make sure he doesn't bother her again. Thanks."

Nell is standing up, dabbing at her mouth, wobbling. I dart across to catch her as she stumbles.

I pick her up, set her on the counter like a child, wrap some ice in a paper towel and press it to her face where he hit her. Fortunately, he wasn't stupid enough to hit her full-force, just a little tap to shut her up. She'll have a bruise, but that's it. She's woozy, bleary-eyed, but she clears up soon.

Dan moans behind me, reminding her of the problem. She straightens in fear at the sound of his voice, peers over my shoulder at the chunk of bloody beef that is Dan Sikorsky.

She looks slowly from him to me. "What did you do?"

I duck my head, embarrassed. "I sort of lost my temper."

"Will he die?" She says it calmly.

I shrug. "Not in your living room."

She narrows her lovely eyes at me. "What's that mean?" A quiet rap on the door has her shrinking against me. "Who's that?"

I pull the tattered remains of her dress closed. "A friend of mine. Go get in the shower, huh?"

"A friend?" She slides off the counter and moves to open the door.

I stop her. "I'll take care of it, okay?"

She narrows her eyes again, vanishes into her room, and closes the door behind her. I let Split in. He's not a big guy, but he's scary. Medium height, lean and toned, skin black as night, vibrantly white teeth and eyes so light brown they're almost khaki. Eyes you can't look at too long or you'll piss yourself. Eyes that see your secrets and threaten to make your nightmares come true. He radiates intensity and exudes threat. I'm glad he's my friend, mainly because I've seen what happens to his enemies: They vanish.

He glances down at Dan. "The fuck happened to him?"

Nell comes out in a clean T-shirt and yoga pants. "Colton was helping me."

"Who're you?" Split says.

"Nell Hawthorne. This is my apartment." She extends her hand to shake Split's.

He looks at her outstretched hand like it's an insect, then cracks a rare smile as he shakes it. "Split." He peers at Nell's face, at the purpling bruise, the finger marks on her throat, the way she clutches her arms around her middle. "He try to rape you?"

Nell nods.

"His name is Dan Sikorsky," I say, knowing Split will put two and two together.

Split's eyes widen slightly, the equivalent of a gasp of surprise from anyone else. "I saw him fight Hank Tremaine a few weeks ago down in Harlem. Fucked Hank up good. You did this?" He kneels down, nudges Dan over onto his back, examines his injuries with a professional eye. "You done a number on him, Colt. He needs a doctor, or he ain't gonna make it."

"He tried to rape her, Split. Then he punched her."

"To be fair," Nell puts in, "he only punched me after I put a knife to his throat."

Split coughs a laugh. "You what? Girl, you crazy. Don't put a knife to a guy like Dan Sikorsky and not kill him. Asking for trouble, pullin' shit like that."

"She's from the Detroit suburbs, Split. Where I grew up. She's vanilla."

He nods. "I getcha. Just saying, in case there's a next time. Don't threaten what you won't finish. Not with motherfuckers like Sikorksy. He'll kill you, even if you are a rich white bitch."

"Excuse me?" Nell straightens in protest.

Split glances at me. I laugh. "He just means a white girl. Not from the hood."

"The hood?" She says it like it's a foreign word. "And you *are* from the hood, Colton?"

Split laughs again. "Colton?" He says the name how she did, clearly enunciating each syllable. "Man, she something else. Where'd you find her?" He looks at Nell. "Yeah, he from the hood. My boy Colt is a OG from way back."

Nell makes a confused face. "OG?"

Split just blows a laugh past his lips, a huff of air. "You something else, man." He pulls out a phone and sends a text, then glances back at Nell. "You holding up all right, white girl?"

Nell's face is impassive. "I'm fine."

Split nods, but I can tell he doesn't believe her any more than I do. I step closer to Nell, and I don't miss the fact that she tenses, even though it's me. "Go take a shower, Nell. It'll help."

"I don't need help." Her voice is hard, stubborn.

I laugh, but not unkindly. "You want to deal with him on your own, then?" I gesture at Dan, who is choking on his blood. Split turns him over so he drools it out on the hardwood floor.

Nell pales, trembles. "Maybe a shower sounds good."

"Yeah. All this will be gone when you get out."

I see panic flit across her face. "You won't be gone, will you?"

"Do you want me to go?" She shakes her head, a tiny, vulnerable motion that makes my heart bleed a little more for her. "Then I'll be here. Just...go take a hot shower."

She nods and disappears into the bedroom. I hear the shower turn on, and I try not to picture her in there. That's not what she needs right now.

Split crouches at Dan's feet. "Get his shoulders, Colt."

I bend and lift him, and we carry him down the stairs and out to Split's waiting car. A couple passes us by, gives us an odd look, but since this is New York, they don't say anything. We toss him ungently in the back seat and close the door. Split opens the driver's-side door and slides in, but doesn't close it.

"She don't belong in this world, Colt." He doesn't look at me as he says it.

"I know."

"Neither do you. You never did."

"I know that, too."

"I like you, white boy. Don't get sucked back in. You'll end up dead, and then who'll fix my ride when it busts?" Split starts the car, and it rumbles to life.

It's a lime green '73 Bonneville with the original engine, restored by yours truly. It's a beauty, and I've always been a bit jealous. He bought it off some little old lady out in Rochester for a thousand dollars, and he and I spent a summer restoring it together. Didn't take much, since the little old lady had barely ever driven it after her husband died.

He brings it to me when he needs a tuneup or something, but really, it's his way of keeping in touch with me.

"I won't, Split."

"What you want me to do with Dickhead Dan?"

"I don't know, and I don't want to know. He deserves to choke to death on his own fucking teeth, but I don't want that on my conscience."

"No shit. You got enough on blood on that bitch."

I laugh. "Thanks for the reminder."

"Just keeping it real." He closes his door and rolls down the window. "I'll stop by the shop and let you know if he makes it."

"Don't. Just make sure he doesn't come back around here."

Split smiles at me, a flash of white teeth in dark skin. "I don't think that'll be a problem." He pulls the gearshift down into "D" but pauses still. "The problem is, he's supposed to fight Alvarez next week, and I had a grand on Alvarez."

I laugh. "Alvarez didn't stand a chance, so I just saved you a grand. He was a dick, but he was a tough motherfucker."

"You missed your calling, Colt. You'd've cleaned up in the UFC."

I shake my head. "I'm well shut of all that shit."

"I know it, I know it. Just saying." He holds his fist out, and I bump it with mine. "Call me, dog. We're past due for some cold ones."

"For sure. Maybe Thursday."

"I could do Thursday. Got some shit early, but that's it."

I nod, and he drives off. I open Nell's door and go in, singing a song so she'd know it was me. The shower is still running, telling me she was probably scrubbing the shit out of her skin. Trying to get the feeling off. She'll be in there till the water runs cold. I've seen too many friends go through this, friends I couldn't be there to save.

I take a new roll of paper towel from under the sink and her bottle of Windex. Fortunately, she has wood floors. It's easier to get blood off wood than carpet. I sop up the blood, spray and scrub the wood, then find an old bottle of Pledge that she must use on her kitchen table. I spray the floor and scrub some more. Then I wipe the walls and everywhere else.

Eventually, the water turns off, and the mess is gone. Nell comes out with wet, stringy hair, clad in only a long Disney T-shirt that barely comes to mid-thigh. I clench my jaw and think of dead puppies and nuns and that time I walked in on my grandma in the shower as a kid. It only helps marginally. She looks more vulnerable than ever, and I'm across the room and wrapping my arms around her before I know what I'm doing.

She doesn't tense this time. She breathes deeply, long, steady, even breaths.

"It's okay to cry," I say.

She shakes her head. "No. It's not."

"You were just assaulted. You're allowed."

"I know. But I won't. I can't." She pushes away from me and goes into the kitchen.

I take the bottle of Jack from her hand before she can drink from it. "I'm not sure that's the best way." She jerks it away and lifts it, but I take it again. "It won't go away forever. It just comes back."

"I know." She reaches for it, and I hold it out of reach, snag a couple juice glasses from her cabinet and pour generous shots. "I need more than that."

"No, you don't."

She turns on me, eyes all gray now, like storm clouds, angry. "Don't tell me what I need! You don't know me."

"But I know about drowning pain with whiskey. It stops working after a while. And then there's not enough whiskey in the world."

"You weren't just raped."

"Almost raped. I stopped him. I'm sorry I wasn't sooner, but there's a huge difference between raped and *almost* raped." Her eyes blaze, and I hold up my hands. "Not saying this is fine. It's not fine. You're allowed to feel what you're feeling. I'm just saying, chugging whiskey won't erase what happened."

"What the fuck do you know?" She slams the shot and presses the glass to her forehead, then holds out the glass for more.

That's when I see the scars. A crosshatch pattern of fine white lines and ridges on her wrists and forearms. Not disguised, not hidden. Some old, some not so old. And some fresh. Still-scabbing fresh.

She sees me see, lifts her chin and dares me to ask. I don't ask. I'm still not wearing a shirt, so I point to my chest, to my pectorals and breastbone and stomach, to a similar field of scars like wind-tangled wheat stalks. I've tattooed over some, utilized others in tattoos, and left others bare and visible. She reaches out with her forefinger, traces them, one scar after another. Some short, like tally marks. Some are tally marks: days survived in the pit, matches won. She traces the scars, the long ones done for the sake of the pain, for the release.

Yeah. I know why she cuts. I just don't know the seed-reason. It's deep inside her, and it'll take time and patience to get it out of her. And I'll probably end up telling her my reasons, too.

Which I really don't want to do.

She looks up at me, and her eyes are soft, full of understanding. "You cut?"

"Used to."

"Why?"

I shake my head. "That's a story for another night, and it comes with a price."

She tenses. "A price?"

"Your story."

She blows out a sigh of relief. "You know the story."

"Not all of it. Not the deep stuff, the shit that comes from beneath, in the shadows in your heart."

"No one knows that." Her voice is barely even a whisper, and goddamn it if it's not seductive and sultry and vulnerable all at once.

"Yeah, well, no one knows about this, either." I tap my chest with my thumb.

"A price. A trade." She's motionless, an inch away from me, each breath causing her breasts to brush my chest, the scars, the ink.

I nod. "But not now. Now, you take one more shot with me, and you watch stupid, mindless TV. And then you fall asleep and you stay home tomorrow."

"I can't. I have class. I have work."

"Call off. Say you're sick."

"I—"

I cut her off. "Call in, Nell."

"You can't stay here all night with me."

"Why not?"

She stares at her toes, chipped pink polish. "You just can't."

"I'll be on the couch. You'll be in your room with the door closed."

"No." Another whisper.

"Why not?"

"It's...part of the trade."

A secret, she means. "Then I'll sleep on the floor outside your apartment. You're not going to be alone tonight."

"I'm fine, Colton."

"Bullshit. You're not fine."

She shrugs. "No. But I'm fine."

I laugh at that. "Look at me."

She shakes her head no, chews her lip, and I want to take that lip in my mouth and suck it until the teeth marks are soothed away. I want to chew her lip for her. I want to taste her tongue. I want to run my hands under the silly, girly, childish, double-XL *Lilo and Stitch* shirt and feel her skin and her curves and her sweet softness.

I do none of this. I just stare at her, then touch her chin with my index finger, lift her head to meet my eyes. She closes her eyes, and I can see the moisture. She's deep-breathing again, and I notice her hands are clutched around the opposing wrists, nails digging in deep, hard, scratching. Pain to replace pain. I use as much gentle force as I possess to pry her fingers out of her skin, turn them so they're gripping my forearms.

I pull her against me, our arms barred vertically between us, and her fingernails dig into my arms. She lets go after a moment and just holds my forearms in her hands.

"It's not the same. Causing you pain doesn't help mine." She whispers the words against my shoulder, the right one, the one with the Japanese dragon breathing fire on kanji.

"It wasn't supposed to. It was just supposed to stop you from hurting yourself."

"It helps—"

"No it doesn't. It just pushes it away temporarily. Just like the booze."

"But I need—"

"You need to let yourself feel. Feel it, own it. Then move on."

"You make it sound so easy." Bitterness drips from each syllable.

"It's not. It's the fucking hardest thing a person can do." I smooth a damp strand out of her face and away from my mouth. "It's the hardest fucking thing. It's why we drink and do drugs and fight. It's why I play music and build engines."

She pulls away from me. "You build engines?"

I laugh. "Yeah. Music is a hobby. A passion. I rebuild engines and restore classic cars. That's what pays the bills. Don't get me wrong, I'm passionate about cars, too, but it's different."

"Do you work for someone?"

"No, I own my own shop in Queens."

"Really?" She sounds surprised, which I actually find a little insulting, but I don't say anything.

"Really."

"Can I see your shop?" Her voice is bright and hopeful.

"Now?"

"Yes, now. I can't be here. I keep seeing Dan. I keep…I keep feeling his hands on me, keep seeing him on the floor right there, bleeding." She points to where he was lying. She's quiet for a long moment, and I know what's coming next. "Is he…is he dead?"

"No. Don't worry about him anymore. He got what he deserved."

"You hurt him really bad."

"I should have killed him. I could have. If he'd…" I shake my head. "It's done. Forget it."

"I should have seen it coming." The words don't surprise me, but they piss me off.

I pull away and glare down at her. "Don't you fucking dare, Nell Hawthorne. Don't you dare put this on yourself. You should never have to see shit like this coming."

She backs away, stunned and afraid by the intensity I know is radiating off me.

"Colton, I just meant he's always shown—"

"Stop. Just stop right there. Granted, you should've never gotten involved with a douchetard like him, but that's no excuse for what he did." I pull her back against me. She resists. "Are you afraid of me now?" I ask, to change the subject.

"A little. You were…scary. You just…you *destroyed* him. Even after he hit you. And I've seen him fight."

I glance down at her in shock. "You mean on TV?"

She shakes her head. "No, the other fights. The underground ones. The ones that your friend was talking about. In Harlem."

"You went to those fights?" I'm shocked. Stunned. Horrified. Those are brutal, vile, vicious fights. Angry, soulless men destroying each other. I should know.

"Yeah. I didn't like it very much."

"I'd hope not. They're evil." I try to keep my voice neutral.

Unsuccessfully, by the click of understanding I see cross her face. "You've fought in them."

"Used to."

"Why?" Her voice is tiny.

I shake my head. "That's part of the trade, babe."

She shudders. *"Don't* call me babe." Her voice is quiet but intense.

"Sorry."

"It's fine. It's just what Dan—"

"I know. I heard." I pull back so we're looking into each other's eyes. "Answer the question, though. Are you afraid of me?"

"I did answer. I said a little. I'm afraid of what you can do. I mean, I feel safe with you, though. I know you'd never hurt me."

I take her face in my hands. It's too familiar, too affectionate, too soon. I can't help it, though. "Just the opposite. I will protect you. From others and from yourself. Always."

"Why?" Barely audible.

"Because I want to. Because…" I struggle to find the right words. "Because you deserve it, and you need it."

"No, I don't."

"Yes, you do."

She shakes her head. "No. I don't deserve it."

I sigh, knowing I won't win by arguing. "Shut up, Nell."

She laughs, a tinkling giggle that makes me smile into her hair. "So. Are you gonna show me your shop?"

"It's four in the morning. We're in Tribeca, and my shop is in Queens. The far side of Queens. Plus, I don't have a car here. I walked here from the bar."

"You *walked* here? You're crazy! That's, like, twenty blocks."

I shrug. "I like to walk."

"So we'll take a cab."

"You really want to see my shop that bad?"

"Yeah. And I really don't want to be here." She shudders again, remembering.

"Well, then, you'll need pants."

She does the giggle again, which I decide to call the Tinkerbell giggle. "Nah. Pants are for sissies." She pulls away and disappears into her room. "No peeking this time, Pervy McGee."

"Then close your door, dumbass."

The door slams in response, and I laugh. I'm glad she can laugh. It means she really is coping. I know she's internalizing a lot, though. Putting on a show for me. She'll have new scars on her wrists soon.

She comes out in a pair of jeans and purple V-neck T-shirt. I have to keep my gaze moving so I don't stare.

She doesn't need my desire right now. Maybe not ever. She grabs her purse from the counter where I'd set it after cleaning up.

I extend my hand to her. "Come on, Tinkerbell."

She takes my hand, then pauses at the nickname. "Tinkerbell?"

"Your laugh. That little giggle you do. It reminds me of Tinkerbell." I shrug.

She does the giggle by accident, then claps a hand over her mouth. "Damn it. Now you have me self-conscious. You can call me Tinkerbell, though."

"Don't be self-conscious. I think it's cute."

She wrinkles her nose at me as she locks her door behind us. "Cute? Is that a good thing?"

I lift an eyebrow at her. "There's a lot of words I could think of for you. Let's just go with cute for now."

"What's that mean?" She's holding my hand platonic-style, palm in palm.

I flag a passing cab with a lit sign, and we slide in. I give him my address and watch him put it into a Tom Tom. When we're moving and the wavery tones of the driver's Arabic music float over us, I turn to Nell.

"Sure you want to ask that?"

She lifts her chin. "Yes."

"You're a lot of things, Nell Hawthorne. You're complex. You're cute. You're lovely. You're funny.

You're strong. You're beautiful." She seems to be struggling with words and emotions. I keep going. "You're tortured. You're hurting. You're amazing. You're talented. You're sexy as fuck."

"Sexy as fuck?" She tilts her head, a small grin tipping her lips.

"Yep."

"Is that more or less than sexy as hell?"

"More. A lot more."

She just nods. "You're sweet. But we must not see the same person when we look at me."

"That's probably true." I look down at our joined hands, then back to her. I shift my fingers, twine mine in hers. "What do you see when you look at yourself?"

"Weak. Scared. Drunk. Angry. Ugly. Running." She turns away from me as she says this, staring out the window. "I see nothing. No one."

I know there aren't words to change how she feels, so I don't offer any. I just hold her hand and let the silence extend through the blocks.

She turns to me eventually. "Why don't you argue with me when I say shit like that? Why don't you try to convince me of my own worth and all that bullshit?"

"Would it work?" I ask. She narrows her eyes, then shakes her head. I shrug. "Well, there you go. That's why. I can tell you what I see. I can tell you what I know about you. I can tell how I feel. I can show you what you really are. But arguing with you won't accomplish anything. I think we've both had our share of people trying to fix us. It doesn't work. We can only fix ourselves. Let ourselves heal."

"But I'm not any of what you said. I'm just not. And I can't heal myself. I can't...I can't be fixed."

"You're committed to being broken forever?"

"Goddamn it, Colton. Why are you doing this? You don't know me."

"I want to." It's the answer to both of her statements.

Chapter 8: Fermented Grief

WE ARRIVE AT MY SHOP, an old garage with the door facing an alley, a little apartment above. I pull my keys from my pocket, open the side door to the shop, and snap on the lights.

Cracked, stained concrete floor; hanging, flickering fluorescent lights in warped cages; stack after stack of red and silver tool chests along the walls; counters with more tools hanging from hooks; chains from the ceiling suspending engines; the metal frame of a '66 Mustang Shelby GT; a couple huge gray plastic garbage cans and overflowing ashtrays and abandoned beer bottles and pizza boxes…

"It's not much, but it's mine." I laugh. "It's really, really not much. I can't believe I brought you here. It's so dirty and ugly."

I'm seeing it for the first time, in a way. I've never brought a girl here before. I've brought girls to my place before, but they never want to see the shop; they're only interested in the bed. I look around, seeing what she must see.

Then she surprises me. "I love it. It…feels like home. It's a place that you obviously love."

I stare at her. "It *is* home. I may sleep upstairs, but this garage is home. More than you know."

I think of all the times I slept in a sleeping bag on the floor where the Mustang is now, before the apartment upstairs was renovated to be livable. I bought this place for a pittance, because it was a dump. Rejected, abandoned, unwanted. Like me. I fixed it up. Made it mine.

She lets go of my hand and wanders around the shop, pulling open drawers and examining tools, which look bulky and awkward and dirty in her clean, delicate hands. She always puts the tools back exactly where they were. I wonder if she realizes how anal I am about that, or if she's just polite. Probably just polite. We really don't know each other at all. She couldn't know about my OCD about the tools.

"Show me what you do," she says.

I shrug. I point at the engine. "That engine there." I walk over and run my finger around the opening of a piston. "I bought it at a junkyard a few weeks ago. It was rusted and dirty and ruined, basically. It was in an old car that had been in a wreck, rear-ended and totaled. A '77 Barracuda. I took the engine, fixed the parts I could fix, replaced the ones I couldn't. I took it apart completely, down to the components."

I pull the tarp off a long, wide table in a corner, showing a dissected motor, each part laid out in a very specific pattern. "Like this. Then I put it all back together, one piece at a time, until you see it there. It's almost done. Just gotta install a few more parts and it's done, ready to be put into a car."

She looks from the table to the reassembled motor. "So you turned that—" she points at the pieces on the table, "into *that?*"

I shrug. "Yeah. Those are completely different engines, but yeah."

"That's amazing. How do you know where all the different parts go? How to fix them?"

I laugh. "Lots of experience. I know from having done it a million times. All engines are basically the same, just with little differences that make each kind of engine unique. I took my first motor apart when I was…thirteen? Of course, once I got it apart, I couldn't get it back together again, but that was part of the learning process. I tinkered with that fucked-up engine for months, figuring out how the thing worked, which parts went where and what they did and how to get them back in. Eventually I did get it back together and running, but it took me, like, I don't know, more than a year of dicking around with it every day. I took it apart again, and put it back together after that. Over and over again, until I could do it without stopping to think about what came next."

She tilts her head. "Where'd you get the engine?"

I stare up at the ceiling, trying to remember. "Hmm. I think I bought it off the shop teacher at the high school. I'd saved my allowance for months." She still looks confused, and I laugh. "I had a tutor at the high school after classes ended at the middle school. I happened to walk by the shop one day and saw the engine, and something just clicked as I watched the shop instructor, Mr. Boyd, puttering with it. He ended up being one of my best friends until I moved out here."

Nell is peering at me as if seeing me for the first time. "You had a tutor?"

I wince, wishing she'd have missed that part. "Yeah. I wasn't very good at the whole school thing."

I turn away and throw the tarp over the table, and lead her to the private stairway leading to my apartment. It's my way of politely indicating I don't want to talk about it, and she seems to get the message.

Saying I wasn't very good at the school thing was a huge understatement, but she doesn't need to know that. I'm hoping to avoid the subject as long as I can.

My apartment isn't much. A galley kitchen I can barely fit in—like, I can't have the stove and the cabinets opposite open at the same time, not that I ever use the stove, but still—a living room in which I can just about touch all four walls standing in the center, and a bedroom that contains my queen bed and nothing else. All my clothes are in the dresser, which is in the living room, and the dresser also doubles as the TV stand. Not that I ever really watch TV.

I throw my arm out to gesture at the apartment. "It's even less than the shop, but it's home. I'd say I would give you the ten-cent tour, but I'd need to give you nine and a half cents back."

She laughs, the Tinkerbell giggle, and my heart lifts. But even with all the normality, the questions, the interest, I can see her fighting for calm. She hides it well, hides it like a pro. It's buried deep, thrust down under the surface.

I respect the hell out of her for how hard she's working to be okay. I just wish she'd let me show her how to let go, how to let herself hurt. I want to take her pain.

She's plopped down onto the couch, and I can see the exhaustion in her eyes, in her posture. I leave her sitting on the couch, head back, legs splayed out. Making sure my room isn't a complete pigsty, I change the sheets and add an extra blanket, then go back out to tell her she can crash in my bed. She's already passed out in the position she sat down in. I lift her easily. She's light as a feather, like an actual, factual fairy, made of glass and magic and fragile porcelain and deceptive strength. I set her in the bed, tug off her shoes, then debate whether to take her pants off for her or not.

Selfishly enough, I decide to go for it. I mean, I know I hate sleeping in pants, so I can't imagine she does, either. I pop the button, slide the zipper down, grip the denim at her hips, and pull. She wriggles, lifts her hips, and I pull them down to her knees. The sight of her thighs and her pale cream skin is almost too much for me to take, especially with her tiny yellow thong, barely disguising the tender "V" in which I want so desperately to bury my face, my body. I can't help my fingers from tracing a featherlight line across her thigh, just a brief touch, but too much. And not nearly enough.

I jerk myself away and scrub my hands over my face, through my hair, fighting for control.

I turn back, close my eyes, and peel her jeans off the rest of the way.

As I'm in the process of pulling them past her toes, she speaks, muzzy and sleepy and ridiculously goddamn cute. "You've already seen me in my panties. Why the shy guy now?"

I settle the blankets at her neck, and she presses them down with her elbows on the outside, staring up at me with long fluttering lashes and tangled strawberry blonde hair wisping across her perfect features. I back away before I give in to the temptation to brush the hair away with my callused fingertips. I can't read the expression on her face. She just looks so fucking vulnerable, as if all the hurt is coming up and boiling over and she's barely keeping it in, now that sleep has nearly claimed her.

"That was an asshole move," I say. "I shouldn't have done that. You were asleep, I didn't want—"

"It was sweet," she says, cutting in over me.

"I'm a lot of things, Tinkerbell. Sweet ain't one of them." I brush my hand through my hair, a nervous gesture. "I only closed my eyes so I wouldn't feel you up in your sleep."

Her eyes widen. "You wanted to feel me up?"

I don't quite succeed in stifling my laugh of disbelief; she doesn't understand how bad I want her. Good for her. She can't know.

I take a step closer to her, next to the bed, and I just can't summon the strength to resist. A strand of hair lies across her high, sculpted cheekbone. I brush it away, mentally cursing my weakness.

"You have no clue, Nell." I back away before my mouth or my hands betray me further. "Sleep, and think of blue."

She snorts. "Think of blue?"

"It's a technique I learned to keep bad dreams away," I tell her. "As I fall asleep, I think of blueness. Not things that are blue, just…an endless, all-encompassing sense of blue. Ocean blue, sky blue."

"Blue like your eyes." Her voice is unreadably soft.

I shake my head, smirking. "If that's what brings you peace, then sure. The point is, think of a soothing color. Picture it floating through you, in you, around you, until you are that color." I shrug. "It helped me."

"What do you dream about?" Her eyes are awake, and piercing.

I turn away and flick the light off, speak facing away from her. "Nothing for you to worry about. Bad things. Old things." I turn back to glance at her, and her eyes are heavy again. "Sleep, Nell."

I close the door behind me and retreat into the kitchen. It's nearly five in the morning by this point, and I'm beyond exhausted. I was up at seven yesterday finishing a Hemi rebuild, and the guys are going to be here to start working on the 'Stang around eight. I end up writing a note and leaving it taped to the frame, saying I won't be in today. They know what to do. Perk of being the boss, I guess. I trudge back up the stairs and slump back on the couch, eyes heavy but brain whirling.

I'll never get to sleep at this rate. I curse under my breath, trying to banish images of Nell's naked thighs, begging to be caressed. It's not working.

Desperate times call for desperate measures. In the top drawer of my dresser is a little white medicine box. I keep it for times like this, when I can't sleep, can't stop thinking. It's a holdover from the bad old days. I roll a pin-thin joint and smoke it slowly, savoring it. I rarely smoke these days. I don't even remember the last time, to be honest.

I gave up hard drinking, gave up cigarettes, gave up pot, gave up a lot of other shit when I decided to get my life straight. But every rare once in a while, a little bit of weed is a necessity. I pinch off the cherry and stow the kit, and I'm finally lying down on the couch, fading away, when I hear it.

Strained, high-pitched humming. An odd noise, scary, tense. As if she's struggling with every fiber of her being not to sob, teeth clenched. I can almost see her rocking back and forth, or curled into a fetal position.

I'm through the door and cradling her in my arms in the space of three heartbeats. She fits on my lap, against my chest, in my arms so perfectly. She's shuddering, trembling, every muscle flexed. I brush her hair back with my fingers, cup her cheek, feel the tension in her jaw. The noise is coming from deep inside her, dragged up from the bottom of her soul. It breaks my heart. Wrecks me.

"Nell. Look at me." I tip her chin up, and she jerks away, burrows against my chest, as if she wants to climb between my ribs and nestle in the spaces between my heart and my lungs. "Okay, fine. Don't look at me. But listen."

She shakes her head, and her fingers grip my bicep so hard I'll have bruises later. She's crazy strong.

"It's not okay," I tell her. This gets her attention; it's not what she was expecting. "You don't have to be okay."

"What do you *want* from me?" Her voice is ragged, desperate.

"I want you to let yourself be broken. Let yourself hurt."

She shakes her head again. "I can't. If I let it out, it'll never stop."

"Yes, it will."

"No, it won't. It won't. There's too much." She judders, sucks in a fast breath, and shakes her head in a fierce denial. "It'll never stop coming out, and I'll be empty."

She tries to climb off me, and I let her. She tumbles off the bed, falls to her hands and knees on the floor, scrambles away, and stumbles into the bathroom. I hear her vomit, retch, and stifle a sob. I move to stand in the doorway and watch her. She's got her forearm gripped in clawed fingers, squeezing so hard trickles of blood drip where nails meet flesh.

Pain to replace pain.

I step in front of her, take her chin in my hand, and force her to look at me. She closes her eyes, jerks away. The sight of her blood makes me panic. I can't watch her hurt herself. I wrestle with her hand, but she won't let go, and if I force her, she'll only hurt herself worse.

I need to know what's driving this girl. What's devouring her.

"Tell me." I whisper the words to her, rough and raw in the unlit bathroom, gray dawn filtering through dirty glass.

"He's dead."

"That's not enough."

"It's everything."

I sigh deeply, glare at the top of her head. She feels it, finally looks up at me with red-laced eyes. Sad, haunted, angry eyes.

"Don't fucking lie to me, Nell." The words are grating and too harsh. I regret them, but keep going. "Tell me."

"*No!*" She shoves me back so hard I stumble.

She sinks backward, shrinking down into a ball in front of the toilet, next to the tub. I kneel down, creep forward as if approaching an injured, skittish sparrow. I am, really. She's clawing her nails up and down her thighs, leaving red, ragged scratch marks. I catch her hands and still them. God, she's strong. I heave another sigh, then scoop her up into my arms again and carry her into the bedroom.

I cradle her against me and settle onto the bed, slide down with her until her head is pillowed on my chest and I'm holding her tight, squeezing hard, clutching her wrists in one of mine.

She's frozen, tensed. I take long, even breaths, stroke her hair with my free hand. Gradually she begins to relax. I count her breaths, feel them even out, and then she's limp on top of me, sleeping, twitching as she delves into slumber.

I wait, stay awake, knowing what's coming.

She moans, writhes, begins to whimper, and then she's awake and making that fucking horrible high-pitched whining noise in her throat again. I hold her tight, refuse to let go. She struggles against me, waking up.

"Let me go!" she growls.

"No."

"Let me fucking go, Colton." Her voice is tiny, scared, vulnerable, and vehement.

"*You* let go."

"Why?" A hitch in her voice.

"Because holding on to it is killing you."

"Good." She's still struggling, thrashing against my hold.

"'There's a shortage of perfect breasts in this world. It would be a pity to ruin yours.'"

She stops thrashing and laughs. "Did you just quote *The Princess Bride* at me?"

"Maybe."

She laughs, and the laugh turns into a sob, quickly choked off.

I sigh. "Fine. How 'bout I start?" I really don't want to do this. "When I came to New York, I was seventeen. I had five dollars in my pocket, a backpack full of clothes, a package of Ritz crackers, a can of Coke, and nothing else. I knew no one. I had a high school diploma, barely, and I knew I could fix any engine put in front of me. I spent the first day I got off the bus looking for a mechanic garage, trying to find a job. No one would even let me apply. I hadn't eaten in two days. I slept on a bench in Central Park that night, at least till the cops made me move."

I have her interest now. She's still in my arms, staring up at me. I'm speaking to the ceiling, because her eyes are too piercing.

"I nearly starved to death, to be honest. I knew nothing. I'd grown up privileged, you know my dad, how much my parents have. I'd never even had to make my own food, wash my own clothes. Suddenly, I'm alone in this insane city where no one gives a shit about anyone else. Dog eat dog, and all that."

"How'd you survive?"

"I got in a fight." I laugh. "I had a nice little spot to sleep beneath a bridge, and this old bum comes along and says it's his spot and I have to move. Well, I hadn't really slept in days, and I wasn't about to move. So we fought. It was sloppy and nasty, since I was hungry and tired and scared, and he was old and tough and hard, but I won. Turns out this guy was watching the whole thing. He came up to me after I won and asks if I wanted to make a quick hundred bucks. I didn't even hesitate. He brings me to this old warehouse in a shitty part of I don't even know where. A back alley in Long Island, maybe. He feeds me, gives me a cold beer. I was a new man after that. He brings me down into the basement of this warehouse where there's a bunch of people in a circle, cheering and shit. I hear the sounds of a fight."

Nell gasps, and I can tell she knows where this is going.

"Yeah. I won. The guy I fought was huge, but slow. I'd been in my share of trouble in high school, so I knew how to fight. This guy was just big and strong, no technique. I did three fights that night, all in a row. Took an awful beating in the last one, but I won. Made four hundred bucks, and that was how I started. Then I met Split. He was at one of the fights and offered me job, sort of. Said he needed someone to be muscle for him, collecting debts, be scary. Well, I could do scary. So I went with Split and I...well, it wasn't bare-knuckle prize fighting. Intimidation, mostly. People owed him for favors, for drugs...I'd solve the problem. That's how I met Split, how I ended up in the Five-One Bishops."

"A gang?"

"Yes, Nell. A gang." I sigh. "They were my family. My friends. They fed me, gave me a bed to sleep in. Gave me booze to drink and pot to smoke and girls to roll. Sorry, but it's the truth. I'm not proud of some of the shit I did, but those guys, they were tight. Honorable, most of 'em, in their own way. They'd never, ever betray me, no matter what. They'd back my play, no questions asked. Even now, years out of the game, living clean and honest, working for myself, if I called them, they'd come, and they wouldn't flinch to do whatever I asked."

"Like Split today."

I nod against her hair. "Exactly."

"Tell me the truth, Colton. Where did he take Dan?"

I shrug. "I honestly don't know. I told him I didn't want to know. I told Split I didn't want a body on my conscience, though, but I also didn't want you to ever have to worry about Dan again. So forget him."

A long silence, and I knew she was formulating a question. "Do you?"

"Do I what?"

"Have bodies on your conscience?"

I don't answer. "Does it matter?"

"Yes. To me it does."

"Yes. I do." I hesitate for a long moment. "You can't understand that life, Nell. You just can't. It was survival."

"I guess I can get that."

"But?"

She sighs. "I don't understand why you came here alone with no money. What about college? Why didn't your parents help you? Do they know about how you survived?"

I shake my head and examine my knuckles. "That's a different conversation."

"My turn?"

"Yes," I say. "Your turn."

"You know the story, Colton. Kyle died."

I growl low in my chest. "There's more." I lift her wrist to trace the scars there. "That's not enough to make you do this."

She doesn't answer for so long I wonder if she's fallen asleep. Eventually she speaks, and when she does it's a raw whisper. I barely breathe, not daring to interrupt.

"We were up north. Your parents' cabin. We'd been dating for over two years, and we were so excited to be taking a vacation together, like adults. Your parents and mine gave Kyle and me the talk about being careful, even though we'd been sleeping together for almost two years by that point. Until then it seemed to be 'don't ask don't tell,' I guess. I don't know. But we had a great time. Swimming, sitting by the fire, having sex. I…god…god…I can't." She's struggling so hard against her emotions. I comb my fingers through her hair and scratch her back. She continues, her voice tight, but a bit stronger. "Sunday, the last day, it was stormy. Rain so hard you couldn't see shit, windy as hell. I mean, I've never seen wind like that, ever, before or since. Those huge pine trees around the cabin were bent nearly double."

She pauses, panting as if exhausted, then continues in a much softer and more vulnerable voice. "A tree fell. It should have hit me…it almost *did* hit me. I saw it falling toward me, and I couldn't move. Some of the nightmares, it's that moment I see, over and over again, the tree coming for me. Those are the nice and easy nightmares. A split second before it hit me, Kyle knocked me out of the way. I mean, he straight-up football-tackled me. Knocked me flying. I landed on my arm. I don't remember hitting the ground, but I remember coming to and feeling pain like a white wave, and seeing bones sticking out of my forearm, the whole bone bent almost at a ninety-degree angle." I barely hear the next words. "I should have died. He saved me. It hit him instead. Broke him. Just…fucking shattered him. A branch broke and—and impaled him. I can still see the blood coming out of his mouth… bubbling on his lips like froth. His breath…it whistled. He—I watched him die. I didn't even know the address of the house, and he, he told me the address as he died for the ambulance that wouldn't get there until after he was dead. I ripped my fingernails off trying to move the damn tree. I broke my arm worse when I fell in the mud. That's the worst dream-memory: lying in the mud, watching him die. Watch—watching the light go out of his eyes. His beautiful chocolate brown eyes. The last words he said were 'I love you.'"

I don't dare speak. She's shaking so hard I'm worried it's almost a seizure. She'll break soon.

"The other thing I see, every goddamn night, is his shoe. We'd gone to dinner at that fancy Italian place. He had on his dress shoes. Black leather. Stupid little tassels on the front. I hated those shoes. When the tree hit him, it hit so hard his shoe was knocked clean off. I see that shoe, in the mud. Smeared with brown mud, like shit. I see that one stupid fucking shoe, with the tassels."

I have to say it. She's gonna get mad, but I have to say it. "It wasn't your fault."

"DON'T SAY THAT! YOU DON'T FUCKING KNOW!" She shrieks it in my ear, so loud my ears ring.

"Then tell me," I whisper.

"I can't. I can't. I can't." She's shaking her head, twisting it side to side, a refusal to break. "It was my fault. I killed him." A sob, then a full, unchecked sob.

"Bullshit. He saved you. He loved you. You didn't kill him."

"You don't understand. I did kill him. We were arguing. If I had just said yes, he'd be alive. You don't understand. You don't—don't. Can't know. No one knows. If I'd just said yes, he'd be alive. But I said no."

"Said yes to what?"

Shuddering, heaving in ragged breaths, still denying the breakdown, she murmurs the words, and I know they break her, once and for all. "He asked me to marry him. I said no."

"You were eighteen."

"I know. I know! That's why I said no. He wanted to go to Stanford, and I wanted to go Syracuse. I would have gone to Stanford with him, just to be with him, but...I couldn't marry him. I wasn't ready to be engaged. To get married."

"Understandable."

"You don't get it, Colton. You don't—you don't get it." Hiccups, now, words coming in stutters. "He asked me to marry him, in the car. I got out, angry that he didn't understand why I said no. He followed me. Stood in the driveway arguing with me. I was on the porch. Minutes like that, him in the driveway, me on the porch. We should've gone inside, but we didn't. The rain had stopped, but the wind was worse than ever. I heard the tree snap. It sounded like a cannon going off."

"You didn't kill him, Nell. You didn't. Saying no didn't mean—"

"Shut up. Just...*shut up*. I said no. He thought it meant I didn't love him, and we wasted so much time out there, in the way of the tree. If I had just said yes, gone inside with him, the tree would have missed us both. Missed me, missed him. He'd be alive. I hesitated, and he died. If I hadn't frozen, if I had just moved out of the way…one jump to the left or the right. I could have. But I froze. And he saved me…and he—he died. He's gone, and it's my fault."

"It's not."

"SHUT UP!" She screams it into my chest. "I killed him. He's gone, and it's my fault…my fault. I want him back." This last, a shattered whisper, and I feel—finally—warm wet tears on my chest.

It's silent, at first. I think maybe she's waiting to be condemned for weakness. I don't, of course. I hold her. I don't tell her it's okay.

"Get mad," I say. "Be hurt. Be broken. Cry."

She shakes her head, tiny side-to-side twisting of her neck, a denial, a futile refusal. Futile, because she's already crying. The high-pitched whining at first, high in her throat. Keening.

I once saw a baby kitten in an alley sitting next to its mother. The mama cat was dead, of age or something, I don't know. The kitten was pawing at the mama's shoulder and mewling, this nonstop sound that was absolutely heartbreaking, heartrending. It was a sound that said, *What do I do? How do I live? How can I go on?*

This sound, from Nell, is that. But infinitely worse. It's so fucking soul-searing, I can't breathe for the pain it causes me to hear. Because I can't do a goddamn thing except hold her.

She starts rocking in my arm, clutching my bare shoulders so hard she's gonna break the skin, but I don't care, because it means she's not hurting herself. Now it's long, jagged sobs, wracking her entire body, and god, she's got two years' worth of pent-up tears coming out all at once. It's violent.

I don't even know how long she sobs. Time ceases to pass, and she cries, cries, cries. Clutches me and makes these sounds of a soul being ripped in two, the grief so long denied taking its toll.

Fermented grief is far more potent.

My chest is slick with her tears. My shoulders are bruised. I'm stiff and sore from holding her, motionless. I'm exhausted. None of this matters. I'll hold her until she passes out.

Finally the sobs subside, and she's just crying softly. Now it's time to comfort.

I only know one way; I sing:

"Quiet your crying voice, lost child.
Let no plea for comfort pass your lips.
You're okay, now.
You're okay, now.
Don't cry anymore, dry your eyes.
Roll the pain away, put it down on the ground and leave it for the birds.

Suffer no more, lost child.

Stand and take the road, move on and seal the hurt behind the miles.

It's not all right, it's not okay.

I know, I know.

The night is long, it's dark and cruel.

I know, I know.

You're not alone. You're not alone.

You are loved. You are held.

Quiet your crying voice, lost child.

You're okay, now.

You're okay, now.

Just hold on, one more day.

Just hold on, one more hour.

Someone will come for you.

Someone will hold you close.

I know, I know.

It's not okay, it's not all right.

But if you just hold on,

One more day, one more hour.

It will be. It will be."

Nell is silent, staring at me with limpid gray-green eyes like moss-flecked stone. She heard every word, heard the cry of a lost boy.

"Did you write that?" she asks. I nod, my chin scraping the top of her scalp. "For who?"

"Me."

"God, Colton." Her voice is hoarse from sobbing, raspy. Sexy. "That's so sad."

"It's how I felt at the time." I shrug. "I had no one to comfort me, so I wrote a song to do it myself."

"Did it work?"

I huff at the ridiculousness of the question. "If I sang it enough, I'd eventually be able to fall asleep, so yeah, kind of."

I finally glance down at her, actually look into her eyes. It's a mistake. She's wide-eyed, intent, full of heartbreak and sadness and compassion. Not pity. I'd flip my shit if I saw pity in her eyes, just like she would if she saw it in me.

Compassion and pity are not the same: Pity is looking down on someone, feeling sorry for them and offering nothing; compassion is seeing their pain and offering them understanding.

She's so goddamn beautiful. I'm lost in her eyes, unable to look away. Her lips, red, chapped, pursed, as if begging me to kiss her, are too close to ignore. I'm suddenly aware of her body against mine, her full breasts crushed against me, her leg, one round thigh, pale as whitest cream, draped over mine. Her palm, long fingers slightly curled, rests on my shoulder, and lightning sizzles my skin where she touches me.

I'm not breathing. Literally, my breath is stuck in my throat, blocked by my heart, which has taken up residence in my trachea.

I want to kiss her. Need to. Or I might never breathe again.

I'm an asshole, so I kiss her. She deserves ultimate gentility, and my lips are feathers against hers, ghosting across hers. I can feel every ridge and ripple of her lips; they're chapped and cracked and rough from crying, from thirst. I moisten them with my own lips, kiss each lip individually. First the upper, caressing it with both of mine, tasting, touching. She breathes a sigh.

I think I'm okay, I think she wants this. I was honestly terrified at first she'll wig out, slap me, scramble away. Tell me she can't stomach a kiss from a blood-soaked monster like me. I don't deserve her, but I'm an asshole, a selfish bastard, so I take what I can get from her, and try to make sure I give her the best I've got.

She doesn't kiss me back, though. She shifts on my body, and her curled fingers tighten on my chest, but her mouth? She just waits, and lets me claim her mouth with mine. I take her lower lip in my teeth, ever so gently. My palm, my rough and callused paw, is grazing her cheek, smoothing a wayward curl back behind her ear. She lets me. Foolish girl. Letting a brute like me kiss her, touch her. I'm afraid the grease under my nails will mar her skin, worried the blood that has been soaked into my bones will seep out of my pores and sully her ivory skin.

She nuzzles her face into my palm. She opens her mouth into mine, kisses me back. Oh, heaven. I mean, god*damn*, the girl can kiss. My breath never really left my throat, and now it rushes out of me in disbelief that she's letting this happen, that she's actively taking part.

I don't know why. It's not like I'm a nice guy. I'm not good. I just held her when she cried. I couldn't do anything else.

I end the kiss before it can turn into something else. She just looks at me, lips slightly parted, wet like cherries now and so, so red. Oh, fuck, I can't resist going in for another kiss, from letting some shred of my raging hunger for her beauty show through in my kiss. She returns it with equal fervor, moving so she's more fully on top of me, and she doesn't stop me when my hand drifts down her scalp, down her nape, down her back, rests on the small just above the swell of her ass. I don't dare touch her there.

This is insane. What the hell am I doing? She just bawled her eyes out, sobbed for hours. She's seeking comfort, seeking forgetting. I can't have her like this.

I pull away again, slide out from beneath her.

"Where are you going?" she asks.

"I can't breathe when you kiss me like that. When you let me kiss you. It's…I'm no good. No good for you. It'd be taking advantage of you." I shake my head and turn away from the confusion in her eyes, the disappointment. I retreat, squeezing my hands into fists, angry with myself. She needs better than me.

I grab my guitar, rip it from the soft case, and head for the rickety, creaking, outside stair to the roof, a bottle of Jameson in hand. I plop down on the busted-ass weather-beaten blue Lay-Z-Boy I lugged up here for this purpose, twist the top off the bottle, and slug it hard. I kick back with my feet up on the roof ledge and watch the gray-to-pink haze of onrushing dawn, guitar on my belly, plucking strings.

Finally, I sit forward and start working on the song I've been learning: "This Girl" by City & Colour. I regret it immediately, because the lyrics remind me of what I don't deserve with Nell. But it's an intoxicating song, so I get lost in it nonetheless, and it barely registers when I hear her on the stairs.

"You are *so* talented, Colton," she says when I'm done.

I roll my eyes. "Thanks."

She's got her jeans back on and one of my spare guitars in her hand. There's a battered orange love seat perpendicular to the Lay-Z-Boy, and she settles cross-legged onto it, cradling her guitar on her lap.

"Play something for me," I say.

She shrugs self-consciously. "I suck. I only know a couple songs."

I frown at her. "You sing like a fucking angel. Seriously. You have the sweetest, clearest voice I've ever heard."

"I can't play the guitar for crap, though." She's strumming, however, even as she says this.

"No," I agree. "But that doesn't matter once you start singing. 'Sides, keep playing, keep practicing, you'll get better."

She rolls her eyes, much like I did, and starts hitting chords. I don't recognize the tune at first. It takes me into the first chorus to figure out what song it is. It's a low, haunting tune, a rolling, sad melody. The lyrics are…archaic, but I understand them. They're sweet and longing. She's singing "My Funny Valentine" by Ella Fitzgerald. At least, that's the version I know. I've heard a dozen versions of it, but I think she was the one who made it famous.

The way Nell sings it…her voice is a little high for how low the song is written, but the strain to hit the lower notes only makes it full of that much more longing. As if the desire was a palpable thing, so thick inside her she couldn't hit the notes right.

She trails off at the end of the song, but I roll my hand in a circle, so she plucks a few strings, thinking, silent, then strikes another slow, bluesy rhythm. Oh, god, so perfect. She sings "Dream a Little Dream of Me." Louis Armstrong and Ella. God, I love that song. I doubt she realizes this. I surprise the shit out of her by coming in right on cue with Louis's part. She smiles broad and happy and keeps singing, and holy shit we sound good together.

I would never have thought of covering jazz numbers in a folksy style. It's so hot, so fresh. I know the song, so I can weave in some fancy picking, over and around her strumming.

We finish the song, and I never want to stop making music with her. I take a risk and start up "Stormy Blues" by Billie Holiday. It's a slow song, and Nell's crystalline voice and my gravelly one make it into a ballad. I can hear Billie's voice as I'm singing, though. I hear it coming out of the open window from the building next to the shop, back when I first bought it. Mrs. Henkel had a thing for jazz. She was old and lonely, and jazz made her think of long-dead Mr. Henkel, so she'd crack all the windows and play Billie and Ella and Count Basie and Benny, and she'd dance and remember. I'd help her bring her groceries up, and she'd pinch my ass and threaten me with sex, if only she was half a century younger. She'd make me tea and spike it with whiskey, and we'd listen to jazz.

I found her in her bed, eyes closed, a photo of Mr. Henkel on her ample chest, a smile on her face. I went to her funeral, which shocked the shit out of her rich, asshole grandson.

My eyes must give away some of my thoughts, because Nell asks me what I'm thinking. So I tell her about Mrs. Henkel. About the long conversations I'd have with her, slowly getting drunk on spiked Earl Grey. How she was always clucking about my tats and my baggy pants. When I went straight and stopped thugging it up, she was over the moon at my tighter jeans.

What I don't say is that my spending time with Mrs. Henkel was typical selfish Colt. I was lonely. I'd walked away from all my boys from the hood, all of them except Split, and I was lonely. Mrs. Henkel was a friend, a chance to be around someone who was a good influence on me. She'd probably have shit her Depends if she knew half the shit I'd done, and I think she knew that, since she never asked.

Finally, I go silent, the subject of dead Mrs. Henkel exhausted.

"Explain what you meant," Nell says.

"About what?" I know exactly what she means, but I can't let on.

"Why aren't you any good? Why would it be taking advantage of me?"

I set the guitar on its side and take a pull off the bottle, hand it to her. "I'm...fucked up, Nell."

"So am I."

"But it's different. I'm not good. I mean, I'm not evil, I have some redeeming qualities, but..." I shake my head, unable to put it into the right words. "I've done bad things. I'm trying to stay out of trouble these days, but that doesn't erase what I've done."

"I think you're a good person." She says it quietly, not looking at me.

"You saw what I did to dickhead Dan."

She snorts. "Dickhead Dan. Fitting. Yeah, I saw, and yeah, it scared me. But you were protecting me. Defending me. And you stopped."

"Didn't want to, though."

"But you did." She yawns behind her hand. "You're selling yourself short, Colton. And you're not giving me enough credit to know what I want."

"What do you mean?" I know what she means, but I want to hear her say it.

"I kissed you back. It's crazy, messed up, and it confuses me. But I did it eyes wide. Knowing. I wasn't drunk." She looks at me past long, dark lashes, eyes saying a thousand things her mouth isn't.

My mouth goes dry. "I shouldn't have kissed you."

"But you did."

"Yeah. I'm an asshole like that. I just can't help it, around you."

"I don't think you're an asshole. I think you're sweet. Gentle." She says it with a little smile.

I shake my head. "Nah. It's just you. You bring that tender shit out of me. I'm a thug, Nell. Straight up."

"Ex-thug," she counters.

I laugh. "Once a thug, always a thug. I may not run the streets anymore, but it's still part of who I am."

"And I like who you are."

I stand up, uncomfortable with where this is going. "It's late. We should sleep."

She glances at the sun, which is peeking between a couple of high-rises across the street. "It's early, but yeah. I'm exhausted."

I take her guitar and hold her hand as she steps onto the stairs. I like how her hand feels in mine. I don't want to let go, so I don't. Neither does she. Nell stops at the bathroom, and I change into running shorts. Finally, I let myself feel the pain from the fight with Dan. I stretch, feeling my ribs twinge, and I probe my loose tooth with my tongue, wince at the dull ache. At that moment, Nell appears beside me with a washcloth. I eye her warily, then pull away when she reaches for my face.

"I'm fine," I growl.

"Shut up and hold still."

I roll my eyes and bring my face back within reach. Her touch is far too gentle for a rough bastard like me. She touches my chin, turns me to the side, brushes the cuts and bruises as if frightened to hurt me further. I stop breathing from her proximity, from the drunk-making wonder of her scent, shampoo and lemons and whiskey and woman. She turns my head again, wipes the other side of my face, eyes narrowed as she focuses on wiping away the crusted blood. I'd cleaned up a bit while she was in the shower at her place, but apparently not well enough. She wipes my upper lip, my chin, my forehead, my cheekbones. Then she lowers the washcloth and runs her fingers over my face, touching each cut gently, exploring.

I hold still and let her touch me. It scares me. She's looking at me as if seeing me for the first time, as if trying to memorize how I look. Her gaze is intense, needy. Her thumbs end up brushing over my lips, and I bite one of her thumbs, a little hard.

Her eyes widen and her nostrils flare, and she sucks in a fast breath as I run my tongue over the pad of her thumb.

What the fuck am I doing? But I can't stop.

This time, she leans in. Pulls her thumb from my mouth and replaces it with her lips. Her tongue. This is so crazy. I shouldn't let it happen.

But I do. My god, I do. I kiss her back with all the hunger inside me. We're in my room, just inside the doorway, inches from the bed. It would be so easy to spin her around and lay her down, peel her clothes off, and…

I pull away. She sighs as I do, and it's a disappointed sound.

"You keep stopping," she says.

I slip back out of her arms, reluctantly. I'm confused, messed up. I want her, but some vague voice in my head tells me it's wrong to have her. Part of me says we belong together, tells me to cradle her close and never let go. She seems to want me, and I want her…but I know—I know—I'm not good enough for her.

"We need to sleep," I say. "You can have the bed."

I turn away, but her hand catches my elbow.

"I don't want to sleep alone," she says. "I've slept alone for so long. I just… I want to be held. Please?" She's vulnerable again suddenly.

I shouldn't. It's tempting, and I haven't figured out what's right or wrong. But I can't say no.

"I could do that," I say. "I would love nothing more, if I'm being honest."

Nell

Chapter 9: Ghosts, One Breath at a Time

EVERY SINGLE FIBER OF MY BEING is screaming at me. I'm liquid in his arms. Fire burns in my veins. Guilt and peace rage in my brain, warring.

I told him. I told Colton my secret guilt. I cried. I sobbed for hours. Hours and hours. I don't even know how long. And god, did that feel good. But the guilt remains. I know it's ridiculous. I *know*, but goddammit, I can't shake the guilt.

And now it's all compounded a million times by Colton's brawny arms around me. God, I still can't fathom the raw, savage, masculine glory of the man. I hadn't seen him in two years, and then I saw him on a bench—singing *that* song, of all things—and he'd bulked up in that time. Hardcore. He'd been a beast at the funeral, stretching the sleeves of his suit coat. Now? Holy hell. My mouth went dry as a desert when I saw him busking outside Central Park. Ink-black hair down around his eyes and curling above his collar, messy, shaggy, perfect. His eyes, those hadn't changed, soul-spearing sapphires. But his body? Oh, god, oh, god…*ohmigod*.

The tattoos turn his torso into a living mural, poetry in script along his ribs, a dragon on his right shoulder breathing fire on Japanese characters, the flames spreading like wildfire down his back and fading into a golden sun on his spine, an archaic-looking thing, like a compass rose, almost. A pinup girl in silhouette on his left arm, more script lettering on his opposing ribs—Latin, it looks like. Music notes scattered over both forearms, stars, suns, skulls and crossbones, iron crosses mixing and merging and joining it all. He's a masterpiece of skin art. A masterpiece of bulky male muscle, hard and heavy and huge.

He's terrifying. A force of violent power, raw brutality. He destroyed Dan. Took a hard beating in the process and seemed completely unfazed by the broken nose, the blows to the ribs and chest, the cuts on his face. Dan was a monster, and Colton ripped him apart easily.

It was the hottest thing I'd ever seen; the scariest thing I'd ever seen. Colton's fury was a primal thing, so thick and hot I could feel it in the air. His eyes were the eyes of a cold, calculating warrior, terrifying for the icy fury.

I'm completely unable to resist him.

He wants me but won't give in to it. Which I get, I really do.

He's my dead boyfriend's brother. It's just… wrong.

How did you two meet? Oh, we met at his brother's funeral. His baby brother, my first love.

Awesome.

But Colton is…I'm safe with him. He draws the truth out of me. He draws the pain out of me. Colton knows pain. He's intimately familiar with it. Lives with it. Guilt, too.

Colton has secrets, and I want to know them all.

I want his mouth on me. His hands on me. I need it. It makes me feel alive. Safe. Protected, treasured. Colton will, literally, kill anyone who might hurt me. He nearly did kill Dan. Might have, actually.

I don't want to know.

I want to know why Colton is alone in New York when his father is a congressman. Why he was forced into back-alley prize fights to survive. Why he ended up in a gang.

I want to know why Colton won't keep kissing me. Why he always pulls back, why he thinks he's no good. No good, when he's the most amazing person I've ever met. So freaking talented. His deep, gravelly, raspy voice, insane guitar skills, his passion when he performs.

That song he sang to me, a cappella? Most beautiful thing I've ever heard. So jarringly sad. The loneliness, the longing in that song was wrenching. I don't think it had a title, I don't think anyone but me has ever heard him sing it.

And now? Oh, now his arms are around me, holding me close. So close. I want to turn in his arms and burrow close, nestle in and let the warm strength of his body wash over me. Like this, spooning, his arm draped over my waist and not touching me too intimately, this is almost platonic. Almost.

I want more. Dare I?

I dare.

I twist in place, and Colton stirs, loosens his grips, makes a low sound in his throat, sleepy. It makes me smile, that little moan. He's on his side, doesn't roll away when I burrow into him. I press my face to the hollow under his chin, slide my palm over his ribs to curl around his back. I breathe in his scent, let the heat of his body warm me. Oh, god. This might have been a mistake, because this feels entirely too perfect. I'll never want to sleep any other way. My other arm is curled beneath the pillow under my head, and his body is a shelter, a fortress I can lose myself in. I can feel his pulse thumping in his throat against my nose, and I count the beats, wait for sleep.

It comes, so sweetly. No dreams. No empty shoe, no red-slick mud, no blood froth. Just sleep, Colton's hand on my hip. I may or may not have put his hand on my hip. Okay, I did. And I love it. I shouldn't, but I do.

I'm going to give in to this. Time heals all wounds, right? Well, maybe I've had enough time, and now I just need to move on, let go. Have something that makes me happy, after so long in misery.

I wake slowly, like drifting to the surface of a lake after diving deep. The first thing I'm aware of is the *thumpthump…thumpthump* of Colton's heartbeat under my ear. God, I love that sound. Then I become aware of his body, hard yet soft beneath me. I'm basically on top of him, half of my torso on his chest and stomach, my leg over his, my foot between his. Then I become aware of my hand.

It's on his belly. Okay…well actually, it's not quite his belly. It's a bit lower than that. A lot lower. And I'm cupping a part of his body that is most definitely awake. Very, *very* awake. And huge. Thick. My hand is *on* it. Holding it.

Oh, god. Oh, shit. Oh, god.

His breathing is even, softly soughing in and out. He's still asleep, then.

The major problem in this situation is that I don't want to move my hand. I want to touch him. It's been so long, and the thought of him, of what my hand is touching...I feel a clench down low in my core, a gush of damp desire.

I can't really help it. I slide my palm down, then back up. He shifts, rolls his hips up, and then relaxes. I do it again, slowly, gently, guiltily. I watch in hungry fascination as his abs ripple, and tense as he rolls his hips again. He moans, a lupine growl deep in his chest. His breathing stutters, and then he takes in a deep breath.

I look down. A sliver of pink shows at the top of his gym shorts. I lick my lips. I'm so awful. This is so wrong, so stupid, so slutty. But I don't stop. His shorts are hiked up around his thighs, and yet tugged down low on his hips by the way he's moving, shifting. So now the very tip of him is peeking out from beneath his shorts.

I glance up at his rugged face, lax and handsome and innocent in repose. He swallows, shifts his face to the side, lifts his lower half up slightly into my touch. I don't know what I'm doing, why, where it's going to go. He's still deeply asleep, sucking in long, even breaths, letting them out on a slight and adorable snore.

His arm is around me, curling over my back and cupping me to him, his other hand on his chest. And now his hand slides down my back, falls limp and lands on my ass. Yes. I like that. I shift up a little so his palm and fingers are clutching my left ass cheek.

What am I doing? I'm such a fucked-up mess. He stopped kissing me while I was upset to avoid taking advantage of me, and here I am fondling him in his sleep, getting cheap thrills off his hand touching my butt while he snores innocently.

It's so wrong, but I tug his shorts a little lower, so more of him peeks out. Now I can see the thick pink mushroom head, the tiny hole at the tip, the groove around the bottom of the head. I squeeze my eyes shut and tell myself to stop. It doesn't work. I touch the pink flesh with my thumb, biting my lip. So soft, like velvet. I can't help stroking his length again, and I swallow hard in appreciation. It takes me a ridiculously long time to stroke him from root to tip.

I bite my lip hard, just to make sure I'm not dreaming. The sharp twinge of pain tells me I'm awake. Awake, and clearly a slut with no morals. I mean, I haven't touched anyone like this since Kyle. I've kissed a few guys in an attempt to force myself to move on, in an attempt to ease the ache of need that I've carried in my belly for so long. But none of the guys I kissed ever ignited any kind of spark in me. Just dead, nothing. Dan tried and tried, and I really did try to get into it. I never could.

I can't accurately say there's a spark with Colton. No, it's way, way beyond a spark. Just looking at him lights a fire. Touching him, being touched, even innocent touches, even his hand in mine creates an inferno.

This? Touching him so intimately, so erotically? You could light a match from the waves of palpable heat radiating from me, flames of desire fanned hotter every second.

I can't stop stroking him. Up and back down, caressing his length, exploring his thickness through the swishy fabric of his shorts. He moves in time with me now, and he's waking up. Moaning, writhing under my touch. I can't stop now. I think he's close.

I press my thumb to his tip again and rub in circles, and I feel his body tense beneath mine. I glance up at his eyes, watch them flick open and waver in confusion, then stutter and blink as he comes. My gaze flits down to watch the white stream cover his belly.

"The fuck?" His voice is muzzy and and puzzled and slow.

He's awake, he's released, but still thick. I slide my hand into his shorts and take him in my hand, and I bite my lip at the satiny hardness of him. His eyes meet mine, and I can tell he's wondering if he's awake, how he should feel, what to say.

"I'm sorry," I whisper. "I woke up touching you by accident. And then I couldn't stop."

"Am I dreaming?" he asks, wary.

I shake my head. "Nope."

He looks down at himself, at the mess on his belly. "So you just…"

I nod. "Yeah."

"While I was sleeping?"

I nod again, and I can't meet his eyes anymore. "Yeah. I don't know—I'm sorry. I—I couldn't help it. I knew I shouldn't, but I just…" I trail off, unable to make a complete sentence. I suck in a deep breath and try again. "You were so hard and big, and it had been so long, and I—"

"Nell," he cuts in. "Shut up."

I shut up.

"Look at me," he orders. I force my eyes to his.

"I'm sorry," I whisper.

"I said shut up."

I wrinkle my face at his harsh tone, but keep my mouth closed and wait for him to continue.

"I don't even know what to say. I thought I was dreaming." His eyes bore into me, blue and hot like a bunsen burner flame. "You want to know what I was dreaming about?"

I nod.

"Answer me. Out loud."

This is a new Colton. Bossy, direct. I'm not sure if I should be pissed at the way he's barking orders, or turned on by it. I settle for both.

"Yes, Colton. I want to know what you were dreaming about." My tone is soft and submissive, but I know my eyes betray my ire.

His face is impassive. "You. I was dreaming of you." His eyes narrow. "I was dreaming of you doing what you apparently were actually doing."

"Was it a good dream?" I ask, daring. "Did you like that dream?" I trail my fingertip through the stickiness on his belly, eyeing him from beneath lowered lashes.

He sucks in a sharp breath, watching my finger tracing patterns on his skin, and then his gaze flicks to me again. "It was a conflicted dream. I shouldn't have wanted it to not be a dream. I shouldn't have wanted it to be real. But I did."

I try to ignore the thunder of my pulse in my ears. "Why shouldn't you?"

He frowns. "Because…because of everything."

"Say it out loud. All of it." I can be bossy, too.

"Because you were in love with Kyle."

"He's gone. It wouldn't be cheating." I swallow hard, because a part of me says that's a very very valid reason why not. Because it would be. I would be cheating on him.

"Your turn to say it all."

"Say what?"

"What you're thinking."

I begin tracing the kanji on his chest, the orange-yellow flames, the dragon's eye. "I'm a liar. It would be cheating. It would be cheating on his memory. But...that's bullshit."

His head sinks back, and he turns aside to stare at the wall. I watch his jaw clench and release, watch the fine black stubble on his tan skin shift.

"How fucked up is that?" He says, barely audible.

He gets out of bed, takes a couple steps across the hall and into the bathroom. I watch him wet a washcloth and clean off his stomach. He comes back and slips back into bed next to me, on his side, facing me.

"That's what I was thinking, too, though," he says. "It's bullshit, but I can't shake the feeling. You and me would be...an affront to his memory. But that's just bullshit, because he's dead and he'd want both of us to be happy."

"Well that's stupid, too. If he was alive, he'd want me."

"But he's not."

"Is this an argument or a discussion?" I ask.

He huffs a laugh. "I don't even know." He turns back to look at me. "What you just did? That changes shit."

"I know." My words aren't even a whisper. "Are you mad?"

He bobbles his head back and forth. "Mad? No. Not mad. Confused. Not gonna lie, it was kinda shady. I couldn't tell you I wanted it, or that I didn't."

I choke. "I know. I know. I'm so sorry. I—I feel disgusted with myself."

"Don't. Just don't. I'm no better. You were asleep and I took your clothes off—"

"You were making me comfortable," I interrupt.

He talks over me. "I wanted to see you again. I wanted to see your sweet, round ass. I touched your thigh."

"But you didn't make me—you didn't do what I did."

He rubs his face with his free hand.

"Is this a competition? Which one of us is more of an asshole?" I ask.

In my head, though, I'm stunned breathless by what he said. He wanted to see my "sweet, round ass." I've always thought I had too much ass. It's an insecurity. Common, I know, but unshakeable. I still run like a fiend, because it's one of the few times I can be free of dreams and memories and nightmares and guilt. Then, when I'm drunk, and when I'm playing music. But no matter how I run, my ass is round and my breasts heavy.

"I'd win that competition, hands down. No question," Colton says. "You had a moment of weakness, or something. I'm an asshole all the time."

"You're wrong." I shift up his body and meet his eyes from a couple inches away. Kissing distance. "It wasn't a moment of weakness. It was a lot of moments of desire. And you're not an asshole."

"What do you want, Nell?"

"I already asked you that question, remember?"

"So neither of us knows what we want?" His eyes search mine, and his hand inscribes circles on the small of my back.

"No. Yes. I know what I want, but I'm not sure if it's right or wrong. I do know that how I went about getting it was wrong, though. So for that, I'm sorry."

"So you're saying you should've done what you did, but while I'm awake?" His palm continues to circle, but moves lower.

I arch my back subtly, but enough. He notices, and his eyes widen, his nostrils flare, his lips thin, his breathing goes deep.

"Yes," I say.

I have to just own what I did, what I want. He was all too right when he said what I did changes things. I can't go back now. I know how he feels in my hand. I know how his body feels beneath me, and I want more of it. I know how his hand feels on my ass. And I know he wants this as much as I do, and we're both conflicted about it.

I meet his eyes and hold his gaze as he explores downward. I bite my lip when he begins up the swell of my ass. When I got in bed, I'd stripped off my jeans, so all I was wearing was a tiny yellow thong. A triangle of silk over my core, strings over my hips, a string down my crack. I took off my bra, too, so I only had on a tiny T-shirt, a fitted thing, blue cotton with a pocket over the right breast, a glittery purple heart on the pocket.

He follows the line of the waistband of my thong around my hip, his eyes locked on mine, and he slowly and deliberately cups my left cheek. I search his eyes, and see my emotions reflected back at me: conflicted desire.

"I forgive you," he says, an ever-so-subtle smirking tilt to the side of his mouth. "After all, it was a really awesome dream."

He explores the line of the string between my cheeks. I'm holding my breath, and I can't seem to catch it. He slides his palm up the other side, then back down, caressing my thigh, then the other. God. Oh, god. Now up my spine, up my bare back, under the shirt. His fingers, his palm on my skin, tracing fire.

His fingers go between my arm and my rib, seeking access frontward. I shift my arm, slide my palm up his chest, hesitate at his shoulder, then do as I've wanted to do for so long, it seems, and scratch over the stubble on his jaw. This action gives him access, and he moves his hand around my ribs to brush the outside curve of my breast smashed against his chest.

"What are we doing here, Nell?" he asks, his voice his voice a raspy whisper.

I shake my head and lift one shoulder. "I have no idea. But I like it."

"Me, too." He pulls me closer, higher. I go with him, shifting so I'm entirely on my side, head propped up on one hand, leg slung over his thighs, free hand on his breastbone.

Now I'm exposed. My shirt is hiked up so the undersides of my breasts peek beneath the hem. I silently dare him, encourage him with my stillness, my steady gaze on his too-blue eyes.

Ohmigod. *God.* He takes the dare. Palm on my belly at first, I think he might go south, and I think he considers it, then moves up north to the hem of my shirt. I was already holding my breath, but my throat gets tighter, my lungs burn, my heart either stops beating or pounds wildly. I can't decide which.

Then his rough and gentle and huge hand cradles my breast beneath the shirt. I haven't taken a breath in at least thirty seconds. Oh, god, oh, god, *ohmigod*. His hand feels so amazing. Scratchy, hard. My breasts are fairly big, C-cups, almost a D, but he can palm one easily. His palm scrapes my nipple, and now my breath blasts in, rushing through me and making me dizzy.

"Colton…" I duck my head and bury my forehead on his shoulder.

"Look at me, Nell," he commands, softly but firmly. I do. His eyes are hooded and serious. "Turning point, right here. You don't want this, you have to tell me now. Get up and go. This'll all be forgotten. I'll be your friend. But say so now. 'Cause any further, we're in it all the way."

I gulp. I nod. I bite my lip and look away.

"God, fuck me. Don't *do* that," he says, his voice ragged.

I'm puzzled. "Do what?"

"Bite your lip. It drives me wild. Bite your lip, and it's over. Your mouth is mine." His voice is so rough now, so raw and raspy it vibrates against me and sizzles deep in my core.

"Good to know," I whisper.

He moves his hand away. "Decide now, Nell. All in, you're mine, or we pretend this never happened."

"I'm yours?" My voice is soft and tremulous.

"You asking? Or telling?"

"I—Colton, I couldn't forget...but we—" I cut myself off, knowing I'm an incoherent mess.

Unconsciously, I bite my lip again, and Colton growls.

"I fucking told you. Don't...*do*...that. I can't take it. My control is in shreds here, and you're biting your lip again."

"Why does it make you so crazy?" I ask, playing for time.

Time for what, I don't know. I know what I want. But now...with Colton becoming the direct and commanding person again, I'm shy, unsure, insecure, afraid. I'm all over the damn place. Molesting him in his sleep, then unable to jump in when he makes it clear he wants me like I do him. I'm a lunatic, clearly.

"I don't know," he says. "It's just a thing. You bite your lip, and I want to take that lip into my mouth and suck on it like a Popsicle. I want to lick your lips and bite them and kiss you until you're fucking lost and gasping and puddled on the floor."

Well...*shit*. I want that.

Nerves? Gone.

I feel my heart doing this weird thing, swelling, hammering, stuttering, aching, and I know I've decided.

I bite my lip, and it's over.

"Fuck. You're crazy, baby." His voice is a feral snarl, spoken through clenched teeth.

I don't even see him move. One second he's over there, the next he's slamming into me, lips crushing mine, and, true to his word, he takes my lower lip into his mouth and sucks on it, tongues it. I'm jarred and shocked by the sudden violence of his kiss, and then I melt as he sucks on my lip. And then I'm pure liquid beneath him, because he's abruptly gentle, taking my face in his hands, gazing at me with our lips barely touching, and then he kisses me slowly and so thoroughly, so deeply, I'm just…lost. His mouth moves on mine, claims me, steals my heart with his lips, takes my body with his mouth.

We'd kissed before, and it was—every time—the best kiss I'd ever had. My heart clenches when I realize this includes, by a landslide, every kiss Kyle ever gave me. There's just no comparison. That hurts, that does. It hurts so sweet, so deep, so strange, I just don't know what to do with it.

This kiss…I'm gone. Gone. I know, in that moment, that I belong to him. It's what he said: I'm his. How it happened, I don't know. I *really* wish I did.

"Last chance, Nelly-baby." His voice is in my ear, not even a whisper, just breathed subvocalization that I feel on my ear. "Tell me you don't want this."

I push him up and I see the hurt in his eyes before I can correct him. He starts to get off, but I catch his bicep and still him in place. I curl my fingers under the hem of my shirt and peel it off. Colton's eyes go wide and he licks his lips.

"I want this." I say it as loud as I can, which is a breathless gasp at most. "I need this."

His eyes change then. They go feral.

Oh, boy, here we go.

"Take off your thong and spread your legs."

"Say 'please.'" I find strength in the game. My terror, my vulnerability abates, and I'm thankful.

He just stares at me. I don't move to comply. He shakes his head and half-blinks in disbelief. And then he tugs on my thong, and it comes apart. He didn't jerk it, he didn't expend any effort. He just put two fingers around the string at my hip, two fingers of the other hand inside the triangle over my core, and tugged. *Rip*. Gone. I'm naked. That easy.

"I liked that thong," I protested.

"Should've listened, then." He slides his fingers down my belly, which clenches, and across my pudendum and down my tight-clamped thighs. "Now, spread your legs and feel free to scream. No one can hear."

"Wha—*oh*." I don't even have time to process my confusion before his tongue is doing something wicked to my clit.

I spread my legs. Wide. I tuck my heels against my buttocks and let my knees fall apart. I'm shameless.

"Yeah, Nelly. Just like that," he breathes onto my folds. "God...*damn*. Sweet as sugar."

I blush at his words, and then I've got no head-space for anything but the screams ripping from my throat. Because god...I've never felt anything like this. Not ever. I writhe on the bed, arch up, buck in time to his tongue's lapping. And then...oh, yeah, it gets better. He slides a finger inside me and curls it, and I just...lose it. I combust. I scream so loud it hurts my own ears, upon which I clamp my teeth together and groan past gritting jaws.

"Trust me?" His voice is a surprise, and I'm so lost in sensation I don't even understand his words.

"Wha—what?"

"Do. You. Trust me." His fingers haven't stopped their curling and swirling and exploring.

"Your fingers are inside me, so yes."

"You might want to bite a pillow."

"Why...?" I start the question, but I never finish it. "Oh...*shit!*"

He laughs, but it's a pleased laugh. He's got two fingers in my folds now, and a third is...oh, hell. I don't even believe it, can't even fathom or understand it, but it's *down there*. Dirty and dark.

I bite a pillow. My entire existence is a vortex of raging ecstasy. I simply cannot contain it. I'm coming apart at the seams, and I'm not even coming yet. Or maybe I am. Maybe this is what lies beyond the edge, and this is the first time I've ever really been here. I don't know. I can't keep it in. I scream into the pillow, and I sob, and I arch, and I buck. I find my fingers tangled in his hair, crushing him wantonly against me, even as I'm begging him.

Begging him to what, I don't know.

"Colton...Colton...please...oh, god, ohgod, *ohmigod*..."

See? Am I asking him to stop? To never ever stop, not even to breathe? I don't know.

It's just a tiny intrusion, really, the very tip of his finger wiggling inside me in my forbidden place. But it's earth-shattering.

"What...what are you doing to me?" I ask.

"Making you come. Fingering your tight, virgin asshole." He returns his mouth to my folds and sucks my turgid nub into his mouth, and I scream, arch into him. "I'm getting you ready."

"Ready for what?" I want to know. God, do I want to know. There's more?

"Come, and I'll show you."

"I thought I was coming?"

He chuckles. "Oh, no." He reaches up with his free hand, and suddenly he's everywhere. Pinching my nipple and rolling it, and fingering me, curling and thrusting, licking, sucking... "Come. Now."

It's a command, and I have no choice to obey. I explode into pieces, liquid and fire and screams and sobs. Actual sobs. Like, with tears.

And then...then he crawls up my body like the predator he is. The stubble around his mouth is wet. From me. I blush, hard.

Holy god, ohmigod, oh, shit. He's so huge. All muscle and broad lines and hard edges, so big above me. His presence blocks out the world. All I see is tattoos and skin and sapphire eyes and sable hair. And then I glance down, and see his...his *him*. His cock.

I like that word. I never use it. I started swearing openly after Kyle died. I just didn't care anymore. But sex? Gone. No part of my life after that. I swore, I cursed, I drank, but I couldn't fathom sex. I buried myself in classes at a community college and worked for Daddy in his office and saw no one, did nothing, was no one. I worked. I studied. I played music. I was the living dead, a guilt-ravaged shell.

Now...I'm alive. So alive. And I like dirty words.

I'm shameless. And I like it. Partially because the guilt of what we're doing is a new kind of pain, and pain centers me.

Back to his cock. It's…glorious. I just…oh, god. I felt it, before. But seeing it all, every thick inch coming for me…I forget to breathe and bite my lip.

"Don't worry. I'll be careful." His voice is so, so tender.

He thought I was afraid, I think. And suddenly, with that realization, I am. I'm terrified. Scared shitless. Another realization washes over me, and it brings wave after wave of pain, guilt, shame, and tears.

"Nell? What is it? Why are you crying?" He falls to the side of me and nuzzles my face with his nose. "Shit. Shit. I did this. Too much. God…*damn* it." He presses his palm to his forehead.

"No…" I choke the word out past gut-racking sobs. "No. Not you…"

"Then what?"

"Well, yeah." I breathe deep and claw my nails down my forearm. The pain does its job and calms me. "It's you, but not…not what you're thinking."

"Make sense, damn it," he growls.

"Sorry. Sorry." I gulp air and tug at my hair, pulling until it hurts. "You're just so much. So *much*. So much more than…anyone. So much more than—than Kyle." And with that last word I'm sobbing again.

"Fuck." He's over me, on an elbow and gazing down at me, but I can barely see him through the blurry burn of salt in my eyes. "Nell, I'm just me. I know I said last chance, but…it's done. Okay? Don't… don't be afraid. Don't…god. I'm such a fucking dick. Look, this is about you, okay? I'm sorry I pushed you into this."

I laugh past sobs. "You're such an idiot," I manage.

At which he tenses, frozen stiff.

"What? What did you call me?" His voice is deadly cold.

I twist to look at him, and I see that he's livid, jaw hard and tensed, neck muscles corded. "Colton, I—I just meant that I wasn't afraid, not of you. And I said you're an idiot because you're acting like you pushed me into this. You didn't. I pushed *you* into this." He's shaking, he's so mad, and I'm confused and terrified. "I'm sorry—I'm—I didn't mean it…please…I—"

"Shut up for a second and let me calm down, 'kay?"

I nod and hold absolutely still.

After a few minutes, he speaks in a much calmer voice. "I have an issue with that word. With being called an idiot, or stupid. Or anything like that. Retard, dumbass, shit like that…it's a button for me. Don't say it. Not ever, not even in a joke. Got it?"

I nod. "Yeah. I got it. I'm sorry. You're not an idiot. You're amazing. You're...so much. That's my point. It's—"

"No need to go overboard trying to make up for it," Colton interrupts.

I can't help snapping my gaze to his, searching him, wondering what happened to him to make that such an issue for him. Obviously, someone used to insult his intelligence regularly. For it to be such a huge problem for Colton, there's only really one probable source. I just can't see Mr. and Mrs. Calloway doing that. They were always so supportive of Kyle, so loving, so kind. Strict, at times, especially as it came to making sure any publicity was positive, but that's understandable.

"I wasn't," I say quietly. "I was explaining why I suddenly started bawling like girl."

"You are a girl," he points out.

"Yeah," I say. "But until you badgered me into talking about things, I hadn't cried at all. I mean...at *all*."

Colton shifts on the bed to look at me. "You never cried about what happened to Kyle?"

"No."

"You never grieved?" He sounds almost incredulous.

"Grieved?" The idea seems foreign. He says it like it's expected.

He lifts up his head to stare at me. "Yeah. Grieved. Went through the stages." He flops back, rubbing between his eyes with his fingers. "Of course you didn't. Probably why you're so fucked up about it."

I throw an arm over my face to hide my irritation and hurt and the onset of stinging eyes. "He died. I dealt with it."

Colton snorts. "No. You didn't deal with shit. You're a *cutter*, Nell."

"I haven't done that in weeks." I'm aware that I'm rubbing the scars with my thumb, but I can't help it.

He takes my hands and forces them apart, traces the pattern of white lines with a fingertip. It's a tender gesture that sears my heart, makes my jaw tremble. His eyes are mournful.

"Good," he says. His eyes meet mine, and they turn firm, hard. "If you ever cut yourself again, I'll be mad. Like, really *really* pissed. You don't want to see that."

No, I sure as hell don't. I don't answer him, though. I can't promise that. I've managed to not cut in a while, simply because I've had Colton on the brain, and that's enough confusion to take my mind off the urge to bleed myself numb.

Colton isn't fooled. He takes my chin in two strong fingers and turns my head to face him. "Promise me,

Nell." His eyes are cerulean intensity. "Fucking promise me. No more cutting. You feel the urge, you call
me. You get me, we deal together, okay?"

I wish I could make that promise. I can't. He
doesn't understand how deep the need is. I hate it, I
really do. I always feel even more guilty after I've cut,
which makes the problem even worse. It's like this habit
I can't shake, but it's not just a habit, like an addiction
I'm ashamed of, smoking or pill popping or whatever.
I know he gets the need to cut, but he doesn't realize
how embedded in me the urge is.

I haven't answered. I'm staring at the ceiling, shaking. I want to promise him. I want to be healed, to
never want to score lines of pain into my wrists, my
forearms again.

Colton sits up, and he's still naked, not hard anymore, and I'm fascinated by his not-erect cock. It's a
distraction, and only momentary. Colton grabs me,
lifts me, and I'm on his lap, in his arms, forced to meet
his angry glare.

"Fucking promise, Nell."

"No!" I wrench myself free, scramble away, off the
bed, away from his hot skin and hard muscles and angry,
piercing eyes. "No! You can't say that to me, you can't
demand that of me. You don't understand! You can't
just appear in my life and try to change it like this."

"Yes, I can." His voice is calm but intense.

He's still on the bed, watching me. I'm hunting the pile of clothes on the floor for mine, but I can't find my shirt or my panties, so I settle for a T-shirt of Colton's. It hangs to mid-thigh, and it's soft and it smells like him, which is confusing and comforting and incredible.

"No. You can't. You don't know me. You don't know what I went through. You don't know how I feel."

"You're right. But I'm trying to."

"Why?"

"Because you should never have been left alone to deal. You should never have been allowed to bury it all and let it fester. Kyle's death is an open wound inside you. It's never healed, never scabbed over. It's all fucking nasty and gangrenous, Nell. It's rotting. You need to let someone in. You need to let me in."

"I can't...I can't..." I'm running, now. Out of his room, into the kitchen.

It's drink or cut. He's bringing it all up, forcing all the shit I've buried to the surface. He knows it, and he's doing it on purpose.

I've kept it all down for so long, and whenever it threatened to come up, come out, I'd drink until it settled back down, or I'd cut and bleed it out rather than feel it, rather than cry or scream or be angry.

I know he has whiskey somewhere, but I can't find it. It's not in the fridge, and I can't reach high enough to look in the cupboard above the fridge where I know it must be. I climb on the counter, reach for it, and lose my balance. I fall, slamming hard into the floor, and the breath is knocked out of me.

It's coming up. It came up when he forced me into tears, when he made me admit I killed Kyle. The guilt came up and out, and that hurt, like knives shredding my heart.

This?

This is the grief. The loss. The knowledge that Kyle is gone. Of course he's gone, I've known that. But this is the grief. The hurt. The loneliness. It's worse than the guilt. I always knew the guilt was wrong and misplaced. The guilt I can't justify away, can't shift or explain or bury any longer.

I'm fighting sobs, fighting the clenching in my stomach and heart.

No.

No.

I won't let it out.

He forced out the guilt. He can't force out the grief. I don't want it. It's too much. It'll shred me.

A drawer slams open, silverware rattles. I'm not aware of moving, but it's me digging in the drawer for a knife. Let him be mad. I don't care. I hear his feet stomping now. He'd been giving me space to calm down, I guess, but now he knows what I'm doing.

He's too late.

The pain is a blessed relief. I watch in guilty satisfaction as a thin line of red wells up on my forearm. The knife wasn't very sharp, so I had to press. It's a deep cut.

"What the *fuck*?" Colton, wearing shorts, rushing at me, angry, scared. "Nell…what the *fuck*?"

I don't bother answering. I'm dizzy. Bleeding. I look down and see the spreading red, and it's too much. I cut deep. Too deep. Good. The grief slides away and slicks across the scratched laminate floor.

I'm in his arms, and there's pressure around my arm. A white towel, turning pink-to-crimson. He's squeezing my arm so hard it hurts past the cut-pain. The towel is wrapped around my arm, and then a belt cinched tight.

I'm between his knees, my back to his front. I feel his hard chest and his frantic, panting breath, his arms around my shoulders. He's holding the belt in one hand, my wrist in the other. His face is pressed to the top of my head. His breath huffs loud in my ear, on my hair.

"Goddamn it, Nell. Why?"

I find my voice. The hurt in his words is palpable, as if I'd cut him rather than myself, and I want to soothe it. Odd. I want to soothe his pain, the hurt over my cut.

"I can't take it," I whisper, because a whisper is all I can manage. "It's too much. He's gone, and he's not coming back. My fault or not…he's gone. He's dead. He's bones in a wood box, a fading memory. Nothing stops that pain. Not even time."

"I know."

"You *don't*." The last word is growled, rabid. "You weren't *there*. You're not in my head. You don't know."

"He was my baby brother, Nell." His voice sounds almost as broken as mine.

"But…you left when we were eleven. You never even came back to visit." That was something that Kyle and I never talked about, but I knew it confused him, hurt him. His parents wouldn't talk about Colton.

"Yeah, well…I didn't have much choice. I was barely surviving. I missed him every single day. I wrote a thousand letters to him in my head while I tried to fall asleep on park benches and in boxes in alleys, covered in newspapers. A thousand letters I'd never be able to write, couldn't write. I couldn't afford food or shelter, much less a bus ticket back to Detroit."

Something in what he said strikes me as odd, but I'm dizzy and weak and foggy and can't place what.

He lets go the pressure of the makeshift tourniquet, gingerly lifts the towel away. Blood seeps out slowly, but sluggishly. I'm lifted and carried, and I let my head flop against his broad chest. He sets me on the bed, vanishes, comes back with a roll of gauze, medical tape, and a tube of Neosporin.

"You probably should have stitches," he says, folding a bandage and placing it over the cut and rolling gauze tightly around my arm. "But I know you won't get them. So this'll have to work."

"How do you know I won't?" I ask.

"Will you?"

"Hell, no. But how'd you know?" I watch as he tapes the edges down.

"I wouldn't have, if it were me. There'd be questions and social services and psychologists and the psych ward. Worst of all, they'd call your parents." He puts two fingers beneath my chin, a thumb along my jaw. "Which is what you'll get if this shit happens again. I'll rush you to the fucking ER and I'll call your goddamn parents myself, like I should this time, but won't."

"Why not?" I whisper.

"Because they'd get it all wrong. It's not a cry for attention or any of that psychobabble bullshit." He tips his forehead to touch mine. "Because I can help you, if you'll let me. We can get you through this."

'We'? Shit. *Shit.* My eyes still and my lip trembles and my chest heaves. My instinct is to cause pain to stop the tears. Colton knows this by now, gathers me close and holds me against his chest. He's determined to do this, to be all supportive and loving. Which is exactly what I've always been terrified of admitting I want so so badly. Except he's tenacious about not letting me hide or lie or retreat or pretend, and he knows all my tricks.

"Let...it...*go*," he whispers, his voice a fierce, harsh sound in my hair.

"No. No!" The last word is screamed.

"You have to. You can't bleed it out. You can't keep pretending, drinking it down."

A shudder, a tremble, my teeth clamping down on my lower lip. My fingers claw into the hard slab of muscle that is his pectoral. I'm not sobbing. I'm not.

Goddammit, yes, I am.

"It hurts so fucking bad, Colton..." The words are nearly lost in a sea of choking sobs and shuddering, body-wracking gasps for breath. "I want him back! I don't want to watch him die anymore."

I sob and sob, and he just holds me. Eventually I pull myself together and let words pour out of me. "Over and over I see it. Every time I close my eyes, I see him die. I know it's not my fault, I always did.

I convinced myself it was my fault because that was better than the pain of him being gone."

"He's gone. You have to accept it."

"I know. It just hurts." Now comes the hardest admission of all. "I find myself forgetting him. I see him dying over and over, but I can't remember what he smelled like. What his arms felt like holding me. What sex with him felt like. What kissing him felt like. I can't remember him. And I wonder sometimes if I ever really loved him. If it was just teenage infatuation. Thinking I loved him because he was my first. Because we'd fucked. I don't know. I don't remember. And now there's you, and you're...better than he was. Stronger. You turn me on in a way I don't remember with him. You make me feel things he never did. The way you kiss me, it's better than I remember his kisses being. When you made me come, I realized I'd never felt anything like it, ever. *Ever.* Not in all the times I was with Kyle in the two years we were together."

A scream of raw impotent pain and self-loathing and anger and grief tears out my throat; Colton clutches me tighter and lets me scream. Doesn't shush me or quiet me or whisper anything or tell me it's okay.

"I've forgotten him, Colton! I never even loved him, and he's gone! And I'll never get him back, and I'll never be okay!"

"Forgetting is the mind's way of helping you heal. Helping you move on. You *did* love him, Nell. He was your first. Your best friend before that. I know that much about you two. You were inseparable from birth. You did love him. Yeah, he's gone, and it fucking sucks more than anything. He was taken from you too soon, from all of us. I can't make that okay. But you *have to* be okay. You have to let yourself heal and move on. You're stuck in the moment of his death, right now. Locked into a cycle with no way out. You have to break the cycle."

"I don't know how."

"Feel. Grieve. Let yourself feel all the anger at the fact that he was taken from you. Feel the loss of him. Feel the sadness and the missing him. Don't block it out, don't cut so it stops, don't drink yourself numb. Just sit and let it all rip you apart. And then get up and keep breathing. One breath at a time. One day at a time. Wake up, and be shredded. Cry for a while. Then stop crying and go about your day. You're not okay, but you're alive, and you will be okay, someday."

"You make it sound easy."

"Fuck no, it's not easy. It's the hardest thing ever. But it's the only way. What you're doing is gonna kill you."

I hear the personal knowledge of this in his voice. "You've done this."

He sighs. "Yeah. More than once."

"Kyle?"

"Him, too."

"Who else?"

He breathes out again, a long frustrated breath. "Friends. Brothers. A girl I…someone I loved."

"Tell me."

"Fuck. Really? You want to hear this now?" I nod, and he growls in his chest. "Fine. The first one was one of my best buddies, Split's and mine. T-Shawn. Split grew up next to him. T-Shawn and Split started the Five-One Bishops together. There was a rumble on a basketball court, a turf thing. Fists mainly, a few chains, one asshole had a bat. Then it escalated. One of the other guys pulled a knife. Stabbed T in the fucking throat. I watched—watched him bleed out all over my hands, my arms. I watched T die, held him in my fucking arms as he bled out…and then I killed the motherfucker. Crushed his goddamn head against the court until I saw brains. Couldn't stop myself. T was a good guy. A good friend. A gentle guy, really. But he had the bad luck to be born in the ghetto. Ain't much you can do but what you gotta do to keep breathing. It ain't even really a choice, for most. It's just life. Life in the hood. How shit works. T was smart, man. Could have gone to college, written some smart shit, been someone, if he'd have had the opportunity. Didn't. Now he's dead."

"I'm sorry."

"Then another brother got shot. Lil Shady. We weren't friends at first. His girl had a thing for me, which he didn't like. I never did nothing with her, but…he didn't like me for it. Eventually we got past that shit, and had each other's backs when things got ugly. Shady took a slug to the head. Didn't see that shit, thank god. But he was gone, and it sucked. Just…gone. I'd smoked a blunt with him an hour before he died, you know? And then Split and Mo were banging in my door, carrying Shady, yelling about some other gang doing a drive-by." He's gone, his eyes vacant, seeing the past. "Couple others through the years, same shit, different day. None as close as Shady and T, though." He trails off, and I realize he's lost in the memory.

I tangle my fingers with his. "You said a girl, too? Someone you loved?"

"That was the worst day of my life. The reason I decided to quit the gang and live straight, buy the shop and try to get away from all that shit." He ducks his head, buries his face into my hair, takes a deep breath. "Her name was India. So fucking beautiful. Her mom was black, her dad was Korean. Almond-shaped eyes, long straight black hair down to her waist, body like—well, a damn fine one. Such a sweet girl. Too sweet to be living in the ghetto, to be caught up in the shit she was caught up in. She was friends with Split's girlfriend. She was around a lot, and I'd noticed her. Seen her, liked her. Seen her looking at me. We finally ended up the last two awake after a party one night, hung out on the fire escape talking till dawn. She wanted to go to beauty school, or maybe be a model, she wasn't sure which. Coulda been great at either."

A long pause then. Too long. I can't fill it, though. I wait for him.

"We dated for a year. Dated isn't really the right word, 'cause it wasn't like I was taking her to Broadway and Little Italy or some shit, you know? We were together for a year, is what I meant. Fuck. I can't talk about this." His voice cracks, he takes a deep breath, lets it out, and continues. "Had some shit go down with a rival gang, a couple rumbles, whatever. Routine shit. It went bad. Got separated from Split and them, chased on foot for fucking miles by more guys than I could take alone. Didn't mean to, but I led them to India. She was hanging with her girlfriends, couple of their guys. Sees me coming down the street, knew I was in trouble. Called the guys out to help. So the guys and I take care of things and I got hit in the shoulder, but whatever, wasn't too bad. Last one was talking shit, but I could see he was ready to run. We let him. Fucking…he ran off, then stopped about a hundred feet away and blasted a shot, like a last 'fuck you.' India was on the porch, took it straight between the fucking eyes. Total freak accident. I could see the guy's face. He was like 'oh shit,' because everybody knew India. Didn't matter who you belonged to, you knew India, you had to love her, respect her ass. She was that sweet. He got capped the next day, not me, but it happened. Didn't matter, though. She was gone. All that beauty, all that sweetness, all that love for everyone, no matter who you were…just gone."

I feel wetness in my hair, hear tears in his voice. I shift, swivel, pull him to me. I hold his face to my chest and finally understand what he meant by letting yourself just be shredded. Colton is a hard-ass, tough and strong and stoic. But he's just…broken by the memories. And this is years later.

"She was the first girl I ever loved. I mean, I had girlfriends before that, you know? I even thought I was in love with a couple of 'em, but it wasn't love. It was *like* love, *almost* love. But when you feel that kind of all-consuming need for someone, a person you'd do fucking anything for, no matter what? They're in your fucking skin, in your soul, like the essence of who they are is imprinted on you so completely that the very air you breathe and each molecule of who you are is tangled together. That's love. I loved her like that." Colton's voice is...shattered. "And she's gone. That's why I have this shit on my chest, the scars. I couldn't deal. I couldn't accept that she was dead for the longest time. It hurt so bad, so deep that I just had to stop it somehow, I had to feel something besides the emotional agony. It was Split who saved me. Made me face what happened and how I felt, and let it go." He laughs, a rough bark. "You don't ever really let go, though. You don't stop. You don't stop hurting, you don't stop loving. It doesn't go away—you just keep living, and eventually shit gets pushed into the background of your life so it's not consuming you every day. And then one day, you know you're okay. It still hurts, you still miss that person. And yeah, you forget the details. The way she smelled, the way her mouth tasted, how her skin felt, the sound of her voice. It's almost like a different life, a different person who loved her, was with her. But on a day-to-day level, you know you're okay. Sort of."

"And you learn to love someone else?" I ask, because I have to know.

He sits up, and now we're facing each other, cross-legged. "I don't know about that." His eyes are vulnerable, letting me in. "I'm working on it, though. I'll let you know."

He means me.

"How do you compete with a ghost, Colton?" I whisper the question into a long silence.

He shrugs. "I don't know. You don't. You just understand that there's a part of you that you can't give away, because it belongs to a dead person. I don't know."

"Can we do this? You and me? You with your ghost of India, me with mine of Kyle?"

He takes my hands, rubs my knuckles with his thumbs. "All we can do is try, do our best. Give as much as we have to give, one day at a time. One breath at a time."

"I don't know how to do this. I'm scared." I'm unable to look at him, unable to meet his eyes.

He does the thing with his fingers on my chin, tilting my face to his. Except this time he does it and leans in, and his lips brush mine. "I don't, either, and so am I. But if we want to live, to not be half-ghosts ourselves, stuck loving the memory of someone who's gone, then we have to try." He kisses me again. "We understand each other, Nelly. We've both lost someone we love. We both have scars and regrets and anger. We can do this together."

I breathe through the fear, the trembling, the desire to escape. "I like it when you call me Nelly. No one has ever called me that before."

He just smiles and holds me closer.

Chapter 10: Silencing the Ghosts
A Month Later

THINGS RETURNED TO SOMETHING LIKE NORMAL, except Colton would come over and hang out. Things reverted to a less physical stage, although I felt just as much attraction to him, if not more, and I felt his eyes on me frequently. We kissed a few times, but we seemed to have put an unspoken hold on physical affection. I'm not sure why this is. I'm not sure if I like it. I want him. I need his touch.

I attend classes at NYU, I run, I work my shifts as a cocktail waitress, and I play music. And I see Colton, but not nearly enough. Above all, I try not to freak out about my impending acceptance or rejection to the college of performing arts. In all the craziness of meeting Colton in the park and the subsequent events, I managed to actually forget the letter was coming.

The letter comes, finally, brought in along with all my other mail by Colton. I'm sitting on my kitchen counter, feet on a chair, practicing a song when Colton knocks on my door, entering even as he knocks. He hands me the stack of envelopes, which I sort through. The letter from NYU is on the bottom, of course. When I get to it, my heart starts pounding, and I drop all the other mail.

"What is it?" Colton asks, seeing my reaction.

"I applied to the college of performing arts at the university. It's not a guaranteed acceptance thing, and this letter tells me if I got in or not." I slide my finger under the flap and pull out the single sheet of paper. At which point my courage fails me and I wig out, flapping my hands and shrieking like a teenager. "I can't look! You read it to me," I say, handing it to him.

Colton takes it, glances at it, then hands it back. "No, it's yours. You read it." There's an odd expression on his face that I can't interpret.

"I'm too nervous," I say. "Please? Read it to me?"

"You should read it yourself, Nelly-baby. It won't be the same as you reading the acceptance yourself."

"You don't know I got in," I say, shoving it at him, curious and irritated now. "Please? Please read it to me?" I shouldn't push this, I know. I can see by the hardening of his features that this is an issue. A button. But now I have it in my teeth, and I'm not letting go.

"No, Nell. I'm not reading it to you. It's your acceptance letter, not mine." He turns away, digging a fist into his pocket and rattling loose change.

He's staring out the window, his shoulders hunched, his jaw tensed.

"Come on, Colton. What's the big deal? I want to share this moment with you."

He whirls on me, eyes hot and pained and angry. "You want to know the big deal? I can't fucking read! Okay? That's the big deal. I can't fucking read." He turns back to the window, fists curled at his sides.

I'm stunned. "Wha-what? You can't read? Like... at all? How—how is that possible?" I approach him from behind and tentatively, gingerly, lay a hand on his shoulder.

His muscular shoulder is a rock beneath my hand. He doesn't turn when he speaks, and his voice is pitched so low I have to strain to hear him.

"I'm dyslexic. Like, *severely*. I *can* read, but really, really bad, and it takes me fucking forever to get through even the simplest sentences. A goddamned first-grader can read better than me, okay? If I sit in an absolutely silent room with no distractions and focus really hard for an hour or two, I might be able to puzzle out one full article in a newspaper, which is written at a fifth-grade level or some shit."

So much clicks into place now. "That's part of why you're here in New York, isn't it? Part of the issue with your parents."

He bobs his head twice, a short, sharp jerk of acknowledgement. "Yeah. It's been a problem my whole life. Back when I was a kid, shit was less figured out than it is now. Nowadays, you got all sorts of resources for 'learning disabled' kids like me." He uses air quotes around the phrase. "They got IEDs and learning labs and tutors and all sorts of nifty shit. When I was a kid, in a rural district like where we grew up, I didn't have none of that. They just thought I was stupid. So did my parents. They had me tested and stuff, but dyslexia wasn't a huge thing on people's radar, or whatever, so they didn't know what to look for, and I didn't know how to explain what my deal was."

"All I really know about dyslexia is that it's got something to do with difficulty reading." I rub my hand in circles on his granite shoulder

He nods and finally turns to me. I swallow hard and decide to push past the barrier between us. I close in against him, push my body flush with his, slide my hands up underneath his arms and clutch his back. I tilt my head up to look at him, resting my chin on his chest. His scent and his heat and his hardness intoxicate me, a heady rush of need bolting through me.

"Yeah, basically, but it's more than that," he says. "It's...nothing written down makes any sense to me. Letters, numbers, sentences, math equations...everything. I can do a shitload of fairly advanced math in my head, I've got a good vocabulary, I understand grammar, but it all has to be orally communicated to me. Tell me a word, what it means, and it's mine. Explain a mathematical idea to me, I got it, no fucking problem. Write it down? Nothing. It's like things just jumble up, rearrange into nonsense. I look at this paper here," he taps the page in my hand with a forefinger, "and I see the letters. I know the alphabet, I can technically read, I can do 'run spot run.' But when I look at the paper, I swear it's all bullshit, just letters that make no sense. I have to focus on each letter at a time, each word, sound it out, figure it out. And then I have to go back and put the sentence all together and the paragraph and the page, and that usually means I have to work it all out all over again. It's fucking laborious as all hell."

"All the songs you write, the lyrics—"

"All in here." He taps his head. "I compose the lyrics, the music, everything, in my head."

I'm stunned. "You don't have any of it written down anywhere?"

He laughs, a harsh cough. "No, baby. Not being able to read is bad enough. I can't write for shit, either. It's just as hard. Harder, actually, because I start out writing what's in my head, but other shit comes out, like random gibberish."

"So you just have it all memorized?"

He shrugs. "It's just how I am. I have a great memory, and musically, I have one of those perfect ears. I hear a piece of music, I can play it. The notes, the chords, it all just makes sense to me as soon as I hear it. Mechanical stuff is the same way. I just get it, instinctively. I mean, I had to learn how to do it, just like I had to learn how to play the guitar and use my voice right, but it comes naturally to me."

"And your parents didn't understand any of this?" I ask.

He sighs, and it's laced with a growl. "God, I hate talking about this shit." He absently brushes my hair back. "No, they really didn't. I was their first kid. They made mistakes. I get that. Doesn't make how it all happened less shitty."

"What happened?"

He looks down into my eyes, and seems to draw strength from something he sees there. "Like I said, they couldn't really understand what my problem was. I clearly wasn't, like, slow or anything. I could talk fine,

I could interact socially and tie my shoes and identify colors and patterns and all that, but when the lessons in kindergarten started requiring me to look at things on the written page, I just couldn't grasp it. It frustrated everyone. My dad was on the rise back then, and he had big aspirations. Big plans for me, his firstborn son. I'd be his successor, a doctor or a lawyer or something great like that. He'd decided that's what my destiny was, and nothing could change his mind. It kept getting harder and harder, because my comprehension of reading and writing was just…nil. I never progressed past the first grade, really. I had to work three times as hard as everyone else to get my homework done, to pass tests, all that. I was barely scraping by, all the way through school. Dad just thought I was lazy. He'd tell me to work harder, to not let anything stop me. He pushed and pushed and pushed, and never really saw how hard I was working just to get by. I barely passed middle school, and I mean *barely*, and that was with me studying and doing homework for literally four or five hours every night. Because everything is centered around writing the answers, reading the textbooks. Like I said, I *can* do it, it's just…so hard as to be nearly impossible, and it takes forever. I was just a fucking kid. I wanted to play football and play with my friends, hang out, all that normal shit. I couldn't, because I was always in my goddamned room, trying to finish reading the ten pages of history or *The Giver*."

I rest my forehead against his chest, aching for him. "God, Colton."

"Yeah, it sucked. And Dad just didn't understand. He's not a bad person. He's great, he really is. When it wasn't all about school, he was great with me. But that began to overshadow everything else as I got older. By high school, I was just *angry*. All the time. I hated school, I hated the teachers and the principal and my parents and everything. It didn't help that by the time I was fifteen, Kyle was already this golden boy, perfectly behaved, athletic, all the friends and charming and shit. And I had to study for six hours a day just to get Cs and Ds. And the fucking worst part is that I knew I understood the basic concepts. I knew I wasn't stupid. I could listen and understand what the lecture was about. I could listen to the lecture and probably recite the damn thing back to the teacher verbatim. If I'd been able to take tests orally, I probably would have been a straight-A student. But that just wasn't an option back then." He traces the line of my jaw with a fingertip, down behind my ear, down my neck, and across my collarbone; I shiver under the heat of his touch. "I got in a lot of trouble at school because I was just so fucking angry, so frustrated. And kids made fun of me, of course, because I was always in trouble and barely passing, so I got in a lot of fights."

"Kids are awful in high school."

"No kidding," he says with a bitter laugh. "I didn't really mind them, honestly. It was the shit with my parents that killed me. They just thought I wasn't trying hard enough, that I was exaggerating my problems to get out of school or something. And they expected me to toe their line, follow their plan. And that plan included college. All I wanted was to work in a garage, build cars. Play my guitar. That wasn't acceptable."

I'm starting to understand. "So when graduation came…"

"My dad was insisting I *had* to apply to all these colleges, Ivy League and everything." He laughs, and this laugh is mirthless, full of bitterness and old rage. "Fucking college? I barely graduated high school. I could barely *read*. I *hated* school. I was fucking done. I told him this, and he just didn't care. He'd pull strings so my bad grades wouldn't matter. Finally, I knew I had to make him understand. I remember the day like it was yesterday. Clear, sunny, beautiful day in June. I'd been graduated for a couple months and was spending all my time in the garage, working on my Camaro. He wanted me to be applying to Harvard and Columbia and Brown, and I wasn't doing it. It was a constant fight. I finally hashed it out with him on the dock. I told him I wasn't going to college, not ever. And Dad's reply? 'Then you're on your own.' He'd pay my way, support me, rent me an apartment and all that, *if* I went to college. If not, he wouldn't give me a red cent." Colton pauses, and I can see this is the hardest part. "It got ugly. He…we fought, like bad. He called me names, told me I was just stupid and lazy. He was angry, I get that, but…it still fucking scarred me for me life. All I ever wanted was his approval, for him to see that I had other skills, that I was smart in other ways. He just couldn't. Like I said, the fight got ugly. Turned physical. He hit me, I hit him. I ran. Left my car, my Camaro I'd spent fucking years building from scratch. Left all my shit. Grabbed a backpack and some clothes and all the money I had. Bought a bus ticket to New York. Never looked back. Of course, the bus cost pretty much every dollar I had, so by the time I got to the city, I was flat broke, a basically illiterate seventeen-year-old kid with anger problems and no plan, no money, no friends, no car, no apartment, nothing. Just a backpack with some crackers and a change of clothes."

The pain in his voice is heartbreaking. I see him in my mind's eye, a scared, angry, lonely kid forced to fight just to survive. Too proud to go back home, even if he could have. Hungry, cold, alone, living on the streets.

"Colton...I'm so sorry you had to go through that." I hear my voice crack.

He lifts my chin. "Hey. No tears. Not for me. I made it, didn't I?"

"Yeah, but you shouldn't have had to suffer like that." He just shrugs dismissively, and I push back to glare at him. "No, don't shrug it off. You've accomplished so much. You survived. You got yourself off the street. You built a successful business from nothing. You did all that on your own, despite your learning disability. I think it's incredible. I think *you're* incredible."

He shrugs again, rolling his eyes, clearly uncomfortable. I put my hands on his face, loving the feel of his rough stubble under my palms.

"You're smart, Colton. You are. You're talented. I'm amazed by who you are."

"You're fucking embarrassing me, Nelly." Colton wraps his arms around me and pulls me roughly against his chest. "But thanks for saying so. It means more than you know. Now. Did you get in or not? I'm sick of talking about my shit."

I hold the letter up behind his back, reading it over his shoulder. "Yeah. I got in."

"There was never a question. Proud of you, Nelly-baby."

I smile into his chest, breathing in his scent.

I swallow hard. I'm not sure if I can do this. I clutch the neck of my guitar and try not to panic.

"Ready?" Colton's voice comes from beside me. His knee nudges mine.

I nod my head. "Yeah. Yeah. I can do this."

"You can do this. Just follow my lead and sing the harmony, okay? Just strum the rhythm like we practiced and let everyone hear that angel voice of yours, okay?"

I nod again, and flex my fingers. I've never performed in public before. I mean, I've busked a few times, alone and with Colton, but that's different. This…this is terrifying. We're on a stage in a bar, and there's close to a hundred people all watching, waiting for us to start. They know Colton, they're here for him, and intrigued as to who I am. No pressure.

"Hey, everybody. I'm Colt, and this is Nell. We're gonna play some music for you, is that all right?" There's applause and some catcalls. Colton glances at me and then back to the crowd. "Yeah, I know she's gorgeous, boys, but she's off limits. We're gonna play some Avett Brothers to start, I think. This is 'I Would Be Sad.'"

He starts off with a complex string-picking arrangement that echoes the banjo of the original. I come in on cue with a simple rhythm-strum and wait for the harmony cue. The rhythm is easy, and I've practiced it so many times I don't even have to think about it, so I hit my cue no problem. They're floored. My voice provides a perfect counterpoint to Colton's, my clear alto weaving around his rough rasp, and together I know we have them in a spell.

I adjust the rhythm as we transition into the next song, which Colton introduces.

"Anybody here like City and Colour?" There's riotous applause of approval, and he grins at them. "Good! Then hopefully you'll like our take on 'Hello, I'm Delaware.'"

I'm strumming as he does the intro and playing it cool, but inside I'm squeeing with excitement. In the back of my head I'm running back to the beginning, when Colton basically announced that I'm his. I like that. Plus, he told them I'm gorgeous. I'm all a-shiver.

I really get into the City and Colour song, because Dallas Green is incredible. I let my voice go; I don't hold anything back. I sing and let the words roll over me, through me. My nerves are gone, and all I know is the music rushing in my veins, the pure beauty of the song and the adrenaline high of knowing I'm killing it.

The next song is all Colton. I've heard him practice it, so I'm looking forward to hearing him perform it live. Our guitars go quiet, and Colton adjusts the tuning on his while he does the next intro.

"Okay, so this one I'm doing solo. You've probably heard the song before, but not like this. It's "99 Problems,' originally by the one and only Jay-Z. This arrangement that I'm doing, though, was put together by an artist named Hugo. I wish I could take the credit for the arrangement, honestly, because it's fucking genius. So yeah. Hope you like it."

There's some applause, which fades when he starts a choppy, drum-like sequence of chords. I'm giddy with excitement and pride when he brings in the verse. The first time I heard him play the song, I wasn't sure what I was hearing, because it was so unique, but then I recognized it and was totally wowed. He's right about the arrangement being brilliant, because it is, completely.

All too soon it's my turn.

"You guys are awesome. The rest of Hugo's stuff is pretty killer, too, but that's my favorite piece by him. So anyway, Nell's gonna do a solo for you next."

He insisted I intro my own piece, so I adjust the mic closer and strum the opening chords as warm-up. "Hey, guys. I've never sung solo like this before, so be

nice, huh? I'm doing 'It's Time' by Imagine Dragons."
I turn to look at Colton. "I'm dedicating this to you,
because it reminds me so much of you."

When I was jogging and listening to my playlist,
trying to figure out what song I wanted to cover for
tonight's solo, I came across this song. It's an awesome
song that seems almost eighties pop-inspired to me,
which I knew would make for an interesting indie-folk
cover. But it was the lyrics that struck me, the empha-
sis on never changing, on being who you are. Colton
had been through so much and had stayed true to who
he was, refusing to change or give in simply because of
the expectations of others.

I struggled with that for a long time. I had chosen
schools and career paths based on what others wanted
for me, what my parents wanted for me. After Kyle's
death, I couldn't choose, couldn't think, couldn't feel
any desire for anything. I worked for my dad and went
to community college simply because it was the path
of least resistance. My dad had always sort of expected
I would major in business and work for him. I'd never
considered anything else. I'd never thought of my tal-
ents or desires—I just went along with their plan without question.

Then Kyle died, and after a few months, I realized
I needed an outlet. I needed something to distract me

from my guilt and pain. The guitar came along almost as a fluke. I saw a flier stapled to a wooden power line pole advertising guitar lessons. The teacher was an older guy, gray-haired and potbellied and genial. He was a talented teacher, patient and understanding. Best of all, he seemed to understand that I wanted a couple hours a week away from everything. He never asked any questions, just drilled me hard, pushed me, kept me busy, leaving me no time for anything but the chord progressions. He gave me an aggressive practice schedule and rode my ass if I didn't keep up with it.

The singing seemed to be a natural extension of playing the guitar. I'd always loved singing, grew up listening to my mom singing. I never took singing seriously, though. It was just something I did in the car and the shower. And then I started taking guitar lessons and music became an obsession, a release, a way of feeling something besides pain. I'd learn a song, and of course I'd sing along with it. Eventually I realized I enjoyed the singing more than the guitar playing, and then the music itself became the outlet. I'd spend hours and hours playing, singing, sitting on the dock, watching the sun set and the stars come out and playing, refusing to think of Kyle, refusing to miss him, refusing to cry for him. I'd play until my fingers bled, sing until my throat hurt.

Now the music is a thread binding me to Colton. The songs we sing to each other are statements. An ongoing discussion in music notes.

So I sing, and I let everything out. I feel the eyes on me, feel Colton's gaze devouring me. I finish the song, and the last note quavers in the air, and my hands tremble, my heart thuds in my chest. There's a moment of silence, all eyes on me, faces shocked. I'm about to freak, since no one's clapping, but then they explode, shrieking, whistling, applauding, and I realize they were stunned silent.

Guess that's a good thing.

When the noise fades a bit, Colton draws his mic down to his lips and speaks facing me but looking at the audience. "God*damn*, Nell. That was incredible. Seriously." I hear the tension in his voice, see the emotion in his eyes. He's hiding it well, but I know him by now, and I can feel it radiating off him.

We both let a tense moment pass in silence then. We both know what song is next, and we're both nervous.

"I've never played this song for anyone before," Colton says, clipping a capo to his strings. "It's…a deeply personal song that I wrote a long, long time ago. Nell's been badgering me—I mean, *encouraging* me—to play this song live for weeks now, and I finally gave in. So…yeah. Here it is. I never gave this a title, but I guess we can call it…'One More Hour.' I hope you like it."

I can see how hard this is for him. The melody he plays on the guitar is slow and heavy and rolling, melancholy. Then he sings the lullaby, and god, the bar goes so silent you could hear a pin drop in between chords and sung notes. No one is moving, no one is even breathing. We practiced this together. He would only play it if I'd do backup and harmony, so that's what I'm doing. I sing some backup vocals for him and play a basic rhythm, but I keep it low and quiet so he's the focus. And he is. Totally. I see eyes shifting, throats constricting. There are tears. You can hear how intensely personal this song is to Colton; it's clear in the passion of his voice. He's singing to himself again. He's the lost boy again, alone on the streets of New York. I ache for him all over again. I want to hold him, kiss him, tell him he's not alone.

Again, the bar is absolutely silent and still when the last note hangs in the air, and then it goes wild.

A few more popular songs Colton taught me, and then we do "Barton Hollow" together, our last number for the set. I'm exhilarated, shaking with excitement. I applied to the college of performing arts on a whim, as an act of rebellion, communicating to my parents that I was going to do things my own way. I'd never actually performed before.

Now...I'm hooked.

Colton gets our payment and hurries us out. I can't read the look on his face, but I can see tension in his body language. I'm nervous as we stand side by side on the subway, guitars in soft cases slung on our backs, hands holding the rail by our heads. He's silent, and I'm not sure if he's upset, angry about something, jazzed from the show. I just can't read him, and it's making me nervous.

I reach out and take his hand in mine, threading our fingers together. He glances at me, at our joined hands, and then back at me. His face softens.

"Sorry, I'm just...playing that song was rough. I'm distracted, I guess. Not very good company."

I sidle closer to him, pressing myself into his side. "I know it was, Colton. I'm proud of you. You were seriously incredible. People were crying."

He lets go of my hand and wraps his arm around my waist, tugging me even closer. His palm rests on the swell of my hip, and suddenly the subway car falls away, replaced by lightning awareness of him, of his heat, his muscle. His touch is fire, singeing away the layers of clothes between us until I can almost feel his skin on mine. I need that. I need flesh to flesh, heat to heat. We've been dancing around it for too long now, and the slight taste I had of him wasn't enough. I need more. I don't know why he's been keeping distance between us, but I'm done with it. I've been playing along, slowing down in our kiss when he does, not pushing it. The kisses have all been nearly platonic recently, quick touches of our lips only occasionally pushing into more, into the realm of heat and need.

Now, my body singing from his nearness, my mind and heart buzzing from the post-show high, all I can think of, all I can feel is him, and my desire for him. His fingers dig into the flesh of my hip, and his eyes burn into mine, cobalt flames locked on me. I know he feels it, too.

I bite my lip, knowing what it does to him. His eyes go half-lidded and his chest swells. His finger tightens on me even more until it's almost painful, thrillingly so.

"You're coming over," he says.

It's an order, not a question. I nod, never taking my eyes from him. "I'm coming over," I affirm. I lean in close, pressing my lips to the shell of his ear. "No holding back tonight."

I hear him hiss, a sucked-in breath. "You're sure?" His voice is a rumble felt in my chest.

"God, yes." I need him to understand. *"Please."*

He laughs, but it's not a humorous laugh. It's a predatory sound, full of erotic promise. "Nelly-baby… you don't need to beg."

I flush with something like shame. "I am begging, though. You've been making me wait for so long now. And I need this."

His eyes are so fiery, so piercingly blue it takes my breath away. "I was giving you space and time. I didn't think you were ready. I wasn't myself, not entirely."

"I get that, and I appreciate it. But now I'm saying…no more space. No more time."

His hand descends, slides around just slightly, and now he's almost but not quite cupping my ass. "I just want you to be sure. No questions, no hesitations. I want it to be right."

I rest my forehead against his shoulder, then lift my face to look up at him. "I'm ready. So ready. Scared, yes. But ready."

He laughs again. "You think you're ready. You're not." His voice goes husky. "But you will be, baby. I'll make sure of that."

And oh, god, *ohmigod*, the threat, the promise in his voice is enough to have me clenching my thighs together to keep the dampness in. I know my eyes are wide, my breath coming in deep gasps.

"Quit biting your goddamn lip before I fucking lose it right here on the train," Colton growls. I slowly

slide my lip out from between my teeth, teasing him
with my compliance. "Why the fuck is that so hot?"
He seems genuinely confused by his own reaction.

I arch my back and take a deep breath, crushing
my breasts against him. We're on a subway surrounded
by people, but they're oblivious, and I just don't care.
I'm caught up in my own need, burning with the fires
of desire. My sense is gone, my restraint burnt away.

"Knock it off, Nell." Colton jerks me against him,
and now I'm crashed front to front with him. I can feel
his desire against my belly, hard and huge. "Quit fucking with me. You're sexy, and I want you. Point made."

I make innocent eyes at him. "I'm not making a
point, Colton." I lean in close, whisper it into his ear,
my breath soft. "I'm horny." I feel cheesy and ridiculous saying that, but it's what comes out, and it's true.

Colton doesn't laugh like I thought he would have.
"*Fuck*, Nell. You're seriously tempting my control. I'm
about to shove my tongue down your throat right here
on the train."

Wide, innocent eyes again. "You wouldn't hear
me complaining." And I bite my lip, just to hammer
it home.

His jaw clenches, and both hands come around
my waist to clutch my ass. Oh, *god*, I like that. I love
his hands on my ass. My ankle-length black pencil skirt

is thin cotton, and I can feel the rough calluses on his hands scratching the fabric. I can feel the raw power in his grip as he grasps me, holds me against his hard body.

His mouth descends on mine, hard and rough, and his teeth take my lower lip, biting, ravenous, devouring. His tongue slides between my teeth, his lips move on mine. I whimper softly, and then I'm alight with lust. I kiss him back, but 'kiss' isn't really the right word. A kiss is lips touching, tongues playing. This...

This is fucking, but with our mouths. It's raw and primal and hungry.

"Get a room, goddammit," an exasperated female voice says from behind us, and it's a testament to the eroticism of the moment that a New Yorker is willing to say something in protest. Not much fazes New Yorkers, I've discovered.

The train stops, and Colton's hand is on the small of my back, propelling me forward. We climb the stairs to street level, and his arm clutches me close to his body. He hustles me down the street and into his darkened shop. On the way through the garage, I'm briefly assaulted by the smell of grease and cigarettes and sweat and all things Colton. It's a wonderful smell, a scent that somehow is beginning to mean *home* to me. The thought is frightening but exhilarating at the same time.

Up the narrow stairwell, his hand on the no-man's-land of the swell of my hip, not quite on my ass, not quite on my waist. His hard heat is close behind me, and my blood is pounding loud in my ear. The stairs seem endless. I'm a heartbeat away from spinning in place and tackling him here on the stairs.

This lust is overwhelming.

It's a starvation, a need thrumming in every pore of my being. I *need* his body, his hands, his mouth, his lips. I need my fingers in his hair, tracing the contours of his huge, solid body, luxuriating in the contrasts that make him up, hard muscles, silky skin, rough calluses, down-soft hair, wet lips and jutting manhood and roaming hands.

I need all of him, and I need it now.

I'm wet and trembling between my thighs, aching, throbbing.

Thank god, *finally* we're through the door and the latch is catching with a definitive snick and I'm caught in his arms, spun, pressed back against the door, crushed between the rough, hard wood of the door and the harder muscle of Colton.

Exactly where I want to be.

I wrap my legs around his waist, take his stubble-rough face in my hands, and marry my mouth to his, delve into a feverish kiss.

I still feel Kyle's ghost banging against my soul, the spirit of my guilt and pain. I ignore it, let it haunt me. Let it rage.

Colton's hands smooth over my back, under my ass, threading through my hair, and the ghost is quieted. Colton pulls back and searches my eyes with his glittering sapphire eyes, and I see his own ghosts trying to push through.

We're both haunted by the specters of our pasts, but we have to move on sometime and force the voice of our guilt to be silent.

Now is that time.

Chapter 11: Falling Into You

COLTON SETS ME DOWN SLOWLY, and I feel his arousal as my front slides against his. We spin again, and I walk backward toward his room, my breath coming in shallow gasps. His hand curls around my waist, but I pull out of his touch. His brow wrinkles in confusion, then clears as I dance a few steps farther back and wrap my fingers around the hem of my shirt. I peel it off quickly, drop it to the floor between us. Colton bends and scoops it up without breaking stride or eye contact, lifts the fabric to his face and sniffs.

I laugh, then reach behind me and slide down the zipper of my skirt, stopping in the doorway to his room. He halts in the hallway, just out of reach, my shirt balled in one fist, his other hand pressed flat against one wall. His broad chest and lean hips are silhouetted by the soft white fluorescent glow from the kitchen, and my mouth goes dry at the sight of him, rugged and masculine and delicious.

I shimmy my hips, biting my lip, and let the skirt fall to pool at my feet, and now I'm clad in only my bra and underwear. I watch as his jeans bulge noticeably at the zipper, strained by his arousal.

His eyes are hooded, half-lidded, primal, hungry.

I unhook my bra, one eyelet at a time, then slide one strap off, letting the bra fall to dangle from one finger in front of me. Colton rumbles deep in his chest, a sound of pure approval.

My skin tightens, my nipples pebble hard under his sweeping gaze. I stand and let him look. He takes a step forward, and I want to back up to the bed, lie down for him, retreat from the raw intensity in his eyes, but I don't. I stay in place and tilt my head up to meet his gaze until he's standing over me. Our lips are centimeters apart, but we don't kiss. I can feel his breath hot on my lips, and I want to feel them on me, but I don't move. I wait.

And then I can't take it anymore. I tug his shirt off, mimicking his action of smelling it, and ohmigod, it does smell incredible, like him, familiar and comforting and exotic. Then I trail my fingers down his chest, stopping on the trail of dark hair on his belly, leading under his jeans. I unsnap the button, lower the zipper, let my knuckles brush his arousal through the cotton of his underwear. I look down now, and my belly shivers at the sight of the gray cotton boxer-briefs stretched by his shaft, a dot of wetness spreading where his tip presses against the fabric.

He kicks off the jeans, and now we're both in just our underwear. Almost there, almost bare to each other.

I slip my fingers under the string of my bright pink thong, lower them slightly.

"Stop. Leave them." Colton's voice is low and growling, halting me.

I comply immediately, letting my hands fall loose at my sides. I'm not sure why, but it's hot when he orders me around like this. I feel a tingle in my belly, a shiver in my thighs. I press my legs together, trying to soothe the ache between them, but it's futile. He closes the gap so my breasts brush his chest, his arousal pressing into my belly. I reach up to touch his shoulders, slide my palms down his spine, pulling him closer. He leans down and kisses me, softly at first, tenderly. It melts me, softens me, leaves me limp and gasping from the delicacy of his kiss. I have to clutch his waist to keep from falling.

My hands are exploring the border of his waist where skin meets cotton; I lift up on my toes to deepen the kiss and push under the elastic to cup his cool hard ass, roaming the globes of muscle with both hands. He growls into the kiss, one of his hands spanning my spine just above my hips, the other touching my waist and drifting up, up, over my ribs…onto my breast. His rough palm covers my nipple, sending thrills spasming through me. I arch into his palm, grip his ass with my fingernails, roaming his mouth with my tongue.

I'm left off-balance and dizzy and gasping when Colton abruptly pulls away. "Hold on to the door-frame," he orders. I obey, and he smiles at me, a predatory baring of teeth. "Now, spread your feet apart… shoulder-width…yeah, just like that. Now, don't move. And hold on."

I think I know what he's planning, and I suddenly can't breathe past my heart hammering in my throat. My hands on the doorframe are all that's holding me up, and I have to grip tight when he sinks to his knees in front of me. His huge hands curl around the backs of my thighs. I bite my lip and gaze down at him, breathless.

Oh, god, oh, god, *ohmigod.*

He presses his nose against my core, nudging the triangle of pink silk. I can't help a moan, and he hasn't even done anything yet. I cry out when he very suddenly reaches up and yanks my panties down. He lifts one of my feet by the ankle, a silent command to step out. I do, and now I'm completely naked, with Colton's face between my thighs.

I'm waiting, waiting, anticipating, but he's just looking up at me, devouring me with his eyes, his hands curled around my thighs once more, just beneath my ass.

Is he going to use his mouth on me? Go down on me? God, I want him to.

There's no warning. He times his assault when I close my eyes in desperation, willing him to do something. Nothing, nothing...and then suddenly his hot wet tongue slides slowly up the crease of my folds. I let my head fall back, and I whimper in delight, relief. I have to clutch the doorframe with all my strength to stay upright.

His fingers are on the insides of my thighs, curling around from behind to pull me apart, spread me open for his mouth. Another soft, slow lick upward, a third, and then he's lapping, lapping, and I'm whimpering nonstop. And then he digs in with his tongue, pressing against the nub of hypersensitive nerves. I dip against his face, my legs giving out.

"Lock your knees, Nelly-baby."

I do it, and then his tongue is inside me once more, circling my clit and pushing hard gasps out of me, soft moans, breathy whimpers.

An inferno of fiery pressure is building inside me, a huge balloon of impending detonation. The edge is approaching, and he's taking me there, taking me past it, into a wonderland of ecstasy. I want to touch him, touch his hair, his skin, but he told me to hold on to the door and if I don't, he might stop what he's doing and that would be the *worst*, so I hold on to the door like I was told and let myself moan as loud as I want. The louder my voice goes, the faster and more fervently he licks me.

And then, just this side of coming, he slows and pulls his tongue away, resumes licking up my folds, and I make a sound of half-pleasure, half-frustration. One of his hands curves around the outside of my thigh, touches the inside of the opposite knee, then drifts up to his chin.

Yes, yes, touch me, there. I need his fingers inside me.

He doesn't, though. "Tell me what you want me to do. I won't do it unless you tell me to."

I groan, then tip my head down to look at him. His mouth and lips glisten with my juices, his blue, blue eyes shining with desire.

"Touch me. Put your fingers inside me. Keep going down on me." I don't stifle my moan when he slides two fingers inside my hot, throbbing, drenched channel. "Make me come."

"Say my name."

I bite my lip, because I can't help it and because it drives him crazy. "Make me come, Colton."

He grumbles in his chest. It's a good sound. "You know," he says, pauses to swipe my folds with his tongue, and then continues, "you're the only person in my life who calls me that. Everyone else calls me Colt."

"Want me to call you Colt instead?" I ask.

"Hell, no. I love the way you say my name."

There aren't any more words then, because his fingers are moving in a way that has me wanting to scream, and his tongue has zeroed in on my clit again, and his hand is caressing my ass. He's all over me, in me, on me, all around me. My world has shrunk down to him, to Colton and the insanely incredible thing he's doing to me.

So close, so close. But then every time I reach the cusp, he seems to know and slows, switches his rhythm and pulls me back from the edge. He's drawing his cues from my voice, I think. He hears the tempo of my moans increase as I reach the edge, and then when I'm gasping and whimpering with need, he stops, and I throw my head back in frustration, but then I tip it forward again to watch him lap at me. Oh, god, he's so sexy doing that. His dark hair glints in the light, his skin dark and dusky in the low light, his bare muscles gleaming and shifting as he moves. His hand is on my ass, holding me against him, and now I've lost all control over myself. I'm dipping on weak knees against his mouth and fingers, and my hands are tangled in his hair, crushing him against me with wanton need, complete abandonment.

"I need to come, Colton," I breathe. "Please, let me come."

He caresses my ass in circles, smoothing the skin over my left cheek, his right hand inside me, rubbing against a spot high on my walls, rubbing in a way that has me panting and whimpering, then pulls his two fingers in and out, in and out, then rubs the spot again. His tongue is relentless, untiring, flicking and circling my clit, brushing it, licking it, sucking it into his mouth and pulling on it with gentle teeth.

Closer, now. So close.

"I'm right there," I hear myself say, panting. "Don't stop. Don't stop."

He doesn't answer, just renews his assault, and now I'm on the edge, hovering, wavering, about to tip forward. My head is thrown back and I'm moaning out loud, pulling his face against my core in the rhythm of my knees' buckling and his tongue's sweeping.

He pulls my clit between his teeth and suckles it hard, rubbing me furiously with his fingers, and then I come. As I gasp a shriek, announcing my orgasm, he slaps my ass, and I come so hard my breath leaves me and my scream is cut off. He slaps my ass again, on the other cheek, withdrawing his fingers and sliding them back in as he smacks me a third time. With each slap of his hand on my ass, he flicks my clit with his tongue, and I come, come, come, bent forward at the waist and mouth wide but silent.

"Scream for me, Nelly." He accompanies the order with one last smack, the hardest, and nips my clit with his teeth, almost too hard, but not quite.

I can't help but obey, screaming loudly and collapsing forward. Colton catches me in his arms as he stands up. I'm twitching with wave after wave of aftershock, but I force my eyes open, watch as Colton moves across the hall into the bathroom, digs around in the cabinet under the sink, pulls out an unopened box of condoms. He opens the flap and withdraws a string of packets, rips one free, and tosses the rest on the floor next to the bed.

Watching him do this drives home what's about to happen. Letting him go down on me, touching him, kissing him, making him come with my hand, all that is one thing. But actual sex, him above me, sliding into me…that's different.

He strips off his boxers and settles onto the bed next to me, leaning over me on one elbow. "Second thoughts?" he asks, having seen the look on my face, probably. "There's no pressure. You don't want to do this, we don't—"

"I do." I lift my hand to caress the knobs of his spine down to his ass. "I really do. It's been so long, I'm nervous. But I want it."

"And the ghosts?"

"There, but I'm working past them." I follow the line of his side, trace his ribs, then back down to his hip. "You?"

"Same." His gaze rakes down my body, then flicks up to meet my eyes. "You're so sexy, Nell. So beautiful. I can't take it, you're so fucking gorgeous. I don't deserve a delicious little angel like you."

And just like that, the nerves are subsumed beneath a tidal wave of tenderness and desire. "I'm no angel," I say, lifting up on one elbow and pushing him onto his back. "And you do deserve me. You deserve someone better than—"

"I deserve exactly you," he cuts in, settling his hands on my hips as I kneel astride his thighs. "Only you. The good and the bad. All you, all beautiful."

I can only stare at him in response, blinking back emotion. Not tears, not really. Just…emotion. I shift my gaze to his torso, the dragon spewing fire, the lettering, the images, all painted across his gloriously muscled physique. I smooth my hands over his chest, down his stomach, trace the V-cut with trembling fingertips. I follow the lines of the "V" downward to the close-trimmed pubic hair, and—*god, he's huge*—his shaft. I lick my lips, and then bite down, hesitating. He doesn't move, just holds my hips loosely.

"Touch me," he says. "This is whatever you want. Your pace."

A fingertip at first. Just the pad of my index finger grazing the very tip of him; he jerks under my touch, and his stomach retracts slightly, then relaxes. My lip hurts, I'm biting it so hard, and his fingers tighten in the flesh of my hip, his self-control exercised. I've done this to him before, but he was sleeping then, not watching. It's different. I want to know how he likes it, what he wants, what feels best. I want to just touch him, hold him. I want to wrap my lips around him and taste him. That's something I've only done once or twice before a long time ago, and I find myself wanting to try it with him.

I shift back on his legs so I'm on my shins, straddling his knees. Then a deep breath, and I'm wrapping my hand around him. He's thick in my palm, hard as a rock, the skin soft and scorching hot. My heart is a wild drum in my throat, and I'm barely breathing. His eyes are on me, his gaze unwavering and unreadable. I slide my hand down to his base, and he's so long I can place my other hand on him, cradle him with both fists. I slip my fists up his length, then down again, and then I've got a rhythm going.

"God, Nell. I love the way you touch me." His voice is husky, slow.

I don't answer, not until I've bent over him so his pink, veined flesh is in front of my face. "I want to taste you."

"Whatever you want," he says. "But I'm not gonna come in your mouth."

"No?" I hesitate, then touch my lips to his head.

"Nope. Not this time, at least. I want to be inside you when I come. I want to be staring into your beautiful eyes when we come together."

He tangles his hand in my hair, then slumps his head back when I find my courage and slip him between my lips. He tastes of skin, salt, and heat, and there's moisture slicking his tip, touching my tongue and tasting of faint musk and salt. He moans, and I take him deeper, pushing him inch by inch into my mouth, running my tongue along him. I've got my fist around him still, and I slide it up and down on his base, and then my lips are touching my fist and he's as far as he can go before I gag. I back away, sliding him out, moving my hand on him, then descend once more. He flutters his hips slightly as he reaches the back of my throat.

"Sorry, didn't mean to gag you."

I pull my mouth off him, but not my hands, and look at him. "It's fine. I like the way you taste." I don't wait for him to answer, but wrap my lips around him again and take him deep.

This time, I gag myself with him on purpose, out of curiosity, to see how far I can go.

"Jesus, Nell." He tries to pull his hips back, but there's nowhere for him to go, and he's hissing, tightening his fingers in my hair. "If you're gonna do that, at least try to relax your throat. Don't do anything you don't want to. Don't do anything 'cause you think I expect it."

I back away, then down again, and this time I relax my throat muscles and take him deeper. Oh, god, oh, god, *ohmigod*. So deep. So huge. Almost too much, but I like it. I don't know what that says about me, and I don't care. He likes it, I can tell. He's holding back, but he really likes it. I set a rhythm, backing away until his tip is at my lips, then take him as deep as I can, sliding my fist on him as I back away.

"Fuck, Nell. Fuck, that's incredible." He's breathless, trembling from the effort to hold still.

"You can move," I tell him. "Don't hold back."

He groans and begins to move into my rhythm. I glance up at him as his head is at my lips, and his face is turned up to the ceiling, a look of pained rapture on his face. I love knowing I'm giving him this pleasure. His fingers are clenched into my hair, tight against my scalp. He pulls on me gently, encouraging me.

He moves, moves, thrusting into my mouth. I take him, take all of him. I know he said he wasn't going to come in my mouth, but I decide to make him. I want it. I want to swallow it, taste it, feel it, feel him lose control in my mouth.

"Touch my sack," he says, the words grated past clenched teeth. "Please."

I cup his balls in one hand, and they're tight, swollen. I massage them as tenderly as I can, moving my other hand at his root, pumping swiftly, bobbing onto him faster and faster. His breathing is ragged, his hips moving in uncontrolled spasms. I take him deep every time, and I don't gag. I'm proud of that. I like feeling him in my throat, knowing he likes it, loves it. He's given me such pleasure doing this to me, and now I can give it back.

He tries to pull away. "I have to—have to stop. I'm too close, Nell." He tugs on my hair, twice.

I only move faster, and then I feel his hips give in and thrust into me again. I feel his balls tense and pulse, and then his hips strain at the apex of a thrust, deep in my throat. I feel a hot rush spurt down my throat. I back away so his tip is between my lips and suck hard. He groans loudly and his hips buck, and another stream jets into my mouth. I taste it this time, thick and hot and salty on my tongue, sliding down my throat as I swallow. I squeeze his base and pump, sucking still, and he unleashes a third time, a lesser amount and a softer spurt. When I feel the spasms subside, I take him deep one last time, then spit him out and slide up his body so I'm resting on his chest. His still-hard tip nudges my folds, and I can't help but wiggle against it, working it in. I want to feel him inside me.

Colton is tensed and trembling, shuddering. "Holy shit, Nell. That was fucking incredible."

I giggle against his shoulder. "Thanks? I wasn't sure if I was doing that right, but you seemed to like it, so…"

He stills. "You've never done that before?"

I shrug. "I *have*, but…it was a long, long time ago, and I only did it a couple times." That's as close to details as I'm willing to go with him in this moment.

He seems to understand, because he just nods. "Gotcha. Well, I can tell you it was the best fucking thing I've ever felt."

I feel a thrill of pride. "Really?" The back of my mind tells me he must have a lot of experience to base it on, which is something I don't want to examine too closely.

"Abso-fucking-lutely."

"You're just saying that."

He laughs. "No, I'm not. It really was that good." He moves, a sudden shift, and I'm on my back and he's above me, lips touching my shoulder, pressing soft kisses to my skin. "And now I get to kiss every incredible inch of your body."

And he does, every single single inch. He starts at my shoulders, kisses slowly across my breastbone, kneeling between my legs, then slides his kisses down between my breasts. I want his mouth there, but he teases me, kissing the swell of each breast but not taking the nipple into his mouth as I want him to. He touches his lips in a series of wet kisses down my stomach, across my belly to my hips, down each thigh. I expect him to put his mouth to my core, but he doesn't. Instead, he kisses dangerously close to each side, above the inside of each thigh with his rough cheeks sandpaper against my sensitive skin, but he never touches his mouth to my folds.

And then he's moving back up after having kissed my shins and my calves and my feet. He gets to my knees, then hesitates, takes my hips in his hands and twists me onto my stomach. I pillow my head on my arms and try not to be self-conscious as he kisses my calves, the backs of my thighs, then, yes, each buttock, wandering over the globes, paying special attention to them, palming the cheeks around his lips, squeezing the muscles, tracing the crease.

His finger delves into the crease, and suddenly the all-over kissing isn't as sweet as it is erotic. His mouth is still moving over my buttocks, but his finger, it's going between my thighs and back up, deeper.

"You liked my finger inside you back here, didn't you?" he asks, his voice rough and demanding.

I can only whimper in response. I did like it. I can't say that, though.

"Answer me, baby." He nudges my thighs open with his knees, spreading me. "Did you like it?"

He keeps pushing my knees until they're bent as far as they can flex, and I'm spread completely for him. His palm circles my backside, and I can sense he's waiting for my answer. I don't. I want to push him, see what he'll do.

He spanks me again, a light but stinging slap. Immediately, my core clenches and I'm wet, dripping. I moan into the pillow.

"Yes, Colton. I liked it."

"Want it again?"

"Uh-huh." I can't make words. His thick forefinger is trailing down my crease and probing in, causing my breath to hitch and my body to tremble.

His other hand slides under me, his fingers curling up to massage my clit. Lightning shoots through me, and I wriggle under his touch. His finger slides up and down still, closing in but not pushing or pressing. His touch on my clit is gentle and soft and slow, questing circles to get me ready. Oh, I'm ready. So ready. I stretch my legs to open more, and now his finger is gone briefly, then back again. I feel something wet and warm against me back there, and then there's pressure.

"Tell me if it's too much."

He pushes in, oh so gently. Oh, god, oh, god, *ohmigod*. Now his circling fingers are swift and accurate, sending heat through me. I shift and arch, bow my back and roll my hips. So good. So good. I lift up onto my knees and push back, liking the fullness of his finger inside me. Oh, god.

"Colton...don't stop."

"No fucking way." He slides his finger deeper, and I'm nearly undone.

It's so intense, fiery and stretching and slightly painful, but pain is familiar and welcome and erotic. So perfect. But no, I realize even as I think it that this isn't perfect. Him inside me would be perfect. Just like this, but his cock instead of his fingers.

"I want you inside me." I turn my head to whisper the words over my shoulder. "Right now."

"Like this?"

"God, yes. Like this." My voice is a fierce whisper.

I hear a packet rip, feel his hand withdraw from my core, and I turn to watch him slide a condom on one-handed. I rest my weight on my elbows, watching him take his shaft in hand and guide it to my entrance. A gentle nudge, and then his eyes on mine as he hesitates.

"Nell, I—" He's so dominating sometimes, giving me orders that I find myself *wanting* to obey, taking me to delirious heights of ecstasy. And then, other times, he's hesitant and unsure, but it's only ever as regards to me, making sure I'm on the same page as he is, making sure I want what's happening.

I can't form words to answer him, so I push back against him, and I feel him slide into me, filling me.

Oh…my…god. I hang my head between my arms and brace my shoulders, thrust back to crush him deep.

"*Fuck*, Nell. God, you're so fucking tight." His voice is strained, thick. His hand grips my hip where it's bent and pulls me against him.

And now he's flush against me, hips to my ass, finger inside me there still.

"You're so *big*, Colton…" I say, then have to stifle a giggle, realizing how that came out. I said it breathily, and it sounded like something from a porno. But it's true. He's huge, stretching me.

"Is it okay? I'm not hurting you?"

I shake my head. "It's perfect."

I feel the pressure building, a volcanic heat inside me. He slides out and out, and then he's poised with the tip inside me, hesitating a heartbeat, then plunges in slowly and I cry out, a breathless shriek. Another slow slide out, and then back in, his finger pulsing inside me, slightly in and out, pushing the pressure to a head, lightning building and crackling in my blood, in my muscles. He hesitates at my entrance again, his tip nestled in my folds, and this time when he thrusts in, it's faster, almost rough.

"Yes, god, yes, Colton. Like that."

He pulls out and pistons deep, hard. "Like that?"

"Yeah…" I gasp.

Again, hard, deep, so deep. "You like it hard?" A rough rhythm now, deep and fast.

"Yes, Colton…I like it hard."

"Oh, my fucking god, Nell." He bends over me, buried deep, rests his head against my spine. "How are you so fucking incredible?"

I have no way to answer that, and I don't have a chance to anyway, because he's pounding into me again. I whimper at each thrust, push into him when he slides deep. There's no thought but this moment, no memory but the previous thrust, no one in the world but Colton. The pressure of impending orgasm is a thundering presence inside me, and I know when it comes, it will be an inundating weight crashing through me.

Then he slows and shallows his thrusts, sliding halfway in, moving in a sinuous rhythm. Oh, *shit*, that's intense. Even more intense than having it rough, in a way. He's hitting inside me in way that strikes a chord, makes me thrum. The edge is near, my climax hovering close. He moves his finger a little deeper, wiggles it in and out, and then abruptly pounds deep, hard, and I break apart. I scream, shove my ass back into his thrusts, coming and coming and coming.

Then I'm moving, I've lost his presence within me, I'm on my back and about to beg him to be inside me again, but he's there, sliding in gently, and I sigh in relief to have him back where he belongs.

"Nell, look at me." His voice snaps my eyes open, and his gaze is intense, vivid blue, rapturous in the way he's gazing at me with such open adoration.

"Hi," I say.

"Hi," he says back. His hands lift me by the shoulders until I'm upright and sitting on his knees, somewhat awkwardly. "Wrap your legs around my waist."

He's cross-legged, sitting upright, holding me, and I curl my heels around his hips. The shift in position effects an immediate difference. He's...deep. So far inside me it's unreal. I gasp, and then I can't even do that, my mouth locked wide in a silent scream as I sink down around him.

"Oh, god, oh, shit," he says. "You're so fucking tight. Have I said that yet?"

"You—you may have," I gasp. "I'm glad I'm tight for you."

"Move for me. Lift yourself up and down. Make yourself come." His voice caresses me; his eyes lock on mine.

I obey, of course I do. I push down with my heels, lift with my thighs, grip his shoulders with my hands and lift. I hover with him barely inside, and then, eyes wide and mouth gaping, I lower myself as slowly as I can. I lift again and his hands slide under my ass, lift me, lower me. My rhythm increases until I'm frantic, climax building to a peak.

He senses it, sees it. "Come for me."

Oh, I do. So hard.

He's holding back, I think.

"Your turn," I say. "I want you to come now."

He growls, tips us so I'm on my back and now he's above me and now, *now* it's perfect. This is perfect heaven, happiness like I've never known before, and I feel no guilt or pain or shame or anything but Colton's body pressed against mine, his mouth pressing fiery kisses to my breast, taking a nipple in his mouth and rolling it, his cock drilling deep...

I lock my legs around him and my hands on the back of his head, pulling him against my breast. He rolls into me slowly at first, almost lazily. His mouth moves from one breast to the other, his hands flat on the bed next to my head. I turn my face to the side and kiss his iron forearm, then stretch my mouth wide in a soft gasp as he increases his pace, biting my nipple hard enough to twinge.

I didn't think it was possible, but I'm nearing climax again, and I don't think I can take another one, not when they keep getting more intense. If that keeps up I'll be ripped in half by this one, and yeah, it's on me now, so close. He's bucking hard now, plunging madly, his weight a heavy pressure on me, his chest sliding against mine, his mouth at my ear.

He's whispering my name over and over again, chanting it as he rocks into me. One of my hands is tangled in the hair at the back of his head, and the other is scratching down his back to clutch his tensing buttocks, pulling him against me.

His voice huffs in my ear, a gasped whisper. "Oh, god...I'm coming, Nell. Come with me. Come with me, baby."

His head lifts, and our eyes lock.

"Yes...yes...now," I say. "Give it all to me right now."

This drives him wild, and he crashes into me, rough and hard and uncontrolled. It's the most incredible thing I've ever experienced, this primal force of a man lost in the throes of ecstasy, crashing into me. He pounds furiously, driving deep, and I dig my fingers into his flesh and his hair, jerk him harder with my legs, feeling my own climax wash over me.

His rhythm falters, stutters, and then he's flexed, every muscle taut as bowstring, buried deep. He pulls back slowly, drawing himself out, and then crashes deep, a second time, a third, and then he goes limp on top of me, his huge weight crushing me wonderfully.

I stroke his back in slow, soothing circles, kiss his shoulder, the shell of his ear, his temple. I smooth my hands down his spine, caress his ass, then trace up his sides, memorizing the feel of his muscles, the way his body feels on mine.

He shifts. "I must be crushing you."

I hold him in place. "No, don't move. I like it. You're fine. I love feeling you like this."

His face is nuzzled into the hollow of my neck and chin, his breathing slow and steady. I've never, ever felt such complete contentment as in this moment. I'm sated, I'm happy. I'm throbbing and tingling all over, flushed with ecstasy, overwhelmed and full in my heart, mind, body, and soul.

And then it hits me. We've both been using the phrase "I love this" or "I love it when you…" and that's a socially acceptable phrase for something you really enjoy. But…the truth is, I think we both mean it in the deeper sense. I know I do.

I wouldn't change this moment for anything. And I certainly would never give up having this with Colton. I want to experience this again and again, as much as possible. I feel closer to Colton in this moment than I have anyone before. This thought brings up a wave of guilt, but I push it away.

"What are you thinking, Nelly-baby?" Colton rolls with me, and now I'm lying nearly on top of him.

I throw my thigh over his leg and roam his torso with a hand, my hair spread beneath me and over his chest. "I'm thinking this is the best moment of my life. Honestly. I feel closer to you right now than anyone… ever. I'm thinking…I want to experience moments like this with you forever." I suck in a deep breath and let it out, then take the plunge. "I'm struggling with feeling guilty over that, because of everything we talked about regarding your brother, but—it's just the truth. I'm closer to you now than I ever was him. I don't know why that is. It hurts—it's confusing. I know I loved him. I did. But…somehow I'm just—things with you and me are just…more. I don't know."

He strokes my hair, smoothes it over my head. "I get it. I feel the same way. I know I loved India. But this with you? It's like…so much more it's almost a completely different kind of thing."

I shift and tilt my head so I'm looking into his eyes. "I'm falling in love with you, Colton. I don't know if it's too soon to say that to you, but…it's true. It's scary, because I don't know if everybody is going to understand, but I don't care right now. I just have to say it to you, because—just because."

He draws me up to him and kisses me, his palm huge against my cheek. I feel so tiny against him, like I could curl up against him and disappear.

"It's not too soon. I was gonna say the same thing, but you beat me to it."

I smile. "Say it anyway. Please?"

He takes a deep breath and lets it out, examining my face almost idly, obviously composing his thoughts.

"I'm not just falling in love with you, Nell. I'm falling into you. You're an ocean, and I'm falling in, drowning in the depths of who you are. Like you said, it's scary in a way, but it's also the most amazing thing I've ever experienced. *You* are the most amazing thing I've ever experienced."

For the first time since Kyle died, I find myself crying happy tears. I'd forgotten what those were.

Chapter 12: Feel You Bare

I WAKE TO GUITAR CHORDS AND COLTON'S VOICE. It's faint, filtering to me from far away. He's on the roof. I wipe the sleep and the tangled curls from my eyes, swing my legs out of his bed—our bed?—and slip on a clean T-shirt from a laundry basket on the floor. It's still dark out, but as I climb the creaking stairs to the roof, guitar in hand, I see slices of gray on the horizon between high-rises and apartment blocks. An hour or two before dawn, then.

Colton is in his chair, wearing loose track pants and a ripped and ragged gray Champion hoodie, the hood drawn down over his brows, a tangle of black hair sweeping across his forehead. His legs are kicked up, bare heels propped on the ledge. His eyes are closed, guitar on his belly, fingers picking a slow, sweet tune that reminds me of something by City & Colour, but isn't. He's singing softly, his face twisting and brows knotting as he hits high notes, his expressions communicating the intensity of his feelings as he sings. A mug of coffee sits on the floor next him within reach, steaming, and a huge thermos is also nearby so he can refill it. I sit on the ledge, feet on the stairs, watching, listening. I can't quite follow the words he's singing, since he's kind of mumbling and singing softly. Every once in a while, he stops, backs up a few chords, and adjusts the melody or phrasing.

He's writing a song, I realize.

He reaches the end of the song and reaches down for his coffee, noticing me in the process. "Oh, hey. Hope I didn't wake you up."

I shrug and move across the roof to sit on the love seat. "You did, but it's fine. I like waking up to your voice." God, that sounds so sappy, but I don't care, especially when I see how Colton's eyes light up. "What are you doing up so early?" I ask.

He passes me the mug of coffee, and I sip it as he answers. "I woke up with this song in my head. I had to write it, get it out, you know?"

"It's beautiful, from what I heard," I say, truthfully.

"It's not done yet, but thanks."

"What's it about?"

He strums the strings with his thumb. "You. Us. It came from something I said to you last night."

"Play it for me?"

He grins and shakes his head. "Nuh-uh. Not till it's done. We've got a gig on Thursday. I'll play it for you then."

I pretend to pout, and Colton only laughs. We share coffee and watch the sun come up between the buildings, working on the songs we're performing.

I'm happy, and I refuse to let anything spoil that, not even the ever-present guilt, and the fact that I still miss Kyle.

I realize I'll always miss Kyle, and a part of me will always feel guilty for being alive when he isn't, and that's something I'll just have to live with.

It's Thursday, and my nerves are at an all-time high. I've got three solo numbers this week, plus Colton is debuting his new song. We get through the requisite duet covers of Mumford & Sons, The Civil Wars, Rosi Golan, and such. I do my solo numbers, "Let It Be Me" by Ray LaMontagne, and my covers of the Ella and Billie songs, which have become a kind of crowd favorite in the weeks that I've been playing with Colton.

And then, immediately after our break, Colton clears his throat into the mic and strums, adjusting his tuning. It's his way of getting the crowd's attention.

"Okay, so I've got this new song," he says. "It's a Colt original. Anyone want to hear it?"

I yell "yes!" into the microphone, then back away and clap with everyone else. He smiles at me, since he knows I want to hear it. I've only pestered him to give me a sneak peek every single day since the rooftop sunrise jam session.

"Guess I'll play it, then." He takes a deep breath and lets it out. "So, yeah. This is called 'Falling Into You,' and it's about Nell here. It is kind of a love song, but don't tell anyone. I've got a reputation as a badass to uphold, after all." The crowd laughs and cheers, encouraging him.

He starts the melody on his guitar, a complicated arrangement of picking and strumming. The tune is more complex now, but I recognize the underlying theme from what I heard on the roof. Then he sings, and he locks eyes with me, and I realize he's singing this to me, only to me. We might be in front of a crowd of a hundred or so people, but we're completely alone.

"All my life it seems
I've been falling,
Failing,

Flailing,
Barely keeping my head above water.
And then one day
I saw you
Standing beneath a spreading tree,
Refusing to weep.
But even then I saw
The weight of pain hiding in your eyes,
And I wished then,
There beneath that tree,
To take it all away.
But I had no words to heal you.
I had no words to heal myself.
And now that Fate has intervened,
Conspired to draw us together,
Despite the years between us,
Despite the weight of pain
Behind both our eyes,
Despite the ghosts trailing all around us
Like a fog of haunting souls,
I'm still trying to find the words to heal you,
To take your pain and make it all my own
So your beautiful eyes can smile,
So you can be at peace.
And now that Fate has intervened,
Conspired to draw us together,

I can't resist the lure of your eyes,
The temptation of your beauty,
The siren song of your voice
Whispering my name
In the dark comfort between my sheets.
I can't resist you, baby,
Because I'm falling still,
I'm falling into you."

By the time he finishes the song, I'm in tears. Good tears, again. The happy, sappy kind. I completely forget that we're onstage. I leap off my stool and crush myself between his legs, his guitar hard between us, and kiss him deeply. He tangles his hand in my hair at my nape, kissing me back until the crowd begins to catcall and cheer, drawing us back to the present.

"I take it you liked it?" Colton asks, whispering in my ear.

I can only nod and try to compose myself so we can do the next number together without losing it.

We're standing on the stoop of my apartment building, my arms around his neck. I'm on the second step, he's on the ground, so I'm eye to eye with him, nibbling on his earlobe as he tries to convince me to just come back to his place with him instead of staying here.

"Colton...this is my apartment, my home. I'm paying rent, a *lot* of rent, so I have to get some use out of it. You can come up with me, though."

"I have work in the morning. The guys are showing up at seven to finish the Hemi we're rebuilding."

"And I have class at eight. We'll just wake up early." I frown, realizing he's doing the thing where he avoids something that makes him uncomfortable but doesn't want to let on. "What's the real deal, here, Colton? Why don't you want to stay at my place?"

He shrugs, but then meets my eyes. "It's just one of those things. After being homeless for as long as I was, it's hard for me to sleep anywhere but my place. I don't know how to explain it. I just...I like being at home. It's not that I don't like your place, or whatever. I just prefer mine."

"Can you try? For me? I want you in my bed." I never really thought about it until now, but almost all of the time we've spent together has been at his place, or out.

"You want me in your bed, huh?" He grins at me salaciously.

I pull him closer against me. "Yes. And I mean that in every sense of the phrase."

"In that case, I might be able to try. For you." He slides his palms down my back to crush my body against his, gripping my ass and lifting me.

I bite his neck and then whisper in his ear, "It'll be worth it, I promise."

"I know it will be. Any time spent with you, anywhere, is worth it. Even if we don't do anything but sleep, it's worth it."

I unlock the door and lead him up the stairs, moving backward. "We'll be doing a *lot* more than sleeping."

"Oh, yeah? Like what?" His voice is deep and dark and full of promise.

"It might involve my mouth, and certain parts of your anatomy."

"I could get into that."

"You could get into me."

He doesn't grin, but his eyes are smiling. "Oh, I'll get into you. I think I'll bend you over the couch and take you from behind."

"Is that so?" I ask.

"It is."

We're at my door. I twist the key in the lock and pull him after me into the darkened apartment. I don't have time to bother with lights. He's got the door locked again, and he's tugging my shirt over my head, pushing my jeans and panties down, and then he's somehow naked, like, instantly, and then his mouth is on mine, glorious and soft and demanding.

His hands are everywhere, on my breasts, in my hair, stroking my folds, caressing my ass, brushing a thumb across my cheek and sweeping hair away from my mouth. I gasp as his fingers probe into my core and circle my clit, noticing distantly as he rips a condom open with his teeth and slides it on himself one-handed, spitting the wrapper onto the floor.

"Ready?" he asks, his voice a rough demand.

"Take me," I whisper. "However you want."

I'm spun in place, and my breath catches, my heart hammering. Oh…shit. He wasn't kidding. He's moved us so I'm facing the arm of my couch from the side and he's pushing me forward gently. His hands slide over my shoulders and twine our fingers, showing me how to brace my weight on the cushion. His toes nudge my feet apart, and I comply until I'm standing with my legs spread wide, bent over at the waist, ass high.

"Oh, god…" I whimper.

"I haven't done anything yet, baby," Colton growls.

"I know," I pant. "I was just saying your name."

He laughs, a low rumble in his chest, then slides one palm over my spine, under my ribs and cups one free-hanging breast in his huge hand. He pinches my nipple, thumbs it, tweaks it, rolls it, and I'm breathless already. Then his other hand slides down between my thighs to stroke my folds, and I'm lost. I arch my back and lift my ass to give him better access, hang my head as he swipes and circles me into climax.

As I come, an initial shudder of ecstasy washing over me, I feel him nudge my entrance with the head of his shaft. I hold my breath, biting my lip, and then a second wave rollicks over me and he feels it, plunging in as the wave crests. I cry out as he drives home, burying himself to the hilt with a soft, satisfied grunt.

"God, Nell. You're fucking incredible. So beautiful. I love the way you lift your ass for me. I love the sounds you make when you come for me. I love your pale skin and strawberry blonde curls." He strokes into me slowly, sliding deep every time he says the word "love."

I push back into his thrusts, crying out softly at each in-thrust, whimpering when he draws out. He continues this way, slow and gentle and rhythmic.

It's not how I want it, and he knows it. He wants me to beg for it. I'll play his game. I turn to look at him over my shoulder, my hair curtaining to one side.

"Harder, Colton."

His eyes go hooded, and he lifts his chin slightly, curling up his lip in a smirk. "You want it harder?"

"Yeah, baby, I do."

"How hard?"

"Really hard."

"Beg me to fuck you harder, Nelly-baby."

I don't recognize myself when I'm like this, lost in the moment. I like this woman, though, this shameless Nell who begs her man to fuck her. It's a far cry from the innocent sixteen-year-old girl who shook all over in a Red Roof Inn as her first boyfriend touched her tentatively.

I bite my lip, just to make him crazy, pull forward as he draws back, then slam my ass onto him, driving him deep, hard. "Fuck me, Colton. Fuck me hard. Fuck me deep. Spank me when you fuck me."

God, that was hot. I almost couldn't get the words out. But it's what I want, truly and madly. Him, all of him. I want him, Colton, as he is. Rough and raw and primal, gentle and loving and careful. I love what he does to me, how he makes me crazy, makes me want things I didn't know I could ever want.

Colton loses it. He grips my hips in both hands, widens his stance, and draws back until he's almost out of me. I suck in a deep breath, anticipating the flesh-trembling drive of his hips.

Instead, he sinks in as slowly as he can, more softly than I thought possible, a caress of his arousal within me. A tease. And then, because I'm not ready for it, he slams into me. I cry out, face contorting in pleasure.

He pulls out slowly, slides in slowly, two and then three more times, gentle as a whisper.

And then, when I open my mouth to speak, he crashes hard, so hard, and my words, my breath leaves me in a rush. I can't even catch my breath, then, because he's done toying with me. He's driving into me, drilling me with savage power. My entire body is jarred forward with each thrust, and broken whimpers release from me at each one. The whimpers turn into yeses, and those turn into his name, chanted in the brutal rhythm of his hips. He jerks me back into him, pushes me away, and I barely register the first orgasm, so lost am I in the pleasure of the pain, the delicious slam of his body into mine, the way he fills me with each thrust, the way he seems to stretch me.

And then he comes, growling and roaring, slamming into me, driving deep in the hardest thrust yet, almost too hard, but not. It can never be too hard. And then…oh, god, oh, shit, *ohmigod*, he's back to the tender sliding, bent over me, kissing my spine, palming my ass, dipping into me in shallow thrusts that hit me in just the right place to make me completely come undone.

I bury my face in the rough fibers of the couch and scream as I shatter, a million jagged bolts of lightning blasting through every cell of my body. He smacks my left ass-cheek as I scream, and the orgasm ruptures into a higher peak, and I'm rocked forward with a slow but powerful thrust into that perfect spot, timed with the spank of his palm. He pulls back, slaps my right cheek in time with another cresting wave and shallow thrust, and I'm sobbing with the intensity, driving back into him, collapsing forward and rocking back in uncontrolled spasms. Volcanic heat and electricity shred my body, earthquake shudders wracking me, all centered on my core, low in my belly, deep inside me.

He strokes slowly then, milking my climax until he's soft within me and I'm a limp puddle of sated woman. He pulls out of me, lifts me in his powerful arms, and carries me to my bed. He's gone briefly and then back, cradling me against him.

"I can't believe you like it rough like that," he says.

"Why not?" I ask, tracing patterns on his skin, drifting my touch downward to take him in my hand, stroking him.

"You just seem so innocent and delicate."

"You know I'm not either of those things, Colton."

"Yeah, I know that, but it's how you seem." He toys with my nipple, circling it with the pad of his index finger. "One minute you're all classy and kind of aloof and beautiful and everything, and then you seem to just…let go, and something wild comes out of you. You turn into this…"

"Shameless slut-beast?" I suggest.

He snorts, but his finger turns my chin up so I'm looking at him. "Funny, but no. You're anything but that, Nell. Never think about yourself like that."

"I don't—I was joking." Sort of, but I won't admit to the deeper truth.

He sees it anyway, damn him. "Nell." His blue eyes sear me.

I have to look away. "I just…it's the same old thing, Colton. Part of me can't get over the idea that this is wrong. You're his older brother. I know, I know. He's gone, and I have to get over it. We—this, with you and me—it's *not* wrong. It's not. But the stupid guilt is always there."

He doesn't answer right away. "I understand, Nell. I do. Just…talk to me about that shit, okay? Don't lock it away or push it down. I'll understand."

I nod against his chest, then smile as I feel him begin to grow hard in my hand. I slide my fingers around him until he's fluttering his hips into my touch, then slide astride him. He's inside me, slipping in easily, perfectly. I'm sitting up on him, lifting with my thighs and sinking down. I've taken him by surprise, and that makes me giddy. He's frozen for a few strokes, and then he takes me by the waist and moves with me.

Then he freezes again. "We need...we gotta put one on, baby." His gaze is strangely intense. "The last thing we need right now is a pregnancy."

I don't slow in my rise and fall. "We're good, honey. I'm on birth control."

"Since when?"

I frown. "Since...always. I never stopped taking it after...what happened." It's an awkward moment. I bend over him and kiss him. "The point is, we're fine. I want it like this, nothing between us."

He cradles my face in his palms and devours my mouth. "Thank god. I've wanted to feel you bare like this so bad."

"Me, too."

And then there's no more space for words between our gasps and kisses and groans. We move together for an eternity in perfect sync, each motion, each breath mated to the other's, until we dissolve together, coming undone together.

When we're tangled breathless and basking in the afterglow, I press my lips to his ear. "I love you, Colton."

"Don't you forget it, baby."

I snort and glare at him.

He kisses me softly. "Kidding, Nell. I love you. So much."

Chapter 13: A Blue Cross
Eight Weeks Later

No.

No.

Hell, no. This isn't happening. It isn't. It can't be. Not now.

My right hand is flat over my mouth, and it's all that's holding in my panic. I'm sitting on the edge of the tub in my bathroom, naked but for a baby-doll T-shirt. Knees pressed together, feet bouncing. Head shaking side to side, eyes wide and hazy and shimmering and stinging.

I look down at my left hand. I'm holding a white plastic stick between thumb and forefinger. A tiny square window in the plastic shows two blue lines in a cross.

I don't even bother packing a bag. I book the first flight back to Detroit, which leaves in three hours. Not enough time, but it'll have to be.

On the way out, I tape my only explanation to Colt on the front of my door: a note containing three words, and the test.

As I ride the taxi to the airport, his words echo in my head, over and over: *The last thing I want right now is a pregnancy.*

I'm back to where I started, emotionally: locked up tight, refusing to cry. Wanting to find some way to hurt, so I don't have to feel the fear and the panic and the knowledge that this is the last thing he wanted.

By the time I reach DTW, my lip is swollen from biting on it so hard.

I nearly let out a sob when I remember how biting my lip drove him crazy.

Colton

Chapter 14: The Unborn Song
Two Days Later

I'M NEARLY RABID WITH WORRY by the time I'm able to leave the shop and catch a cab to Nell's Tribeca apartment. It's been two days, and I haven't heard shit from her. No calls, no texts. She was supposed to come over after her Theory class, but she never showed. Phone goes straight to voicemail. Texts don't get delivered. Her boss at the little dive bar where she works a couple nights a week says she never showed up for her shift. I contacted her on FB Messenger, no answer. Finally, I leave Hector to lock up the shop, because I just can't take it anymore.

I toss a bill over the seat of the cab and don't wait for change. I have to take a few deep breaths before

I'm calm enough to unlock her door with the key she gave me.

We just exchanged keys last week; I thought things were great.

Up the stairs three at a time, nearly knocking over a little old lady in the process. There's a piece of paper folded in half and taped to the door. Shit, no. Fuck, no. What is this?

I rip the note off the door, and it's oddly heavy for a piece of paper. There's a plastic baggy inside the paper, and inside the bag is a pregnancy test. Oh, *hell* no.

Oh, hell yes.

Positive.

And no Nell. I search her tiny apartment more than once, as if it'd reveal her hiding in a cupboard or something.

Just the test in the stupid baggie, and three scrawled words: *I'm so sorry.*

She fucking *ran.* I'm angry, I'm panicked. I'm so many things it's all a jumble in my heart and head, and I can't think straight. I'm on a plane suddenly, with no memory of having gone to the airport or buying a ticket or anything. I'm in a bad, bad place.

Memories are surfacing, things I've never told anyone, ever, not even Nell, and I've told Nell pretty much every sordid detail of my fucked up life…except *that.*

A couple long, brooding hours later, the plane has landed and I'm in a rental car—I don't even know what kind—and flying far too fast north on I-75. I've shut down. I'm a blank, empty. No thoughts. Thoughts are dangerous. I can't feel. All I can do is act, move, be.

I have to find her.

Fucking *have* to.

Miles flash, stoplights change too soon and slow me down. I barrel through more than one red light, earning blaring horns and flashing middle fingers. Then I'm approaching my parents' house and it's dusk, but I know she's not there, why would she be? I skid to a stop in the middle of the road in front of Nell's parents' house. I leave the car door open, leave the engine running. Unreasoning panic drives me, panic so deep I don't understand it, but I can't stop it. I can only move with it, let it have reign over me.

I burst through the Hawthornes' front door, slamming it open violently. I hear a glass shatter and a woman scream.

"Colt! What the hell—what are you doing here?" Rachel Hawthorne has her back to the sink and has a hand pressed to her chest, confusion and fright in her eyes.

"Where is she?"

"Who? What—what are you doing here?"

"Where...is...*Nell?*" My voice is low and deadly.

She hears the threat in my voice and pales, begins to shake and back away. "Colt...I don't know what you're—she's out running. She went for a run."

"Where does she go when she runs?" I demand.

"Why do you want to know? Are you two..."

"Where does she *go*, Rachel?" I'm standing inches from her, towering over her, glaring. I should back down, but I can't.

Rachel is trembling, white as a sheet. "She's—the old county line road. North. It goes in a big arc and she—she cuts across Farrell's field back this way."

I'm out the door and running, full-on sprinting. Terror claws at me, and I can't fathom it, can't get out of its grip. It's hounding me, pushing me. She's pregnant, and she ran from me rather than talking about it, but that's not enough for the kind of reaction that's driven me since this morning. It's coming from way deep inside me, a kind of psychological foreknowledge that something is horribly, horribly wrong and I have to find her.

My feet stomp in the dirt, pushing mile after behind me. Dark now. Stars out, moon low and round. My blood is on fire; my heart pounds and my head throbs and my hands are clenched into fists.

I'm shaking, I've been flat-out running for at least two miles and I'm not in that kind of shape, but I can't stop. Can't.

Not won't…

Can't.

Another mile, and I know I've slowed, but I'm pushing myself, because I have to find her.

Farrell's property, a wide expanse of high grass and old fallow fields and lines of trees subdividing properties. If she fell in the grass out here, I could pass right by her and never know it.

But there she is. Jesus, thank you.

She's just sitting, hunched over, face in her hands. She's sobbing. Even when she told me everything and cut loose with years' worth of pent-up grief, she didn't weep like this. It's…god, it's the single most awful sound I've ever heard.

Worse even than the wet *thunk* of the bullet into India's head.

Nell has been absolutely broken, and I don't know by what.

I crouch beside her, touch her shoulder. She doesn't even respond, doesn't look at me. I scoop her in my arms, and something hot and wet coats my arms.

The ground where she was sitting is wet, black in the dim light. A huge swath of grass is blackened with dark liquid.

Blood.

Fuck.

"Nell? Baby?"

"Don't *call* me that!" A sudden, vicious scream. She wrenches out of my grip and falls to the grass, crawls away, heaving so hard she's close to vomiting. "It's gone…it's gone, it died…"

And I know what happened but I can't even think the word.

I scoop her up again, feel hot sticky wet flowing from her. She's still bleeding. "Nell, love, I'm here."

"No, no…you don't understand. You don't—don't get it. I *lost* it. The baby…I lost the baby."

"I know, sweetheart. I know. I've got you, I'm here." I can't keep my voice from cracking. I'm as shattered as she is, but I can't let on.

She hears anyway. She finally seems to realize it's me. She's limp in my arms, twists her head to look at me. Her face is streaked with red and sweat, hair tangled and plastered to her forehead. "Colton? Oh, god…*god*. You weren't supposed to follow me."

Anger billows out of me. "What the fuck, Nell? Why'd you run? I love you. You think I wouldn't—wouldn't…shit…what did you think I'd say?"

She pounds my shoulder with a weak fist. "It's what you *did* say. A baby is the last thing you wanted. And that's what I was going to have. A baby. A fucking baby."

"No, Nell. No. That's not what I said. I said a *pregnancy* is the last thing we *need*. I did *not* say a baby is the last thing I wanted. And regardless, running was... so wrong. You're mine. The baby would—would have been *mine*. I'd take care of you. I'll always take care of you." I'm crying. Like a fucking girl, I'm just openly crying as I carry Nell across the field, stumbling over roots and branches and hillocks. "I'm here...I'm here."

She's too quiet. Looking up at me, half-lidded, weak eyes. Unfocused. Shimmering wet in the moonlight. Bleeding onto me. "I'm sorry. I'm sorry. I was just so scared. I'm scared, Colt."

It's the first time she's ever called me Colt. "I know, Nelly-baby. I've got you. You'll be okay."

"No...no. It's *not* okay. I *lost the baby*, Colton." Her voice hitches, breaks.

"I know..." So does mine. "I know."

"I didn't want a baby. I didn't want to be a mother. I'm too young. It was too soon. I begged to not be pregnant all the way here. But—but I didn't mean this. I swear. I didn't want this. I'm sorry... Not this way." She's barely audible, rambling.

She's lost a lot of blood. I'm covered from the chest down. My arms are trembling, my legs are jelly. I ran so far, so fast, and I'm operating on adrenaline right now, pure determination. I'm half-running with her, stumbling in the darkness.

Then the yellow glow of the Hawthornes' backyard appears, and I'm fumbling at the sliding door with bloody fingers. Rachel Hawthorne is frantic, begging, demanding to know what happened. Jim Hawthorne is on the phone.

"Colt, what happened?" Rachel's voice from far away.

I won't let go of her, can't. She's unconscious. Still bleeding on me.

A hand shakes my shoulder, brings me to reality. "Colton, what *happened*? Why is she bleeding?" Jim, harsh and demanding and angry.

"Miscarriage—" It's all I can manage.

"Mis—she was *pregnant*? With your baby?" He's even angrier now.

"I didn't…didn't know. She didn't tell me. She ran. Came here…" I look down at her lovely, slack face. "Please, Nell. Wake up. Wake up."

She doesn't wake up. Her head lolls to one side, her hand falls free and swing. She's barely breathing… or not at all.

Blue-gloved hands take her from me, gently but firmly. I try to fight them, but other hands pull me away. Rougher, harder hands, too many hands keeping me from her. I turn. Dad. Jim, Mom, Rachel. All pulling me away. Yelling at me, but there's no sound. Just a roaring in my ears. A uniformed body steps into view, a young guy from EMS.

His eyes are brown and hard, but compassionate. Sound returns. "...Gonna be okay, Colton. She's lost a lot of blood, but you got her help in time. I need you calm or I'll have to have you detained, and you won't do Nell any good like that."

I'm panting. I meet his eyes. Hope swells in my chest. "She's not dead? She'll be okay?"

"She's alive, yes. Unconscious, but alive."

"So much blood..." I stumble backward, fall to my ass on a couch, hit the edge and tumble to the floor as if drunk.

"She's hemorrhaging pretty bad, but the doctors will be able to stop it, I'm sure."

I don't hear anything else. I'm back in time, back in a hospital in Harlem and a doctor is explaining something to me, but I don't hear him, either, since I tuned out after the words *lost the baby*. I'm back on the cold tile of the hospital waiting room, sobbing. India... dead. She never told me. Or she didn't know she was pregnant. Either way, she's gone, and so is the baby I never even knew about.

Hands move me, push me, pull me. Peel my sopping shirt off, wipe my torso with a hot, damp towel. I let them. I'm in so many places. Torn, mixed, shredded, broken.

Another baby I never got to know or hold, gone. I would have been there. But I never got the chance. No one asks me what I want. Just assumes because I'm a thug who can't read that I wouldn't want a baby.

Not fair, though. India didn't get a chance, either. Maybe she would have told me. Let me be a father. We talked about kids, India and I. She wanted them. I kept quiet and let her talk, didn't tell her what I thought. Didn't tell her I would have loved the child and let him be whoever he wanted to be, even if he couldn't read. It's all I wanted, all my life, and never got.

And now it's been taken from me again.

Sudden rage burns through me, white-hot, blasting and beyond powerful.

It's not fucking *fair*.

I'm not me, suddenly. I'm an observer watching as someone who looks like me heaves to his feet, picks up the nearest object—a heavy, thickly-padded leather armchair—and heaves it through the sliding door. Glass shatters, scatters, the frame cracks.

Familiar yet foreign hands touch my shoulder. "It's going to be okay, Colton." My father's voice, murmuring low in my ear. "Just calm down."

But he doesn't know. He doesn't know me. He doesn't know jack-shit about my life or anything I've gone through. I shove him away and stalk out the front door. My rental has been moved, and I climb behind the wheel. Jim Hawthorne slides in next to me.

"Sure you should be driving, son?" His voice is carefully neutral.

"I'm fine. And I'm not your fucking son." I'm not fine, but it doesn't matter.

I force myself to drive halfway normally to the hospital. Before I can get out of the car, though, Jim puts his hand on my forearm.

"Wait a sec, Colt."

I know what this is about. "Not the time, Jim."

"It *is* the time." His fingers tighten on my arm, and I'm close to ripping his hand off, but don't. He's not afraid of me, but he should be. "She's my daughter. My only child."

I hang my head, drawing deep on my tapped-out reserves of calm. "I love her, Jim. I swear to you on my fucking soul, I didn't know. I wouldn't have let her go anywhere alone if I'd known. She…she ran. She was scared."

"How could you put her in that position after what she went through?" He's hurt too, scared and angry.

I get it.

"We were getting through it. Together. Things between us just happened, and I'm not gonna fucking explain shit to you right now, or ever. She's an adult, she made her choice. We're good for each other." I force my eyes to his, and damn it if his eyes don't look so much like hers it hurts. "I'll take care of her. Now and always."

He doesn't answer, just sits and stares at me, eyes boring into me. I see the father in him, but I also see the shrewd businessman, the piercing, searching eyes of a man used to judging character quickly and accurately.

"She may be an adult, but she's still my baby. My little girl." His voice goes deep and low and threatening. "You better take care of her. She's been through enough. Now this? You goddamn better take care of her. Or I swear to god I'll kill you."

It's a threat he doesn't need, but I understand him. I meet him stare for stare, let him see a bit of the darker side of me. The thug who learned early on never to back down, ever, for anyone. He nods, after a long time. I get out and enter the hospital, ask the desk nurse for her room number.

One-four-one. The ICU.

My boots squeak on the tile. Antiseptic tang stings my nostrils. A vaguely female-sounding voice squawks indistinctly on the PA. A young brunette in maroon scrubs hustles past me, tablet computer in her hands.

Then I'm counting rooms, one-three-seven, one-three-nine…one-four-one. The curtain is drawn. A monitor beeps steadily. I pause at the split in the curtain, my hand on the fabric, shaking.

An older, stick-thin woman with pale blonde hair pulled up in a severe bun appears next to me. "She's asleep right now. They ran a few tests, and they're going to do more later."

"She still bleeding?"

"She's not hemorrhaging anymore, but yes, she's still bleeding." She looks up at me, tapping the chart against her palm. "You're the father?"

I nearly choke at the term. "I'm her boyfriend, yes." My voice is low, nearly a whisper.

She realizes her gaffe. "I—I'm sorry. That was insensitive of me." She pushes past me. "You can go in with her, but let her sleep."

God, she's white as snow. So frail-looking, like this. Tubes in her nose, needles in her wrist.

I sit. And sit. And sit. I don't talk to her because I don't know what to say.

They come and wheel her bed away while she's still asleep. Unconscious, not asleep. Don't need any euphemisms. Will she wake up? They won't say, which tells me maybe not.

I end up in the chapel, not to pray, but to feel the silence, to be away from the smell of the hospital, the stench of sickness and death, the sounds of the sneakers on tile and echoing voices and beeping monitors. Away from the faces like mine, serious, sad, concerned, afraid.

The stained glass gleams purple and red and blue and yellow, depicting something I don't care to know about. The cross is huge and empty and mud-brown wood, machine-tooled.

My dad finds me in the chapel, and he has my first guitar in his hand. Battered, scratched case, no-name brand, tan wood and steel strings, left behind along with all my other shit. I don't know why he brought the guitar, but I'm grateful.

We're alone in the chapel. He doesn't look at me when he speaks. "I owe you a lifetime of apologies, Colt. You're a good man."

"You don't know me, Dad. You never have. You don't know the shit I done."

"I know. But you're here, and you clearly love her. You've made it on your own, without any help from us. We should've been there for you, but we weren't. So…I'm sorry."

I know how much it took for him to say that, but it's nowhere near enough. It's a start, though. "Thanks, Dad. I wish you'd said that to me a long time ago, but thanks."

"I know it doesn't make up for how we treated you growing up, for letting you go off on your own like we did. You were too young, but I just—I was—"

"Focused on your career, and your golden child." I scrub my hair with my palm. "I get it. I don't want to talk about this shit. It's over and done and old news. I'm here for Nell, not to mend fences broken decades ago."

I click open the case and lift the guitar out. It's hideously out of tune. I flip open the little cubby in the case where the neck sits, pull out a packet of strings. I busy myself restringing the guitar, tuning it. Dad just watches, lost in thoughts, or memories, or regrets.

I honestly don't give a fuck which.

He leaves eventually, without a word.

Then I start playing. The music just comes out unbidden, like a river. I'm hunched over my guitar, siting on a hard pew in the middle of the chapel, staring at my scuffed, oil-stained Timberland boots. I'm singing under my breath, and I'm lost in the songwriting haze, where the music is a flood taking me over, searing the words and the melody into me.

"Mr. Calloway?" A timid female voice comes from the door of the chapel. I turn my head slightly to acknowledge her. "Ms. Hawthorne is awake. She's asking for you."

I nod, pack up my guitar, and carry it as I follow the nurse back to the room.

She's biting her lip when I walk in, scratching at her cut-scars with a forefinger. I pull the hard plastic visitor's chair next to the bed and take her fingers in my huge paw. Kiss her palm, each knuckle. Try not to cry like a fucking girl again.

She looks at me, and her eyes are red-rimmed, gray-green, so beautiful and so broken. "Colt—Colton. I—"

I touch her lips. "Sshh. I love you. Always."

She still sees through me. "You're not okay, either, are you?"

I shake my head. "No, not really." I see the question in her eyes, so I sigh and tell her the story. "I told you about India, how she died."

"Yeah?" She's hesitant, as if she can guess where this is going.

"I was at the hospital, because some of my boys were hurt in the whole mess and I had to see to them. Make sure everyone was okay. Somehow one of the nurses knew me, knew I was with India. I think she lived in the same building as India or something." I have to breathe deeply to keep my voice steady, even after all these years. "She told me…god—*shit*. She—she told me India was pregnant when she died. I didn't even know. I don't know if India knew. She wasn't far, just like six weeks or something. But…yeah. Pregnant. I never even got to…she never got the chance to tell me."

"Oh, god, Colton. I'm so sorry. I'm—oh, my god, Colton."

"Yeah." I can't look at her, can only stare intently at my grease-stained fingernails. "I understand why you ran, Nell. I do. Just—just promise you won't run from me ever again. You have to fucking promise me. Especially for shit like that. I know I'm—I know I'm just an illiterate grease monkey, but I can take care of you. I can love you and if you—if we—if…I'd take care of you, no matter what."

She sobs. "Oh, god, Colton. That's not why I ran. You're so much more than an illiterate grease monkey, Colton. You're not a thug. You're not any of the things you think you are. You're so much more. I was scared. I panicked." She tries to breathe through the tears. "I shouldn't have. I'm so sorry. It's my fault, Colton. I shouldn't have left, I shouldn't have been running, I should have—"

I squeeze her hand hard. "No, Nell. *No*. Don't you *fucking* dare. This isn't your fault."

A doctor comes in at that moment. "I couldn't help overhearing," he says. He's middle-aged, Indian, exuding practiced compassion and efficiency. "It is not your fault in any kind of way, Nell. Such things sometimes happen, and we have no way of knowing the why, no way of preventing it." His gaze and his

344344344

voice go intensely serious. "You must not fall victim to blaming yourself. The fact that you were running at the time did not cause the miscarriage. Nothing you did do or did not do caused it. It simply happened, and it is no one's fault."

She nods at him, but I can tell she's going to blame herself anyway. The doctor tells her to rest and that they're holding her overnight for observation. When he's gone, I stand up and lean over her and kiss her as gently as I can.

"Please don't take this on yourself, Nelly-baby. You heard the doctor. It just happened."

"I know. I know. I'm trying." She glances at my guitar case. "Play something for me, please."

"What do you want to hear? Something happy?" I take the guitar out and settle it on my knee.

She shakes her head. "No, just…something. Whatever you want. Play a song that means something to you."

I start with "Rocketship" by Guster, because that song has always struck a chord with me. I listened to that song all the time, on Repeat. I'll play it over and over and over again, almost as much as my lullaby to myself. The idea of a rocket ship taking me away, bound for something new…yeah. I could identify.

I feel people behind us, but I don't care. Let them listen.

"Play something else," Nell says. "Anything."

I sigh. "I wrote a song while you were sleeping. It's…a goodbye, I guess you could say."

"Play it. Please."

"We're both gonna cry like fucking babies," I say.

"Yeah, I know. Play it anyway."

I nod, strum the opening chords. It's a simple song, almost a lullaby. I sigh, close my eyes, and let it all come out.

"You've never had a name.
You've never had a face.
A thousand breaths you'll never take
Echo in my mind,
My child, child, child.
The questions blink like stars,
Numberless in the night sky.
Did you dream?
Did you have a soul?
Who could you have been?
You've never known my arms,
You've never known your mother's arms,
My child, child, child.
I'll dream for you,
I'll breathe for you,
I'll question God for you,
I'll shake my fists and scream and cry for you.

This song is for you,
It's all I've got.
It doesn't give you a name.
It doesn't give you a face.
But it's all I've got to give.
All my love is in these words I sing,
In each haunted note from my guitar,
My child, child, child.
You're not gone,
Because you never were.
But that doesn't mean
You passed unloved.
It doesn't mean you're forgotten,
Unborn child, child, child.
I bury you
With this song.
I mourn you
With this song."

The last note hangs in the air. Nell is sobbing into her hands. I hear a choked cough from behind me, turn to see a crowd around the door, nurses, doctors, orderlies, patients and visitors, all of them clearly affected. My cheeks are wet, and my eyes sting. For once, I let it out, let myself be weak.

Nell scrambles off the bed, wires and tubes tripping her, and crawls onto my lap. I cradle her into me, hold her against me, and we cry together. I comfort her the only way I know: with my silence, my arms, my lips on her skin. There aren't words for this, and the ones I did have, I sang.

Chapter 15: A Song of Single Breaths
Two and a Half Weeks Later

WATER CHUCKS AND LAPS AGAINST THE DOCK PILINGS. The moon is missing a sliver from the side, and gleams silver on the black ripples of the lake. We're back where we started, on the dock, a bottle of Jameson and my guitar.

She's sitting on the edge, pants rolled up to her knees, feet kicking in the blood-warm water. I'm playing "Don't Drink the Water" by Dave Matthews Band, and she's just sitting, listening. I'm leaning back against the corner post, one foot in the water, the other across her thighs. She's rubbing my calf with her fingers, staring at the water. We haven't said much since we came down here at midnight, two hours ago. We're both kind of sloppy, and the loose numbness is welcome.

There've been a lot of hospital visits to make sure she's fine, long-term, physically, plus a whole lot more therapy appointments and grief counseling and all sorts of other long-past due shit. I've been staying with my parents, talking to my dad. I haven't told him much, but enough for him to understand a little of what I went through. He hasn't apologized again, which is probably good since apologies don't mean shit, but I can tell he's trying with me. Whatever. One day at a time, and don't hold grudges. That last part is hard.

Nell is…not okay, but getting there. I'm not okay, but I'm getting there.

And now we're drunk and alone on the dock.

"Don't Drink the Water" turns into "Blackbird," and I'm not sure if I'm doing Sarah McLachlan's version or Paul McCartney's, but it doesn't matter. I'm singing it, and the words have never meant so much. It's not really an epiphany, just a knowledge that we'll be okay, somehow, someday.

She hears what I'm saying behind the song. She turns and looks at me, and her eyes are bright in the moon-silver darkness.

"You were only waiting for this moment to arise…" She sings the last line with me. "God, I love that song. How'd you know?"

I shrug and set the guitar aside. "I didn't, really. I just knew, because it's always meant a lot to me, and now more than ever."

"Are we?"

"Are we what?"

She slides closer to me until her back is to my front. "Waiting for this moment?"

I give a kind-of laugh. "I'm not sure what you're asking, but I'm gonna go with yes. There's been a lot of heavy shit in our lives. And this…this latest business has been hell." I still can't even say the word for what happened; it's too hard. "But we have to learn to be free. We have to, Nell. Doesn't mean happy all the time, or okay all the time. It's okay not to be okay. I told you that, but I'm relearning it myself. But not being okay doesn't mean you stop living."

She leans back, tilts her head to press her lips to mine. She tastes of Jameson, and the lemon-lime tang from the Sprite she's chasing it with. Whiskey and Sprite? Blech. But she likes it, so whatever. She tastes like Nell, and that's all that matters.

Her tongue sweeps my mouth, and I realize where she's going with this. Her hand lifts to brush the back of my head, cup my nape, and pull me against her. My fingers trail across her belly, find the gap between her shirt and pants, touch the silky heat of her skin. I tug the shirt up, and she pushes away from me so I can pull it free. We came down to the dock late at night, after she'd taken a shower, so she's not wearing a bra. I like it. I can smooth my palms across her belly, up her ribs, slide my fingers around her taut nipple and cup the heavy weight of her breast. She moans into my mouth, and I know she needs this.

I do, too.

I kiss her, explore her mouth, relearn the curve of her hips and the swell of her breasts and the shower-damp curls of her hair. She kisses me, lets me touch her. Each caress brings her healing, I think. Shows her she's more than the sum of her grief.

It does the same for me.

Finally, she twists in place, and we slide so the dock is beneath my back and she's pillowed on top of me, body pressed flush to body, softness merging with hardness. She lets all her weight rest on me, cradles my face in her hands and kisses me into oblivion, and sweet Jesus, her mouth is my heaven.

Nell

I DIDN'T REALIZE HOW BADLY I CRAVED THIS until his hands came up over my thighs to knead the muscle of my ass. Up until that point, kissing him was just…sweet and perfect and all the things I needed to forget. But then, something in the way his fingers dug hungrily into my backside unleashed a need inside me.

I need him. I mean, yeah, emotionally, mentally, I need him, too. He's my rock. He's there, just…always *there*, exactly how I need him. Calming, comforting, protecting, and distracting me. But this…I have to have his arms around me, his hands on me, his fingers blazing a trail of heat on my skin and his mouth wreaking wonderful havoc on my senses. I absolutely cannot live without that another minute. It's a madness in me.

I think he senses this in the way I suddenly attack him. We were just kissing, making out, touching a bit, and then I rear back and look down at him and see his vibrant sapphire eyes sparkling in the starlight and moonbeams, and his eyes are taking me in like I'm the most beautiful thing he's ever seen, and I just…lose it.

I dig at his jeans, fumbling frantically at the button and at the elastic of his boxers and at his shirt. I'm panting with need, crazed.

He stills both of my wrists in one of his hands and lifts my chin with the other. "Relax, Nell. Slow down."

"I can't, I can't." My voice is not mine; it's almost a squeak, and I don't squeak. "I need you. Right now."

His eyes are calm but hungry. "I need you, too. But slow down. I'm here. I'm here."

He pulls me down against him so I can feel his hot flesh and hard muscle and his arousal against my thigh.

"It's not enough. I need you inside me, Colton. Please."

He brushes a wayward curl aside with his thumb. "I know, baby. But breathe for me, okay? It's all right."

I realize I'm hyperventilating. I'm not okay. But Colton makes me okay, not because he fixes me, just because he's him. He's unchanging. He's raw and rough and kind and smart and nearly illiterate but so brilliant and so talented and so fucking hot it's absurd, and he's *mine*. And all that makes me okay, because he loves me, even when I run away and even when I'm hyperventilating.

I breathe. I slow myself down, one breath at a time, like I've been learning in therapy, and slowly, I begin to find a semblance of sanity.

And then Colton stands up easily, lifting me in his arms, and carries me to the spare bedroom in his parents' house where he's been sleeping. The house is empty, silent in the way that only empty houses can be. His mom and dad are gone, finally taking a much-needed weekend away together.

Colton lowers me to the bed, and I catch a scent of his cologne and shampoo and whiskey. I watch him, stare at him, drinking in his rugged, masculine beauty. He strips his shirt off, doing that sexy guy thing where he peels it straight up over his head, stretching the slabs of muscle on his stomach and chest. Then he flicks open his jeans button, and I'm a trembling mess watching him unzip achingly slowly, teasing me. The jeans slip off to the floor, and his underwear are tented. He's not self-conscious at all. He hooks his thumbs in the gray elastic waistband and draws the black cotton over the head, baring himself to me.

God, yes.

I can't help biting my lip and smiling at the sight of him standing straight up, tip glistening. He's naked, standing over me. I reach out and grasp him, pull him to me. He climbs onto the bed and kneels above me.

"You're wearing too many clothes," he murmurs.

"You should fix that," I say.

He grins and draws my yoga pants off, then my panties. His mouth descends on mine, and this kiss isn't delicate or gentle; it's needy. Demanding. I stroke him, caress him, slide my thumb over the wetness at his tip, explore the veins and ridges and the silk-and-steel contrast of him.

I keep expecting him to slide into me, but he doesn't.

"The doctor cleared you for this, right?" He whispers it gently.

I just nod and try to pull him down to me. He resists, though, staring down at me, eyes inscrutable. I don't know what his hesitation is—I think I've made my need clear.

Then he's rolling to his back and drawing me onto him, except he lifts me so I'm lying on him back to front. He shimmies upward, adjusts the pillows so we're reclining, and god, this is fucking incredibly comfortable and sexy as hell at the same time. I'm lying on top of him, and he's nudging my entrance. I lean back to press kisses to his jaw, and get lost in the taste of his skin while he leans away to dig in the drawer for something. I hear a packet ripping, and he rolls it on smoothly. I barely register this, tasting the salt on his neck, but then his hands are on me, arcing across my ribs and pinching my nipples so I'm gasping and moaning and reaching down between our legs for him, guiding him where he needs to be, pressing him into me. Oh…oh, god.

I keep my fingers on the joining of our flesh while he slides in, and the feeling of his latex-coated flesh moving against my desire-wet folds is intoxicating, sexy as anything I've ever felt. I can feel us moving, feel my petals stretching from his thickness, feel the moisture slicking us both, and then my fingers join his at my clit and we're stimulating me together. My other hand is at his jaw, and he turns his face into my palm to kiss it. He's kneading and caressing my breasts while he fondles my swollen nub, and his thighs are tensing, turning to rock, and my legs are draped to either side of his and lifting me up and sinking me down. I can just barely reach his sack, so I caress him there, cup him, stretch a bit farther to rub my finger on the tiny slice of muscle just behind it.

His breath is hot on my neck, and his voice murmurs my name, chants his love for me, repeats how beautiful I am, how perfect, how amazing. Each word from his lips is poetry, a song rhythmed to the sinuous grind of our bodies.

There's no start, no stop, no him or me; there is only us, only perfection, only meshed souls and merged bodies and dizzy pleasure.

At some point, I come, and the release is endless, wave after wave of delicious pressure and wafting heat and billowing ecstasy and a rush of love so powerful I can't breathe past it, can only rest my head on his shoulder and keep coming around him and whisper his name as my prayer to our love.

There's no magical healing in this. I won't wake up tomorrow fixed and joyful. I'll still hurt and grieve.

But moments like this, with Colton? They make it all bearable. He doesn't fix me, doesn't heal me. He just makes life worthwhile. He helps me remember to breathe, shows me how to smile again. He kisses me, and I can forget pain, forget the urges I still have to cut for the pain that erases the emotions.

He slides his body into mine, and I can moan with him, breathe with him, moan, each single breath a song, and for the minutes and hours spent devouring his love for me, his love inside me, I can only be his Nell, the one without scars and ghosts.

When he comes, I come again, and I whisper the words that have come to almost replace *I love you* between us: "I'm falling into you."

So true. When we come together, when we kiss, when we drowse into sleep side by side, we're falling into each other, and that's when I'm okay. When I'm falling into him.

The End

Featured Music Playlist

"Danny's Song" by Kenny Loggins

"Reminder" by Mumford & Sons

"Barton Hollow" by The Civil Wars

"Like a Bridge Over Troubled Waters" by Simon and Garfunkel

"I and Love and You" by The Avett Brothers

"Make You Feel My Love" by Adele

"Can't Break Her Fall" by Matt Kearney

"Stillborn" by Black Label Society

"Come On Get Higher" by Matt Nathanson

"I Won't Give Up" by Jason Mraz

"This Girl" by City & Colour

"My Funny Valentine" by Ella Fitzgerald

"Dream a Little Dream of Me" by Ella Fitzgerald and Louis Armstrong

"Stormy Blues" by Billie Holiday

"I would be Sad" by The Avett Brothers

"Hello, I'm Delaware" by City & Colour

"99 Problems" by Hugo (originally written and performed by Jay-Z)

"It's Time" by Imagine Dragons
"Let It Be Me" by Ray LaMontagne
"Rocketship" by Guster
"Don't Drink The Water" by Dave Matthews Band
"Blackbird" by The Beatles

I would like to take a moment to thank all of these artists. Music is an integral part of my writing process, and this novel wouldn't exist without these songs, and many more not listed. I encourage you to try these artists, if you haven't listened to them already. And also… don't be pirates. Buy the music legitimately. Support artists, whether they're writers, poets, painters, musicians, sculptors, photographers…buy their work and support their talent. Art makes the world a better place.

About the Author

JASINDA WILDER is a Michigan native with a penchant for titillating tales about sexy men and strong women. When she's not writing, she's probably shopping, baking, or reading. She loves to travel, and some of her favorite vacations spots are Las Vegas, New York City, and Toledo, Ohio. You can often find Jasinda drinking sweet red wine with frozen berries.

To find out more about Jasinda and her other titles, visit her website: www.JasindaWilder.com.

CPSIA information can be obtained at www.ICGtesting.com
Printed in the USA
LVOW101432100513

333272LV00001B/86/P